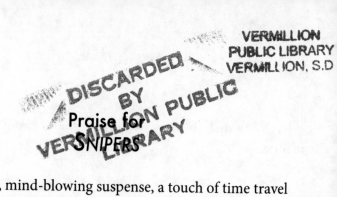
Praise for SNIPERS

Chilling murders, mind-blowing suspense, a touch of time travel and a bit of romance combine to a thought-provoking, entertaining vacation from reality.

—*RT Book Reviews*

Snipers is an excellent amalgamation of history, thriller, mystery & science fiction. Rusch lays out the period in meticulous detail, as only she can.

—Dave Dickinson, *Astroguyz*

This is a fast-moving thriller, and the ending implies that a sequel is in the works. I'll be reading it.

—*Bill Crider's Pop Culture Magazine*

Praise for THE RETRIEVAL ARTIST SERIES

One of the top ten greatest science fiction detectives of all time.

—*io9*

The SF thriller is alive and well, and today's leading practitioner is Kristine Kathryn Rusch.

—*Analog*

[Miles Flint is] one of 14 great sci-fi and fantasy detectives who out-Sherlock'd Holmes. [Flint] is a candidate for the title of greatest fictional detective of all time.

—*Blastr*

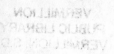

If there's any such thing as a sci-fi *CSI*, the Retrieval Artist novels set the tone.

—*The Edge Boston*

What links [Miles Flint] to his most memorable literary ancestors is his hard-won ability to perceive the complex nature of morality and live with the burden of his own inevitable failure.

—*Locus*

Readers of police procedurals as well as fans of SF should enjoy this mystery series.

—*Kliatt*

Praise for
"G-MEN"

Rusch brings out the mad opportunism and bleak acquiescence of her characters very deftly.

—Nick Gevers, *Locus* [recommended story]

["G-Men"] is a sadly cynical story, very well crafted, well resolved.

—Rich Horton, *Locus* [recommended story]

If you liked E.L. Doctorow's *Ragtime* or the writing of Caleb Carr (*The Alienist*), you'll enjoy this tale.

—*New York Times* bestselling author Jeffrey Deaver

Praise for
HITLER'S ANGEL

…a short, powerful novel that proves the always impressive Rusch can successfully tackle any genre she sets her sights on.

—BarnesandNoble.com (Editor's Pick)

Oregon author Rusch [writes] a fine historical thriller that takes an intriguing incident from the early life of Adolf Hitler and runs with it…. It's a great story, cleanly told.

—*The Oregonian*

What the author finally stirs together is a fascinating concoction of historical speculation, moral compass calibration, and an account of tough police work. Much as with Caleb Carr and Thomas Harris, Kris Rusch sails under her own flag.

—Edward Bryant, *Locus*

The question of whether Geli's death was suicide or murder, and if the latter, who committed the crime, is at the core of Kris Rusch's *Hitler's Angel*…a serious novel structured around the reminiscence of a long-since retired Munich detective, Fritz Stecher, famed for solving one notorious murder, but trapped in the politics surrounding Geli's death.

—*Crime Time*

Deeply evocative, it breathes menace from every page and memorably conveys what Rusch calls the "casual evil" that suffused Germany as the Nazis came to power.

—*The Daily Mail* (London)

Also by
KRISTINE KATHRYN RUSCH:

The Retrieval Artist series (novels and novellas)
The Diving series (novels and novellas)

Recovering Apollo 8 (novella)
The Tower (novella)
Show Trial (novella)

The War and After: Five Stories of Magic & Revenge (collection)
Five Female Sleuths (collection)
Five Diverse Detectives (collection)

SNIPERS

KRISTINE KATHRYN RUSCH

WMG PUBLISHING

Snipers

Published 2013 by WMG Publishing
www.wmgpublishing.com
Cover and Layout copyright © 2013 by WMG Publishing
Cover design by Allyson Longueira/WMG Publishing
Cover art copyright © Udvarházi Irén/Dreamstime,
Rasà Messina Francesca/Dreamstime
ISBN-13: 978-0-615-76205-0
ISBN-10: 0-615-76205-0

SNIPERS

1913

THE ASSASSIN GOT LOST in the corridors of Ferstel Palace. He stood near a dark, dank stairwell, and allowed himself a moment of panic.

Maybe the prototype had malfunctioned again. Maybe he wasn't in 1913 at all. Maybe he was in some other year, some other century.

Then he took a deep breath and made himself take stock. The walls were covered with soot from the gaslights, and the air smelled faintly of oil. The heat was low, and he was cold. His hands, wrapped in woolen gloves with the fingers cut out so that he could handle his Glock, were clenched into fists.

He relaxed the fists one finger at a time. Gaslights were correct. Not all of Vienna had gotten electricity by 1913. And he had no real map of Ferstel's corridors. The building had been long gone—nearly a century gone—when he estimated where it had been and activated the prototype.

Then he ended up here, several stories up, uncertain and terrified that his memory had betrayed him.

The Ferstel Palace of the old photographs had bright rounded windows, decorated on the sides with multicolored electric lights. It had never been a palace, nor had it belonged to the Ferstel family, although it had been designed by Heinrich Ferstel.

Once it had been a bank and stock exchange, but by now, it had been converted into something else. The assassin had thought he would find a conference center, filled with shops.

But there were no shops. Only stairwells and more stairwells, doors after doors, and narrow little corridors that were so dark they seemed like the night outside.

He knew that the Café Central had to be inside Ferstel Palace. He had read more about Vienna in 1913 than he had about the history of the twentieth century. And he was an expert in that history.

He knew Vienna, even though he hadn't been able to check his details before this trip.

The Café Central had to be here. The question was where.

The assassin wrapped his woolen scarf tighter around his neck. The wool scratched his soft skin. Despite his chill, he was sweating beneath the four layers of clothing—the woolen overcoat covering a vested woolen suit, the heavily woven shirt as scratchy as the rest of it, not to mention the long underwear, also made of wool.

No wonder no one bathed in this era. Getting out of the clothing was a nightmare. He should have practiced shooting the Glock with his arms bundled in thick material. His aim might be off. Even a millimeter would make a horrible difference.

He stopped at the end of a corridor, near a wooden door with a brass knob, and forced himself to pause, to calm down.

It was different in the past. Of course it was.

And like always, he had been a fool not to expect it.

2005

SOFIE BRANSTADTER STOOD as close to the open grave as she could. Three men, none of them young, had been working for more than an hour now, using shovels to uncover the coffin.

The dirt here was hard-packed and old—it clearly hadn't been disturbed in more than a century. The diggers struggled to make clean holes in the soil, as the forensic anthropologist, Karl Morganthau, had instructed.

They had been near the grave since dawn. The sexton had put up the privacy screens—if that was what the white, six-foot-high barriers could be called—the night before. Two reporters had camped out all night, hoping to get some sort of story, but the local police had chased them away at dawn.

Even though Zentralfriedhof, Vienna's Central Cemetery, was open to the public, the gates closed at posted hours. No visitors were allowed between ten p.m. and eight a.m. There were too many valuable statues here, too many famous graves, and too many legends about ghosts haunting this, Europe's largest cemetery.

Sofie didn't believe in ghosts. But, as a historian, she understood that the past had a significant influence on the present. That knowledge provided the basis for every book she had written, and it would for this one as well.

Morganthau crouched near the foot of the grave, filtering the dirt through his fingers. He was supervising this part of the process only because he'd done it before. Sofie had never before seen a coffin disinterred.

The process was making her very uncomfortable. The last time she had seen an open grave, she had been five. She had stood in a Munich cemetery, clinging to her grandmother while undertakers poured dirt on her parents' coffins.

Her parents. Murdered thirty years ago by a sniper who had never been caught.

Sofie pulled her sweater tightly around her shoulders. Maybe the press had been right: Maybe this project did tie to her parents somehow. How appropriate, the London *Times* had written when her book deal was announced, that one of the few surviving victims of an anonymous sniper should write a history of the Carnival Sniper, the world's very first sniper/serial killer.

Sofie had been offended when she saw that. She felt her interest was purely intellectual. But the deeper she got into this project, the more she wondered if the papers didn't see her more clearly than she saw herself.

The photographer, Greta Thaler, circled the grave, taking candid shots of the diggers, of Morganthau, of Sofie. Greta was in her midthirties, the same age as Sofie, but dressed like a teenager. Greta wore blue jeans and a T-shirt. She pulled her blond hair back with a leather thong and she wore no makeup.

Sofie's only concession to the location were her flat shoes. Her tan slacks were too light for work in such dirt, and her summer sweater too ornate. She felt out of place here, as if she had been invited to watch other people work instead of paying them to do her bidding.

Greta had two other cameras around her neck: Whenever the diggers reached a new soil level, they called her over, and she took indepth shots of the grave itself. She continued to circle, looking as interested as Sofie felt.

Sofie wasn't sure what she'd find, or whether this disinterment was even worthwhile, but she was playing her hunches, and so far, her hunches had served her well.

Still, it had taken her most of a year to get the permission of the heirs and the City of Vienna to disinter Viktor Adler. Finally, she had to cite anomalies in the autopsy report, anomalies that had been a subject of controversy for over ninety years.

Of course, the press had latched onto her request. Interest in the Carnival Sniper had grown with each successive year—which, generally speaking, was good for her. She wouldn't have gotten that excessively large advance if St. Petersburg Press Worldwide—the largest publisher in the world—hadn't believed they could make a fortune off her book. And SPPW wouldn't have offered to split the bill for Sofie's expenses with Dragon Entertainment Ltd., who held the motion picture rights, either, if it weren't for the possibilities of great profit.

Sofie couldn't have afforded to investigate the Carnival Sniper on her own. Her popular history books did well, but not well enough to pay for the top-of-the-line forensic analysts, the world's best crime labs, and crime scene reconstruction experts.

She was fortunate that the world was as interested in the Carnival Sniper as she was, and even more fortunate that the Sniper had become a mini-industry.

But that good fortune also created problems for her. The press kept an eye on her, trying to scoop her on her own story, and so she had to make plans in secret. She also had a hard and firm deadline eighteen months away. Ironically, the deadline was in the middle of Vienna's Fasching, or Carnival, the very season in which the Sniper had committed his crimes.

At first, Sofie had seen the deadline as a positive omen. Now she wasn't so sure. She still hadn't finished her research, nor had she found anything the other Sniper historians hadn't found. So far, even with all the modern investigative tools available to her, she still hadn't found what her publisher liked to call "the smoking gun."

Viktor Adler was one of the Carnival Sniper's first victims, and only one of two whose grave Sofie could locate. Most of the Sniper's victims were impoverished expatriates with few friends in Vienna. So the victims, for the most part, had been buried in paupers' graves, often with other poor.

Sofie suspected that the body of at least one of the victims had been sold to a local medical college for study. She had meant to trace that, hoping to find the skeleton, but then the city had, to her surprise, granted her request to disinter Adler.

She had never thought anyone would approve. Adler had a place of honor in the cemetery, although he was not buried in the main avenue between the gate and the church. That area was reserved for the truly famous Viennese—the Strausses, Beethoven, Brahms, as well as the presidents of the Austrian Republic and other luminaries. The city often considered those buried in places of honor untouchable.

But Adler had a checkered history, and wasn't as revered as the Sniper's only other Viennese victim. Adler had been the leader of the Social Democratic Party around the turn of the last century. He had founded the workers' May Day Parade, and had been very active in socialist circles. He had received his burial with honors shortly after his untimely death, although there had been some controversy about those honors three years later, when his son murdered Minister-President Count Karl Stürgkh in a misguided ploy to stop the Great War.

After the assassination, people wanted Adler's grave moved because his family was in disgrace. But the effort to punish him posthumously ended quickly, as the press and the public lost interest in the assassination. The decade-long war preoccupied everyone, and the city moved on, leaving Adler here, easy to find, and with a slightly tarnished reputation.

The reputation that let Sofie disturb his grave.

She didn't know exactly what she was looking for but, as she told Morganthau, she would know it when she saw it. If Adler's body yielded up its secrets, it could tell her a number of things: how many times he was shot; whether or not he'd been about to die anyway (some conspiracy theorists believed that Adler had hired the Sniper to take out his enemies while helping him commit suicide); and the chance to settle the biggest controversy of all—whether or not the body was Adler's in the first place.

A thousand theories abounded about the Carnival Sniper. Sofie's least favorite was that Adler had faked his own death so that he could assist in the war effort as a spy for socialist elements in the Russian army. That theory forced historians to make huge leaps—first of all, that there were socialist elements in an army still commanded by the Tzar; second, that Adler cared more about Russia than his native Vienna; and third, that Adler, who was in his sixties at the time, had the energy for a prolonged undercover operation.

The clang of metal against rock caught Sofie's attention. She looked at the grave. So did Morganthau. He let the last of the dirt filter through his gloved fingers, and turned his thin, aesthetic face toward the diggers.

Two of them leaned against their shovels. The third, a thickly built, middle-aged man, tossed his shovel to the ground, then followed it down, resting his ribcage against the edge of the grave. At first he peered into the square hole the diggers had made, then he plunged his arms inside.

Greta grabbed a different camera—not the one she had been using for candid shots, but the black-and-white she had taken for the artistic shots that Sofie hoped would grace the book—and stood near the digger's hips, apparently trying to catch his head, torso, and point-of-view all in one photograph.

Morganthau beckoned Sofie to join him. She walked behind the two standing grave diggers. The third digger was pushing dirt aside, his hands so filthy that they seemed almost part of the earth itself. Sweat dripped off his face into the hole. Sofie couldn't believe he was that warm; she was still freezing in the early morning air.

"If we're lucky," Morganthau whispered when Sofie reached his side, "there'll be a metal identification tag on the outside of the coffin."

She frowned. "I thought that was a late-century innovation."

Morganthau shook his head. "Not if Adler's family paid extra for this plot. Stamping the coffin was a good way to prevent the undertaker from using an economy coffin."

Sofie winced. She had seen an economy coffin in the Undertaker's Museum. The coffin had a flap on its bottom that opened easily. After the funeral itself, the coffin would be placed on top of the grave, the undertaker would open the flap, and the body would fall—unprotected—into the soil below. Then the coffin could be reused, saving the next family some of the death costs.

"The economy coffin was banned in the eighteenth century," Sofie whispered back.

The gravedigger was scraping frantically at the coffin's top. His companions were leaning on their shovels, watching.

Greta was moving around the wide hole, using all three cameras to take different shots.

"Just because it was banned doesn't mean it went out of use," Morganthau whispered. "Adler would be a prime case for the coffin. He didn't have a lot of money, and he was famous enough."

"But there's a coffin there," Sofie said, no longer whispering.

One gravedigger smiled at her. He had apparently overheard her.

"Doesn't mean much, *Fräulein*," he said, his tone friendly. "We find lots of these folks with a warped board over them, simulating a coffin, I'm afraid."

"Good ideas are never wasted," Morganthau said, his blue eyes twinkling.

Usually Sofie liked his mordant sense of humor, but not at the moment. Adler was too important to her. If the body had been lying unprotected in soil for nearly a century, she doubted there'd be much left—certainly not enough for her purposes.

The gravedigger felt around the edges of the wood. Sofie held her breath. After a moment, he looked up.

"It's a coffin," the gravedigger said.

Sofie let out a small sigh of relief. Just because they had located a coffin didn't mean the body was in good shape. But it was a start.

The gravedigger pushed himself farther over the grave and shoved the last crumbs of dirt aside. Sofie watched avidly.

There were a lot of tricks economizing undertakers made, especially in those unregulated days at the turn of the last century. The worst for her now would be discovering more than one body buried in that casket. She'd have to spring for countless DNA tests on each useful piece of fabric, each bit of bone.

She was planning to pay for at least one DNA test anyway, provided that there was something useful about the body. The test would compare the Adler heirs' DNA to the body. She was trying to cover all contingencies. The last thing she wanted was someone to accuse her of masquerading another body for Adler's just to prove her theories.

Not that she had any theories yet. She had purposely avoided forming any, so that her research would be as pure as possible.

Sofie's hands were threaded together. She had been twisting them nervously, not realizing what she was doing. She untangled her fingers and dropped her hands to her sides. She made herself concentrate on the scene before her.

Greta was kneeling beside the digger. She looked petite next to him, her lanky frame half the width of his. But Greta seemed as focused as he did, only she was doing her concentrating through the lens of her camera.

She kept zooming in for closer and closer shots. Sofie assumed Greta was focusing on his hands, but she wouldn't know for certain until she saw the contact sheet.

Sofie took a step closer to the grave. Morganthau caught her arm and held her in place, nodding toward the small pile of dirt he had already sifted through.

"Let's not have you mixing up the evidence," he said.

He was looking for things that had fallen near the grave at the time of burial. He also was looking for things that had left the coffin, particularly if the coffin had disintegrated over time. So far, it was clear he had found nothing.

Sofie nodded. She crouched, and watched the gravedigger.

The digger had pushed himself farther over the grave, balancing one hand on the coffin top and using the other to brush dirt off the center section of the lid.

"We have a plate here." The digger's voice sounded strangled, probably from his position. He no longer rested his chest on the side of the grave, but his stomach. His diaphragm was probably restricted.

"An identification plate?" Morganthau asked.

"I think so." The digger kept brushing.

Morganthau moved around Sofie, and lay on the other side of the grave. As he did, he pulled a small brush from his breast pocket.

His posture imitated the digger's. Morganthau used his small brush to clear dirt out of the engraving.

Sofie's mouth went dry. If anything on that plate indicated the body belonged to someone other than Viktor Adler, she would have to quit digging now. The Viennese government had given her permission to disinter based on the written records that the body in this gravesite belonged to Viktor Adler.

It was in her agreement that if someone or something indicated that the body was not that of Viktor Adler, the disinterment had to stop until the identity of the body could be proven.

She had tried to get that clause changed, but she hadn't been able to. The government was already bending the rules for her. Normally, inspectors would be graveside to verify identity themselves.

But Sofie wanted as few people here as possible. Confidentiality agreements only went so far. If the witness pool were large, someone would break the agreement and leak information, assuming—quite rightly—that it would take too much work to figure out who the source of the leak had been.

Sofie had provided double- and triple-documentation to the authorities. She had also backed up her research with a newspaper drawing of the coffin being lowered into the grave. Although the trees were differ-ent, the nearby sculptures were not.

If the body in that grave did not belong to Viktor Adler, then some-one had made the switch before the body got buried.

"I have a 'd,'" Morganthau said. "And an 'e.' I think."

"First letter's gone, though," the digger said.

"Not gone, necessarily, but hard to read." Morganthau pulled him-self farther forward. He continued brushing the engraving. "That third letter could be an 'l' or a one. Can't tell."

"That's enough for me," Sofie said. "Let's continue."

The digger looked up at her. His eyes were dark, and the laugh lines were brown with dirt. "That's not regulation, miss."

"We're not following standard procedure," Sofie said. "The govern-ment has already vouched for the veracity of the records, and the family has signed off. We could proceed even if there wasn't an identification tag."

The digger's mouth thinned. He turned back to the coffin lid, brushed some more dirt off, then pushed himself up. After a moment, so did Morganthau.

He grinned at Sofie as he shook the dirt off his brush. "Impatient, are we?"

"Protecting my interests," she said. "We don't need any more de-lays, especially following a procedure that's already been waived."

He stuck the brush back in his breast pocket. His grin had faded. "I thought you wanted a good document trail."

"I do," Sofie said. "But we'll get better pictures of that plate in the lab. And if there's a problem, we'll deal with it then. Let's finish remov-ing the coffin."

And getting out of the cold. The June morning wasn't warming up. She shivered again, and stepped away from the small dirt mound. Greta took a picture of her with the black-and-white, probably catch-ing Sofie's nervousness.

Sofie wasn't sure what she'd do if there was nothing of use in the Adler coffin. She didn't want to think about that. Not yet, anyway.

She stepped closer to the privacy screens, and watched as the other two diggers carried their shovels graveside. One of them climbed in the hole, standing on the coffin lid as he made chopping motions in the earth.

Greta started to take a picture, but Sofie waved her away. The entire disinterment was controversial enough. She didn't need a photograph of a gravedigger being inadvertently disrespectful hitting the press at the same time as the book did.

Or, God forbid, before.

Sofie felt her breath catch. An elation she hadn't expected filled her. Finally, this long, involved project was moving forward.

2005

ANTON RUNGE LEANED against the trunk of an ancient oak tree near the central path. His sweat was drying in the slight breeze, and he was beginning to get a chill.

He'd run his three miles this morning, and somehow they had brought him here, to Zentralfriedhof. And not just to the cemetery, but off the main path, away from the tombs of the famous, into the cemetery itself, toward the grave he had visited too many times—the grave of Viktor Adler.

At the moment, the grave, with its simple marker, was impossible to see. The official in charge of the cemetery had put up barriers to keep prying eyes away from this important disinterment.

And there were a lot of prying eyes. Anton counted at least five paparazzi, two of them in nearby trees, using telephoto lenses to get pictures of the work going on behind those barriers.

The paparazzi were going to get run off. As he'd come into the cemetery, he'd overheard a police officer speaking to the dispatch, confirming that he—or someone—would check this part of the cemetery every twenty minutes.

Apparently Miss High-and-Mighty Branstadter had paid a lot of money for her privacy.

Anton sighed, crossed his arms, and rested the top of his head against the tree's scratchy bark. He knew he shouldn't begrudge her anything. Sofie Branstadter's very public interest in the Carnival Sniper meant that the sales of *Death at Fasching* had increased by nearly fifty thousand copies in the past year alone.

The royalties from the book, written by Anton's great-grandfather, had helped Anton through some lean years, and helped him make the difficult transition from solo artist to composer. Now he didn't have to parade in front of crowds to earn a living. He could remain in the privacy of his own home and write down the music that had haunted him since he was a child.

Anton's father would be appalled that Anton was spending the money instead of saving it for future generations. But Anton was thirty-five, with no marriage prospects on the horizon. His only marriage, which had been no less unpleasant for all its brevity, had left him childless, and he didn't see that state changing any time soon.

So there would be no future Runges, and therefore no need for Anton to bank the money the way his father and grandfather had.

His father wouldn't have approved of Anton's presence here in the Central Cemetery, either. Both Anton's father and his grandfather had been embarrassed by *Death at Fasching*. But the book had once fascinated Anton.

When Anton had been a young man, the Carnival Sniper had become an obsession for him. He had read *Death at Fasching*, and then all the articles and the other books on the subject. In most, Anton's great-grandfather, Johann Runge, starred as an almost romantic figure—a man on a never-ending quest for the truth.

Anton had trouble remembering how he felt about the books, the Sniper, and his great-grandfather as his own fame grew. He had won several important international piano competitions, and all the press wanted to talk about was the Carnival Sniper.

Headlines all over Europe proclaimed that the great-grandson of the Sniper detective had won the prized Chopin Competition. Only Vienna had the grace to remember that Anton was the first Viennese to win since the competition started twenty years before.

Interviews were always about the Sniper, never just about Anton's music. Even after Anton had stopped his solo performances, reporters would show up at his door, wanting yet another Sniper story.

The nuisances had grown worse since Miss Branstadter got her outrageous book deal.

Anton wondered how she would play it. Books often had to make up new points of view, new conspiracy theories, just to have new material on this ninety-two-year-old case.

Some of the books actually blamed Johann Runge's unusual detecting methods for the bungling of the case. A few claimed that if the Carnival Sniper had been caught, the devastating Great War—the most important event of the twentieth century—would never have happened. And one recent book actually accused Johann Runge of incompetence that let the Carnival Sniper go free.

Anton knew his great-grandfather hadn't been incompetent. He had been, in the words of Anton's father, too irascible for that. But the man had become an enigma, obsessed about the Sniper, afraid that the Sniper still lived decades after the killings.

Somewhere in the middle of all those theories lay the truth, and Anton doubted Miss High-and-Mighty Branstadter would find it. For all her pronouncements, she was just another sensationalist writer, trying to make money off someone else's life.

At least Miss Branstadter had the resources to pursue a few new avenues. Although Anton did not believe that she would find any new evidence in the graves of the Sniper's victims.

What could decomposing corpses tell her? That they had been shot, yes, and that they had died. But there were no bits of paper tucked into the pockets revealing the identity of the killer.

That was the problem with a gunman who chose his victims at random: Finding a unifying thread was impossible. Anton believed that the Sniper had snapped one morning, taken his pistol, and shot five people in the next twenty-four hours.

Then he had boarded a train and disappeared from Vienna forever.

The story wasn't even that unusual. Snipers had taken out victims all over the world. From clock towers in London to airports in Madrid, snipers had been using their guns to enforce their crazy beliefs for decades now.

The only reason the world wanted to know about the Carnival Sniper was because he was the first. The first to use a gun to shoot more than one victim, and the first to do it at random.

No matter how many conspiracy theories people wrote, no matter how many graves they dug up, the Sniper would still remain anonymous because he had no agenda, no plan, and there had been no logic in his actions outside of his own twisted mind.

Still, Anton wished he could be inside those barriers and see the body that his great-grandfather had stood over in the Café Central.

Time barely existed in Zentralfriedhof.

Anton almost felt as if he could reach through the early morning mist, and touch the past.

1913

THE ASSASSIN DECIDED to leave Ferstel Palace. He was too panicked and too confused. He wasn't even certain he had been inside the right building. Nothing on the walls mentioned the name of the building, and he couldn't remember who the other 1913 occupants of the building had been.

He knew there was a street entrance into the Café Central. He had just not planned to use it. In his imagination, he had seen himself appearing in the café, shooting Bronstein, and escaping before anyone realized the assassin was there.

But, of course, he had imagined the scene all wrong. Now he would have to enter the café like any other customer and try to find his target.

The assassin found a ground-level door and stepped outside. Instantly, the bitter January cold hit him. Arctic air blanketed the city, made worse by the presence of the sun.

It seemed to make the cold damper, and his lungs ached.

The street seemed nothing like any of the photographs he had seen. The buildings rose higher than he expected, and even though all of them had ornamentation—tiny statues, baroque decorations, beautiful stonework above the windows—they looked grimy, soot-covered and dark.

The sunlight didn't add brightness. Instead, it emphasized the filth around him.

The streets weren't crowded, but there were more people than the assassin would have liked. People crossed the ice- and snow-covered street, dodging piles of horse manure. Most of these people were men, all wearing woolen suits and woolen overcoats, their hats covering full heads of hair. As they moved quickly, their faces were indistinguishable, hidden by scarves or neatly trimmed beards.

A few horses clip-clopped by, and so did some horse-drawn carriages. The stench, even in the cold, was more than the assassin could bear. Manure, cigar smoke, human sweat, and perfume hung in the air.

Trams also moved through the crowd, and people seemed to avoid them. A single Model A putted by. The driver clutched the wheel as if he were afraid it was going to bite him. He bent forward, looking at the passersby, apparently hoping they would avoid him.

The assassin stood and watched, his heart still pounding.

The Model A helped his confidence. Automobiles and horses co-existed on Viennese streets well into World War I. The clothing was right, too. The assassin's outfit was just the same as the others he had seen.

Apparently, working backwards, the prototype had no problems.

He sighed, his breath frosting out of him, visible in the chill air. He pulled his coat tighter around him, then thought the better of it. The tight coat revealed his shoulder holster and, if he moved just right, the Glock would also be visible against his frame.

The Glock, modified to fit his needs, wasn't like any handgun someone from this decade had ever seen, but the general shape hadn't changed.

It was still recognizable as a gun.

He shoved his hands in his outside pockets and decided to follow the crowd. Maybe he could ask someone where the Café Central was. If he kept the question simple, he would not run the risk of being memorable.

He walked until he realized he had reached a square. It looked completely unfamiliar. The buildings were tall and made of stone, and they were brown in the unusual January sunlight. Snow topped their roofs.

A fountain stood in the middle of the square, but he didn't recognize the sculptures on it. And the fact that there was a fountain meant nothing; a number of squares in Vienna had had fountains.

The assassin had to figure out where he was. Then he saw the cross atop one of the square towers of a building across the square. The building looked familiar. He closed his eyes, tried to imagine the Vienna he had once known, and the pieces fell together.

The Schottenkirche. He opened his eyes, and now the building did look familiar. The Scottish Church, even though it had actually been founded by Irish Benedictine monks. He had always loved that irony. Strange he hadn't recognized the Schottenkirche before that.

He hadn't realized how much a building's setting determined the building's appearance. The shape of the Schottenkirche, so familiar to him from his original time period, was hidden by the nearby buildings.

He shivered, closed his eyes once more, and let his faulty memory help him. Some of the descriptions he'd read of the old Café Central said it was off Herrengasse. If he was in Freyung Square, Herrengasse was behind him.

He had come out on the wrong side of Ferstel Palace.

The assassin exhaled, feeling slightly dizzy with relief.

He might get this done after all.

2005

OF ALL THE PROTECTIVE GEAR that Sofie had to wear in Autopsy Room Number 4, the breathing mask bothered her the most. Twice now, she had raised her gloved hand to adjust the mask, and twice, she had let her hand fall.

What the staff of the coroner's office called "protective gear" was really no more than a thin plastic suit pulled over clothing. Booties went over Sofie's shoes, and a cap, which resembled a shower cap, covered her hair.

She wasn't the only one dressed so ridiculously. Greta's protective gear made her look like a refugee from a bad French film. Her camera was the only thing that hadn't been wrapped, but she had been warned that it might have to go through special cleaning should something contaminate it.

Only Morganthau looked comfortable in his protective gear, probably because he wore it often. He was bent over the body, categorizing, examining, logging. A small cassette recorder sat on the table next to him, picking up every word.

Sofie had stood in on forensic anthropological autopsies before, as practice for this moment. But none of the bodies had been as old as this one.

She had already made her own notes about the coffin and the process of removing the body. She and Morganthau had used a specialized sling to lift the corpse onto the autopsy table. Later, they would inspect the coffin's interior for any secrets it might yield up.

Until then, the coffin rested on the floor near the far wall, looking surprisingly firm and modern considering how many years it had been underground.

There was no doubt that the body was Adler's. Once the identification tag had been cleaned, the words V. Adler appeared in a beautiful, hand-lettered script. Someone had spent extra time on the engraving, just as, it seemed, someone had paid a lot of money for a fine and lasting coffin.

Sofie was just a bit surprised that the body hadn't fared as well.

None of the flesh remained on Viktor Adler, although much of the clothing did. His bones had turned brown with age, but the skeleton had remained intact, even with all the movement that the coffin had suffered that day.

The unusual aspect of this corpse, however, was the hair. Apparently, it had slid off the scalp along with its flesh, and had dried toward the back of Adler's head. The hair, along with the damaged reading glasses that had come to rest on the yellowish cheekbones, and the very fussy suit, still buttoned as if the corpse were heading to an important state dinner, made Adler seem real to Sofie in a way she hadn't expected.

Perhaps, too, the scent of loam mixed with a faint hint of ancient rot, also made him real. Until this moment, Adler had been a victim. A historical figure with an interesting past who just happened to end up dead at the hands of the most famous sniper of the twentieth century.

Sofie had never thought of Adler as a person before.

"How preserved do you want the clothing?" Morganthau's voice sounded muffled.

It took Sofie a moment to realize he was talking to her, and not making notes for the recordings.

"Why?" she asked.

"Because I can't unbutton this damn vest," he said. "I'd like to cut it off."

"Let me try." Sofie's fingers were smaller and slimmer. She reached onto the autopsy table and touched the top button. It had retained its chill, but she couldn't get a sense of texture through her gloves.

She managed to slip her thumb and forefinger underneath the button, twisting it enough to pull it through the small opening in the vest.

"Good," Morganthau said.

A click echoed nearby. Greta was standing just to the side of Sofie, photographing her fingers.

Sofie continued unbuttoning the vest, trying not to think about how intimate the movement felt. No one had undone these buttons in more than ninety years. No one had touched Viktor Adler in all that time.

Sofie let out a small breath and continued working, feeling the tension in the buttons and something soft beneath.

As she reached the bottom of the vest, Morganthau grabbed the sides and gently peeled the vest back.

The shirt and undershirt had meshed into a single garment. The garment was a yellowish-green color, and beneath it, were still some putrefied remains.

That rot smell rose again, and this time, Sofie had to swallow down bile. Her eyes watered. She looked up at Morganthau.

"I was afraid of that." His expression was apologetic. "I knew the moment we opened this casket that he either wasn't embalmed or embalmed badly. I should have warned you."

Sofie had to swallow again before she spoke. "Are we going to go through this everywhere he was covered in clothing?"

"Possibly," Morganthau said. "But the torso is always the worst. There's so much liquid in the human body, and most of it exists in the center. There isn't a lot of bone mass to hold it in here, so it finds something else if it can."

"The clothing," Sofie said.

"And it probably wouldn't have been like this if he had worn a normal amount. But styles of the day meant at least four layers, maybe more, all of them natural, heavy fabrics."

Sofie nodded, not sure exactly how that made a difference, and not willing to ask. Those details weren't that important to her book. She would have to put gory descriptions into the text, but there'd be as few as possible, and most of them would center on the killings themselves.

"I'm going to have to cut this mess open," Morganthau said.

Sofie supposed he could peel it back, but she wasn't about to help him. Now she couldn't believe that she had touched that corpse so casually.

"Cut away," she said.

He used a special pair of scissors and sliced as deftly as if he were working in a fabric store. The material split open, and so did the liquefied contents of the middle. Actually, the contents didn't look like they had liquefied; they looked like they had jelled. They mostly clung to the fabric, and pulled away with it, revealing the spinal column beneath.

Something thudded against the steel of the table.

"Interesting," Morganthau said, not stopping. He continued to snip until the shirt and undershirt were completely cut in half.

Sofie, however, peered over the body, hoping to see the source of the thud.

"It's probably a loose part of the spinal column," Morganthau said, setting the scissors in a nearby tray. Still, he leaned over the body as well, and used his fingers to probe the interior.

Sofie tried not to wince. She couldn't imagine touching that mess of stuff.

"We're going to have to boil the ribcage," Morganthau said. "There's too much tissue still attached to tell us if the bullets hit anything here, and not enough skin left to show us a trajectory."

Morganthau spoke while he was probing the body's main cavity. Then he paused, frowned, and pushed. After a moment, he lifted an intact bullet out of the interior.

"Well," he said, putting the bullet into one of the evidence trays. "I guess now we know he was shot."

Sofie smiled at him. That part was never in doubt. Whether or not the shots actually killed him ahead of his time was.

"I would have thought you would find more bullets than that," Sofie said.

"Me, too," Morganthau said. "But we're not done. We might find fragments adhering to bone, we might find some in the coffin, and we might find some in the clothing. Patience, Sofie. Remember?"

She did remember. Morganthau had taught her that when she had insisted, all those months ago, on standing beside him for other anthropological autopsies.

The body reveals its secrets slowly, he had said that first day. *Even more slowly if the body has had a lot of time alone.*

His conversation was often mystical. He seemed to believe that the corpses had a spirit all their own. That made him a difficult witness in court—a lot of prosecutors preferred not to use Morganthau because he wasn't dry and pedantic—but it also made him popular with juries and the press.

Morganthau's work, for all his strangeness, was unassailable. No one had ever found fault with his factual conclusions. Only with his personal way of presenting those conclusions.

Morganthau continued to probe, one hand holding the shirt back, the other near the spinal column.

Sofie's stomach roiled. Between the rising stench, the squishing sound of Morganthau's fingers, and the whitish-green mass that had been Adler, she felt sicker than she had at her first autopsy.

She knew she didn't dare watch any longer, so she turned to her first piece of original evidence: the bullet.

Sofie had to walk around the body to get to the evidence tray. The stainless steel tray sat on top of a stainless steel table. The bullet rolled around inside.

She picked up the tray in her gloved hand and peered at the bullet. It was longer than she expected, its end pointier than any bullet she had ever seen before.

"Is this bullet supposed to be green?" she asked.

Morganthau didn't even look. He was still bent over the body. "If it's copper, it might have turned green."

"I don't think it's a copper bullet," Sofie said. "The base is a silver-gray."

"Hmm." Morganthau didn't sound interested. "A million chemical reactions took place inside this casket. Who knows what interacted with the metal and caused some kind of change? It's not my area of expertise."

It wasn't Sofie's, either, but she had never seen a bullet that looked like this one.

"This green isn't oxidation," she said again. "It seems to be the color of the metal."

"What?" This time, Morganthau did turn. He kept his hands outstretched, the gloves covered with the jellied substance that had been Adler's interior.

Sofie didn't allow herself to look at them for more than a moment. She held the tray up so that Morganthau could study the bullet on the steel surface.

"Son of a bitch," Morganthau said. "I think you might be right. Why would someone make a green bullet?"

"You got me," Sofie said. "Maybe it's fluke."

"Or maybe not. How many times did you say this guy got shot?"

"At least five, maybe more. He was shot at such close range that his body was a mess." Sofie could recite some facts as if she'd witnessed them herself. It was the others she didn't know, the ones everyone else disagreed over as well.

"Then there might be another bullet—or enough of one that we can see if it's also green." Morganthau shook his head. "You're going to have to get that to the lab guys."

"I plan to," Sofie said.

"You know," Morganthau said, turning back toward the body, "when you came to me, I thought reopening this case was weird. But the deeper I get involved, the more intrigued I am. A green bullet. Who'd have thought?"

Certainly not Sofie. She stared at it for a moment longer, then set the tray down.

Morganthau was deep inside the body again. "Chipped rib bones," he said. "Shattered clavicle, and a nice circular hole through the left wrist bone. These bullets were powerful."

"The investigating detective figured it was the range," Sofie said.

"Bone usually stops bullets," Morganthau said. "So far, I haven't found any bullets near the bones. Just that one, which, I assume, was trapped in the abdomen and then, eventually, fell loose as the body decayed."

Sofie sighed and walked back to her spot. "I'd love to have a second one for comparison's sake."

"I'm not promising anything," Morganthau said. He was still working in the center part of the body.

Greta had her camera in her hands, but was watching Morganthau instead of taking pictures. Sofie glanced at her.

"Did you get shots of that bullet?" she asked.

Greta nodded. "One."

"Get some more. From different angles. Make sure you have as many photographs of that bullet as you can."

"But don't touch it," Morganthau said. "That's for the lab guys to do."

Sofie looked at him, as she had a realization. He had touched the bullet. He had held it between the thumb and forefinger of his right hand as he placed the bullet in the tray.

If the green color had been a coating, Morganthau's fingers should have smeared it. And yet there were not visible smears on the bullet itself.

Sofie didn't say anything. She clasped her hands behind her back, and watched Morganthau work.

But her mind was with that bullet. An unusual bullet would be a gift. Evidence that would be easy to track. Imagine—an unusual bullet, a single manufacturer, a way—perhaps!—to finally get a real lead on the Carnival Sniper.

Even if she could say that the Sniper was from a particular country, that he bought his weapon and his bullets from a particular place, that would help her with her book. That and the novelty of the disinterment, the photographs, the crime lab work.

She smiled softly to herself.

Maybe this project would be original after all.

1913

WILLIAM DID NOT THINK OF HIMSELF as a mad bomber. In fact, he usually thought of himself as quite sane. But he felt vaguely mad as he stood in the narrow aisle between the seats of the crowded train, his coat weighted down by a tactical nuke the size of a baseball in his right pocket.

His mouth was dry. The stench of tobacco and unwashed bodies didn't help. He felt like he didn't belong, even though he had been here, one-hundred-and-fifty years in the past, for nearly a week.

The tips of his ears were frostbitten. He'd lost his hat shortly after he arrived. The muffler he wrapped around his neck was too modern, but he hadn't known it until he got here. His coat was too new, and his boots too shiny.

He'd taken care of all of that, preparing for this moment—scraping his boots with mud, ripping his coat, searching for a new hat. He had finally found one, but it cost too much. If he bought a hat, he would have no money left for food.

So he spent the week cold and miserable, waiting at the Krakow train station for the right train to Vienna—nothing in the histories told him which one he needed—and finally he saw his target.

The target was traveling under the name Stavros Papadopoulos. William had practiced the name, so that if he had to talk to the man, he wouldn't let his knowledge of the man's other identities slip.

That had been William's greatest preparation. He had thought his PhD in history, with his specialty on nineteenth- and twentieth-century Europe, would have been enough. He had treated this mission like a research paper, making certain he spoke enough Polish to get by; brushing up on his German, Russian, and French; and checking the facts, as history had recorded them.

He should have checked on the details. The details, he had learned in this long week, were what was truly important.

William swayed with the train. He kept his gaze on Papadopoulos.

Papadopoulos had garnered a seat, and was sitting on its very edge, his hands resting on top of a wooden box. His right hand covered his left, but not enough. Just enough of the left was visible to show that the hand was indeed withered.

The seats nearby were full. William couldn't continue standing—a conductor would ask him to sit down, just like one had in the other car.

However, there was a seat a few rows back. William would be able to see Papadopoulos's mud-covered boots, even from that distance.

William sat down, grateful to be off his feet. This trip had taken a lot of energy. Initially, he had thought of it as a vacation in the past—an adventure before he completed his private mission.

But the vacation had been strenuous. Krakow was not as sophisticated a city as he had thought it would be. He should have started in Vienna after all, or maybe, as some of his friends suggested, simply time-traveled in, planted the bomb in a public place, and time-traveled out.

William stuck his hand in his pocket. The nuke was there, small and smooth against his hip. In his other pocket, he had the detonating remote and his handheld time-travel device. The pockets on this coat had button-down flaps, and he was grateful. If he lost any of those three items, he would fail or be stranded here in the past.

He hated it here. He missed bullet trains that would have traveled from Krakow to Vienna in fifteen minutes—and ten of those would have been spent loading and unloading. He missed hydropower, and fresh air, and even, comfortable heat.

Whoever claimed that the past was romantic had obviously never been there.

His shrink had warned him that he would get disillusioned. *It's your nature, William*, the shrink said. *You have delusions of grandeur, and when reality confronts those delusions, you blame everything around you, but not yourself.*

William doubted the shrink would say the same thing now. William had successfully traveled to 1913, and lived here for a week without suspicion.

Of course the shrink, with his precious by-the-book Freudian methods ("What did you dream last night, William? Was it about your mother?"), believed in nothing except his own brilliance. The shrink said William was controlled by his subconscious. This trip would prove the shrink wrong. William's intelligence controlled him. If it hadn't, he wouldn't have been able to execute this extremely complicated plan.

The plan began its last stages when William had trailed Papadopoulos through the train station and onto the train without getting caught.

That was the part that had had William the most worried. Papadopoulos was known for his cunning and his paranoia. William had expected Papadopoulos to see him in Krakow, but Papadopoulos hadn't.

No one had understood the importance of the symbolism. William suspected the shrink would have understood, because the shrink had given him the idea in the first place.

People think symbolically, the shrink had told William one afternoon. They had been talking about William's obsession with history, and the shrink kept asking William what the past symbolized. William didn't even get a chance to answer before the shrink answered for him.

The shrink said that for William, the past symbolized even more. Within the past lay all of William's hurts, all of his unacknowledged pain. The shrink believed that William studied history in order to understand himself.

William shook away that thought. It wasn't because of the past that he wanted this bit of symbolism. He figured he was going to get revenge for millions of lives.

Papadopoulos would be ground zero because he had always been ground zero. Only this time, Papadopoulos would literally be at ground zero, instead of protected by his cronies and his friends. He had few cronies in 1913, and almost no friends.

William would get his revenge, and everything would change.

For the better.

2005

THAT NIGHT, SOFIE returned to her home, tired and alone. She owned her apartment, which was a narrow, three-story corner in a historic building not far from the Ring. The apartment was old enough to have servants' quarters on the main floor, office space on the second, and living quarters on the third. But she inverted the upper two stories after her second history book hit the bestseller lists.

Now her office took up the entire third floor, with nooks and crannies jammed with library shelves. She used most of the second floor for relaxation, and the first served only as an entry. She had no servants, and had even closed off the servants' kitchen, including the dumbwaiter.

She had become paranoid in the last few years, afraid someone would break into the apartment and steal the secrets of the Carnival Sniper book. Her paranoia had a basis in fact: Her publisher's office had been broken into—twice—after the London *Star* had erroneously reported that she had turned in a preliminary manuscript. Her files had been the only ones taken during the break-in. Obviously the thief had been hoping to scoop her book.

She climbed the stairs to the second story and unlocked the main inner door. Since the break-in at SPPW, she had kept all of her inner doors locked, just as a precaution.

Then she kicked off her shoes and left them on the mat, walking across the polished hardwood. The living room was sparsely furnished—bookcases covering all the walls, of course, but only a couch, an easy chair, and an oak table that had once belonged to her grandmother. No knickknacks, no photos.

She had none. For some reason, her grandparents had decided that Sofie needed no reminders of her parents. She had no photographs of them at all, and when her grandmother died, she found none in the attic or anywhere else.

At university, she had finally gone into the newspaper archives and looked up the records of her parents' murder. A sniper had hidden in one of Munich's parks and shot at random passersby. Fifteen people had died that day, the sniper had never been caught, and the police had run out of leads.

Once, on one of her research trips, she had gone to Munich and talked with the detective who now handled the case. He quizzed her about her own memory of the events, but they both knew she had added nothing new.

At least she got to see some more photographs of her parents—alive—which the department had had. She looked like her mother, but she had her father's eyes. She could remember those eyes, crinkling as they smiled at her. She could even remember his voice, deep and warm.

She had almost no memories of her mother.

Sofie believed her own inability to sustain intimate relationships came from a lack of intimacy in her past. Sometimes she thought that if she could have some answers about her parents, about their murder, about their lives, she could move forward with her own life.

But she knew that would never happen.

Sofie wandered into the large, eat-in kitchen that she had specially designed for her own love of baking, and set the bag containing her dinner on the counter.

Usually she cooked for herself, but she knew on this night she wouldn't be able to tolerate looking at raw meat. So she had purchased a sandwich at one of the nearby shops. She doubted she'd have enough appetite for that, either, but she would try. She usually loved the food she got there.

She poured herself a glass of burgundy—an indulgence she rarely partook of alone—and put an album on the stereo. Brahms, nice and soothing. The day had been long, and had taken more out of her than she had expected.

She sank into her chair, letting the rich tones of a cello fill her senses. For a moment, she closed her eyes, but all she could see was the center of Adler's body—the jellied skin, the thin flakes of flesh on brown bone.

Morganthau had told her that nothing in the preliminary results suggested that Adler would have died any time soon if he hadn't been shot by the Sniper. Morganthau would know more when he completed all his testing, but he could almost guarantee that Adler would have lived another few years, maybe even a decade, if the Sniper hadn't interfered.

That was something, at least. That and the bullet would make the book worthwhile.

Sofie rubbed her wineglass on her forehead. She didn't have a headache—not yet—but she could feel one building behind her eyes. Exhaustion and worry were combining into something lethal.

Exhaustion, worry, and ambition. She didn't want to add one or two new details to the Sniper case. She wanted to break it open, make discoveries that no one could argue with. Ideally, she wanted to solve the case.

She had claimed, when she got the book contract in the first place, that modern science would find out who the Sniper was. At the time, she had thought there was more evidence on the Sniper than there was.

The lead detective on the case, Johann Runge, had listed several items in his book, items that Sofie hadn't been able to find. The evidence boxes for the case had apparently gone missing, and no one knew when or how.

The missing evidence was one more thing for Sofie to solve, and she had been trying—going to the police archives once a week for months, seeing if the evidence boxes had been misfiled.

So far, she was only to the 1930s, and she had found nothing. She had found a few other misfiled cases, but not the one she was looking for.

And in this instance, she couldn't hire help. She didn't want to risk having the evidence stolen right out from underneath her.

Sofie sipped the wine, grimaced, and set the glass down. The liquid tasted bitter, but that might simply be her mood.

Her fingertips still tingled from touching Adler's vest and then discovering what had been beneath it. All the way home, she had been unable to get the image of the man out of her mind.

Morganthau had given her facts she hadn't known: Adler had scoliosis of the spine—whether it had been caused by a disease or by bone loss as he aged, Morganthau couldn't say. Adler's right hand was slightly larger than his left, signifying right-handedness, and his teeth were so bad that he must have been in constant pain.

That had been enough to make him seem human, but the two facts that caught Sofie were more mundane.

Adler had been buried with his glasses on, and his wedding ring in his vest pocket.

Someone had sent him to the grave believing that the man still needed to see, and that he needed a token of his family along with him. That the glasses were broken didn't seem to matter. They had been carefully cleaned and placed on the body before the casket was closed.

Sofie stood, set the wine on the counter, and grabbed her sandwich. She took half of it out of the bag and left the other half inside. Then she put the bag in the refrigerator.

The sandwich was a cold turkey on salt rye, with hot mustard, cheese, pickles, and a tomato. She'd had them leave off the lettuce because, for some reason, it reminded her of the grassy patches of earth she had seen that morning.

She put the half sandwich on a plate, and carried it through the kitchen to the TV room. The Brahms still played in the kitchen behind her, a kind of white noise.

She had made great progress today, but it was only a start. She wouldn't be able to disinter any more graves in the Sniper case.

So she had to find another way to prove that the green bullet wasn't an anomaly.

And that meant finding the evidence files in the archive.

It meant more research of a kind that had nothing to do with history, and everything to do with human incompetence.

1913

THE CAFÉ CENTRAL was a pleasant surprise. It was a large open space, with a great domed ceiling and marvelous windows. Samovars stood on square tables beside the walls, tall clear glasses piled high so that some patrons could help themselves.

Men sat at round tables, sometimes alone, sometimes with others. Several played chess. Many read newspapers from around the world, but most people were engaged in soft, heated conversation.

As the assassin stepped inside, a waiter smiled at him. The assassin started. He hadn't expected to be noticed—at least not yet.

"Would you like me to take your coat, sir?" the waiter asked in Viennese German.

The Viennese spoke German as if it were a romance language, running the consonants together, chanting the vowels, and giving the language a lilt rarely heard in such a guttural tongue.

"Thank you, no." The assassin's accent marked him as a foreigner, which wouldn't create a problem in Vienna. The city was a crossroads—and in 1913, those roads met at the Café Central.

The assassin stepped deeper into the café, warmed by the scents of cigars and Turkish coffee, mixed with the smell of freshly baking bread.

He surreptitiously peered at faces.

Somehow, he had expected to see Lev Bronstein sitting in the center of the café, a shining light on him. But Bronstein wasn't immediately visible. A lot of men had dark hair, pince-nez, and a neatly trimmed goatee and mustache. The men all seemed intense as well, having serious discussions in a variety of languages.

The assassin headed deeper into the room, sweat breaking out on his forehead. His clothing was too warm for the café.

Finally, he saw Bronstein. The man sat at a table near one of the large, arched windows. He looked exactly like his photographs. The high Slavic cheekbones, the Asiatic eyes, the puffed-up black hair that looked as if it needed a trim, all accented the delicate lower features, the Romanesque nose, and tiny, determined mouth that marked him as different, but only subtly.

Bronstein wore a gray suit that looked expensive and clean, odd combinations in this part of Vienna. His vest was neatly buttoned, and a gold watch hung from a chain next to his heart. His white shirt had been starched and his tie precisely knotted.

He leaned over a chessboard, studying the pieces. Beside him sat a clear glass cup filled with a light brown liquid (probably coffee with a touch of cream), a glass of water, and a half-eaten croissant.

On the chair beside him, a copy of the London *Times* sprawled, and pages of the Berlin *Vorwärts* had fallen onto the floor. Next to the chair, a case stood half open, papers spilling out.

The assassin didn't recognize the other man at the table. He, too, had pale features and a three-piece suit, but his didn't look as expensive and he wasn't as neatly dressed as Bronstein. The other man had uncombed gray hair and thick glasses that fell to the end of his nose. He studied the chess board and stroked his large gray mustache as he contemplated his next move.

The assassin glanced over his shoulder at the path he had just traversed. The door seemed very far away. A window, however, stood just a few meters from him.

He would never make it out the door, but the window would work. The window would work very well indeed.

He had to be quick, just like he had practiced.

Quick and accurate.

The assassin pulled the Glock from beneath his coat, braced his trembling right hand with his left, spread his legs and took a brief second to aim.

No one seemed to notice him. The conversations continued around him.

He took a deep breath—and fired.

The shot hit Bronstein in the chest. His head snapped back and his arms rose up, one hand still clutching his queen. The quick movement unbalanced the chair, and he toppled sideways.

The assassin took a step closer—he had to make sure Bronstein was dead—and caught a movement out of the corner of his eye.

The man who had been playing chess with Bronstein—the sloppy man with graying hair—had come out of his seat and was lunging toward the assassin.

The assassin turned and fired several times, his breath whistling out of his clenched teeth. He had stopped shaking but he was rooted to the ground, unable to run away from the man who was trying to attack him.

The man who was doing a small, inadvertent dance as the bullets plowed into him.

Bronstein moaned and reached up, his head turning toward the assassin. The other man fell, landing with a thud against the wooden floor.

Other patrons were getting up. They would come after the assassin, too, and there'd be too many deaths; he couldn't be responsible for more deaths, the wrong deaths, that wasn't what this mission was about.

He stepped forward, shot Bronstein in the face, and then winced as blood and brains splattered the area around him.

The assassin's stomach churned. He hadn't expected this to be a mess. In his imagination, everything had been so clean, so right.

But this wasn't clean. It wasn't clean at all.

And his mission had only just begun.

2005

THE NEXT DAY, SOFIE visited the evidence archives in the Süh-nhaus on the Ring. The Sühnhaus had once been police headquarters, and a small presence remained there, but for the most part, the force had moved to larger, more modern facilities closer to the Danube Canal.

A police museum graced the main floor of the building, but the rest of the place was devoted to archives for cases that went back for nearly 150 years.

The Carnival Sniper Case still had a number, and according to an administrative file from 1925, the evidence boxes were to be kept under lock and key. There hadn't been that great an interest in the Sniper in those days—the country was still dealing with the effects of the Great War, which had ended the year before—but the interest would build. By 1930, as the post-war period settled into normality, the still-open Sniper case had become a popular item for discussion in the press.

The concern, according to the 1925 administrative note, was that the Sniper was still working and killing throughout Europe, and that this evidence would some day become important. The war had destroyed communications all over Europe, and no one had records of the Sniper. Some assumed that he fought during the long conflict; others assumed he was dead.

As the post-war violence grew, however, and snipings became more common, other people believed the Sniper was still alive and carrying out a vendetta that no one understood.

Sofie had been searching for the original police files off and on for the past eighteen months, and was doing so alone. The archivist in charge of the old evidence looked sometimes, but for the most part, she didn't have time to keep the current cold cases in the best order, so she certainly didn't have a chance with the Carnival Sniper case.

In his book, *Death at Fasching*, Johann Runge had talked about finding unusual evidence, but he hadn't said what the evidence was. His unwillingness to tell all about the case was one of the many reasons *Death at Fasching* had received such harsh criticism from official quarters. But Runge, in an interview given before his death, said he still considered the files open, so he wasn't going to give away all the important information.

Later, the interviewer reported that he had a sense Runge had a personal reason for hiding the information. The interviewer never stated what gave him that sense, nor did he discuss Runge's demeanor during the interview.

Sofie hoped, after the bullet she had found the day before, that the unusual evidence Runge spoke of was another green bullet.

She pulled down a box and sorted through it. 1930s evidence was kept in manila folders, smaller boxes, and envelopes. She would be happy when she reached the days of plastic bags and more sanitary files.

She always left the archives feeling like she had the dust of a thousand crimes on her skin—and she probably did.

This part of the archive was old, with rusted metal shelves so high that she had to stand on a sizeable ladder to get some of the boxes down. A narrow table stood at the end of each aisle, making her have to walk several feet with the heavy boxes.

She often felt exhausted and discouraged after a day in the archive.

She was beginning to lose hope. Misfiling happened a lot, especially with so many records in such a small space. But the misfiling she'd

found concerning other cases—and she'd found a few while searching for the Sniper records—usually happened near the regular file. The
mistakes were predictable—a case with the same number, or one with
a similar M.O.

Connected cases—or cases the detectives initially believed connected—also had a lot of cross-filing. Sofie had searched those cases
first and had found nothing. In fact, in some of those cases, she had
found very little material at all.

At the time, more than eighteen months ago, the fact that she had
found little didn't bother her.

But she had now been through countless records, and most of them
were voluminous—carbon copies of typed reports, as well as bags and
bags of decaying evidence. The report records were also filed in standard file cabinets, usually after the case was closed or had been moved
to the inactive list.

She had found the Sniper files in that cabinet, and had gotten the
police department's permission to make copies, which she was using for her book. But, based on those records, there should have been
more than ten boxes of evidence—at least two for each victim—and
she had found none.

Sofie leaned on the box she had been sorting through. At some
point, she would have to end this part of her investigation. At some
point, she would have to admit that the evidence in the Sniper case
had gone missing.

She didn't want to. First of all, she would have to go through department procedures to prove that the files were gone. Then she would have
to suffer through the press allegations, which she could already imagine: They would accuse her of taking the files for her multimillion-dollar
book deal, so that no one could see the evidence and prove that she had
been wrong.

The thing was, none of the other writers who had penned Carnival
Sniper books had ever tried to look at the evidence. According to the
evidence logs—and those existed all the way back—no one, not even

the so-called Sniper experts, had ever visited the archives, let alone requested the logs.

No one, of course, except Johann Runge.

Sofie froze, feeling her stomach clench. Johann Runge wouldn't have taken evidence; he was too good a cop for that. But Johann Runge had become a man on a mission—a man determined to prove that the Carnival Sniper was still out there and still working—and perhaps he had acted like any other fanatic.

Perhaps Runge had bent rules.

Sofie closed the box she had been looking through and put it back on the shelf. Before she went any further, she would review Runge's books and reports and see if he had made notes about the evidence.

Maybe he had moved the evidence to another location. Maybe he had filed it with other cases.

She needed to double-check. With luck, she would find something she had missed.

1913

THE ASSASSIN HURRIED along Herrengasse, heading northwest. At least, he hoped it was northwest. Everything had an unfamiliar feel to it.

He could see his breath. He was gasping as if he were having a heart attack. He forced himself to slow down, brush the glass off himself, make sure the gun's safety was back on and the gun was in its interior pocket in his overcoat.

If he walked casually, he would look like any other man on the street.

The images were stuck in his head. In his checkered past, he had killed countless people; yet somehow, these two were the worst. The blood, the brains, that look on Bronstein's face. The explosive sound of shattering glass as the assassin had shot out the window...

In that moment, he realized how silent the killings had been. Grunts, the slap of metal against skin, the splattering of blood and gray matter, and gasps from the people nearby.

He had never been so terrified in all his life.

By the time Herrengasse became Freyung, the assassin had slowed and his breath had become even. He managed to keep his head down, looking like a man on a mission.

Fortunately, the blood had sprayed away from him. He might have stepped in some as he vaulted for the window, but that would be off his shoes by now, leaving a small trail on the ice-covered street.

The trail wouldn't matter. Police procedures were inept in this time period. Even if the police found him, no one would think to look at his shoes. And even if they did, they wouldn't know what they found. They wouldn't be able to test for it, wouldn't be able to prove he had been at that scene, with those men, and with that gun.

Well, they'd be able to prove the gun. But he wouldn't let anyone catch him.

He didn't dare.

The assassin had reached the Ring, the wide boulevard that surrounded the old city. The historic buildings looked new, and he realized with a start that most of them had been in place less than fifty years. The trees in the middle of the boulevard were small and bare, the leaves long gone. Someone had shoveled the snow off the cobblestone, but snow still decorated the statuary that topped most of the nearby buildings.

He rubbed his hands together, feeling the cold in his gloveless fingertips. Maybe after his next stop, he would find another coffeehouse, sit for a few hours, and warm his hands. He had no idea how long the cafés were open, but he would have to get warm—and stop shaking.

Somehow.

Part of him knew, as he dodged women in long skirts and men in deep conversation, that his shaking hadn't come from the cold. His route took him right past police headquarters. He had known that when he planned it, and he had thought at the time that it was best to take that route. No one would look for an assassin near the police headquarters.

No one in his right mind.

But that was because no assassin had been dumb enough to try this—not until now.

Maybe he should avoid his next stop altogether. This next killing was personal. It was for the person he had once been, for the person he would be in the alternate timeline created by what he was doing. He would save himself years of agony, suffering, and misunderstanding.

He would save others from it, too.

The changes wouldn't be as obvious as they would from the death of Bronstein, but there would be changes.

And they would be for the best.

They would have to be, to get him to pull the trigger again.

Bile rose in his throat. He made himself focus on the spires of the Votivkirche a few blocks away.

He had only a few blocks to get to his next target.

Only a few blocks before he killed again.

2005

WHEN SOFIE GOT HOME in the middle of the afternoon, she was covered with dust and feeling discouraged. She peeled off her clothes as she let herself into the second floor of her apartment, and left her shoes on the rug near the door. As she headed to the shower, she noticed three messages on her answering machine.

She almost didn't play them; she wanted a shower more than she ever had in her life. But she hit the button as she passed, and a male voice introduced itself as Max Kolisko with Crime Research Labs, the private criminology lab she had hired to test much of the evidence she found.

In the first message, Kolisko just left his phone number. In the second, which came only an hour later, he asked her to call him as soon as she got the message. In the third message, he sounded almost plaintive—begging her to call him at either work or at home, no matter what the hour.

Intrigued, Sofie picked up the phone and dialed the work number. She leaned on her phone table, unwilling to sit her dusty body down on one of the nearby chairs.

The phone rang for a long time, and she was afraid no one would answer. Just as she was about to hang up, someone picked up.

"Kolisko." The voice didn't quite sound the same, and it took Sofie a moment to realize that the excitement was missing.

"Hello, Dr. Kolisko." Sofie felt her cheeks heat. She hated talking on the phone. "I'm Sofie Branstadter—"

"Miss Branstadter!" The excitement was back in his voice. "I am so pleased that you returned my call."

She wiped her face, then inspected the back of her hand. It was covered with black streaks, but whether they were from her forehead or had already been there, she didn't know.

"You made this sound urgent," she said.

"Yes," he said. "Yes, it is. I am the person who has been testing your bullet."

She felt a surge of irritation. She was paying Crime Research Labs an extraordinary amount of money; she would have hoped more than one person would examine that bullet.

"Is there a problem?" she asked.

"Well, I don't know exactly. Where did you say this bullet was found?"

"I didn't." She had been very cautious about that. She didn't want to influence anyone else with unreasonable expectations.

"But you are working on the Carnival Sniper case, correct?"

She cursed silently. The case that she had brought to Crime Research Labs had only been labeled with a number.

"What makes you think that?" she asked, even though she knew.

"The papers. Am I wrong, then?" he asked. "Isn't this the Carnival Sniper case?"

He was probably a closet expert. There were thousands of them in Vienna; millions of them worldwide.

"Yes," she said, "it is."

She was already computing the costs of finding a new lab, one that wasn't tainted by publicity. Second tests, on at least three items, would also add to the price.

"That's fascinating," he said. "Where did you get the bullet?"

"I can't tell you, Dr. Kolisko," she said. "To do so would compromise the work you're doing. Why do you need to know?"

"Because I've never seen anything like it."

47

Sofie froze. That had been her thought when she saw the green bullet with the silver-gray base.

"Neither have I," she said cautiously. "What are you finding different about this?"

"A lot, actually," he said. "It's got a very dense core, made of tungsten, which I've never seen before."

"Is that steel?" Sofie asked.

"No," he said. "It's a metal alloy, often used in high-speed steel. But it's used other places as well. Those filaments you find in light bulbs, they're usually made of tungsten."

"I don't understand," she said. "If it's a common material, then what's to stop someone from making a bullet out of it? Bullets can be made out of any metal, or so I thought."

"They can," Kolisko said. "Actually, they can be made out of anything that can be melted and poured into a mold. But that's not the point here. The point is that this bullet has been manufactured with tungsten in the middle."

Sofie frowned. Something about that truly intrigued him. "So?"

"So," he said. "Tungsten has the highest melting point of all metals, which makes it very hard. I would think that it would damage any weapon's barrel, making the weapon, after the first shot, inaccurate at best, and impossible to use at worst."

"And that's why you asked if this is the Carnival Sniper case?" Sofie asked, still not quite sure why he was so excited.

"No," he said. "Someone coated this hard core with a substance I've never seen before. It's some kind of polymer, and it appears to be inert. I'm not a chemist. I'm going to give it to one of our chemists who can really examine this thing."

Sofie wasn't a chemist either. She wasn't even a scientist. Her background in math and science was relatively weak—just strong enough to allow her to get her undergraduate degree in history.

"I don't understand," she said. "Why is all this important?"

"For a bunch of reasons," he said. "First of all, this appears to be a synthetic substance—manmade. So far, my tests have shown that it's moisture resistant and it doesn't seem to react to extreme heat or cold. But as I said, I'm not a chemist and—"

"Okay, I get that it's a strange substance," Sofie said. "But we are talking about the Carnival Sniper. Maybe he made the bullets himself, for whatever purpose."

"No." Kolisko spoke with such emphasis that Sofie had to move the phone away from her ear. "As I said before, this bullet was clearly manufactured. It even has a manufacturer's stamp on the base, although it's one I don't recognize."

"All right." Sofie rubbed her eyes with her thumb and forefinger, then wished she hadn't. She got some dust in her left eye, and it teared. "You said there were several things."

"Yes," he said. "The technology to make this bullet, in particular the coating—I don't think it existed in 1913. This is some kind of fluorocarbon plastic, unless I miss my guess, and they weren't widely used until the 1940s."

"Plastic?" Sofie said. "Someone covered the bullet with plastic, and that's why it's green?"

"That's why it's green. The color is natural to the coating," Kolisko said. "I did that test, at least. The bullet didn't change color in the intervening ninety-odd years. Provided that this comes from Sniper evidence. Does it? Can you trace it?"

She almost told him that it came from Adler's body, that she'd seen the bullet herself, but she didn't. She hadn't seen Kolisko's report, and for all she knew, he would leak this information, even though everyone at Crime Research Labs had signed a confidentiality agreement.

"You think this bullet might date from a later period," Sofie said, as much to deflect his line of questioning as well as double-check the information.

"Based on the coating alone," Kolisko said. "But there are other elements to consider. If you have a projectile this hard, it's going to bore through most materials—bone, steel, anything you can think of. I have no idea why anyone would make a bullet this powerful when a regular bullet will do."

She ignored that for a moment. He was throwing too many details at her in her tired state.

"So can you trace this bullet?" she asked. "Just because you don't recognize the manufacturer doesn't mean that it didn't exist somewhere. Maybe the stamp changed over the years. Maybe the company went out of business before the war. Maybe the bullet was modified by the shooter himself."

"I suppose that's possible," Kolisko said. "But I don't see the flaws that I would usually find on a self-made bullet. And if this one's been fired—which I assume it has, since it made its way into your evidence bin—then the external substance is really tough because it hasn't flaked or peeled or lost any of its consistency. And if it is over ninety years old, then that's even more remarkable."

"But you can trace this?" Sofie asked again.

"I can try," Kolisko said. "I can't promise results."

Sofie sighed. She needed results.

"I was wondering if you had another bullet," he said.

Sofie blinked. Her left eye was still tearing. She wiped at it with the back of her hand. "Why?"

"Because, if there are two like this from the case, then it's not a fluke."

"But if there's only one, it's a fluke?" Sofie asked, feeling testy. Of course he would want more. Evidence, the one thing she lacked.

"Maybe it was planted or got misplaced or—you know. You know how these things work," he said.

She bit back her answer, nearly revealing for a second time that the bullet had come from Adler's body. But if Kolisko followed the Carnival Sniper press coverage as closely as she suspected he did, he already knew that.

Not that the press knew she had recovered a bullet. But everyone knew she had disinterred Adler, and then the bullet appeared shortly thereafter.

The timing was suspect.

"This is the bullet I want Crime Research Labs to work on," she said, deliberately implying that she had another bullet and that a different lab was working on it.

Kolisko let out a sigh so heavy it echoed into the phone. He had clearly understood the implications.

"Would you mind if I give this to a chemist?" he asked again.

"In-house?" she asked.

"Yes," he said.

"So long as he has signed our confidentiality agreement," Sofie said.

"She," Kolisko said, "and we all have. Signed the agreement, that is."

"Good," Sofie said. "Can you get me a preliminary report on all this? You threw a lot of information at me, and I'm not sure I processed all of it. Maybe put some of it in layman's terms for the non-scientist."

"I'll do what I can." Kolisko's voice sounded more relaxed, almost as if he were smiling. He was a smart man. He knew that the non-scientist she was referring to was herself.

"Dr. Kolisko," she said. "If this bullet does turn out to be untraceable, and this material is something unfamiliar even to your chemist, what does that mean?"

"I'm not sure I understand," he said.

"For the Sniper case. What does this unusual bullet mean?"

"I don't know," he said. "I deal in facts, not speculation."

"But if you had to speculate," she said, "what would you say?"

"I don't know." Kolisko paused for a moment. "There's nothing to say. If this really is from the Sniper case, then it's even weirder than I thought."

Weird. That about summed it up.

Sofie hung up and walked toward the bathroom, reflecting on what he had told her. An unusual alloy in the center of the bullet, an unrecognizable substance coating it, and an unknown manufacturer.

Whatever she had expected, it wasn't this.

She had expected to find answers as she dug into this case. Not more questions.

1913

JOHANN RUNGE RAN toward the Café Central. He had heard of the shooting shortly after it happened. It took him less than five minutes to make it from the police station to the café, but already the assassin was gone.

The café was a mess. Chairs and tables overturned, the coffee mixing with blood. Two bodies were crumpled on the floor, and the head waiter stood over them, wringing his hands.

The other patrons were long gone. Runge had hurried, and yet he had missed them.

He had known that people would disappear, guilty or not. Half the people who came to the Café Central were wanted for political crimes in other countries; no one would remain to show him their papers.

Runge shoved his hands in the pocket of his greatcoat, careful to look before he touched. He was a small man whom people often underestimated, even other men on his own force.

But he was glad to be here alone. The others didn't understand the value of caution at a crime scene. He would get a chance to look before they destroyed the tableau.

He memorized it—the chess pieces still standing in the center of the table, the newspapers sopping up blood on the floor, the open case with notepaper stuffed inside of it, a French novel crammed against the side.

The café was cold. The air coming through the shattered window was quickly overcoming the two stoves that made Café Central one of the warmest cafés in the winter.

Runge sighed, and his breath appeared before him, pale as a ghost. If he didn't act soon, the crime scene would be frozen in place.

The first body was sprawled on its side, half of its hair blown away. The other corpse was lying on his back. The force of his landing had shattered a chair, but not as Runge would have initially thought. The man's head had cracked the seat from the side—the chair had already fallen before the man had landed on it.

So something had happened before the man had been shot. Something quick, because the table and its chess pieces still stood.

But as Runge got closer, he realized that not all of the pieces remained on the table. A knight had fallen on its side, and the queen had tumbled to the floor. She rested beside the other body, the body of the man with only half a head.

Cracked pince-nez lay beside the queen. The man's hand rested near her, as if he had taken her with him when he fell. He had been playing chess; maybe hadn't even seen his assailant. The assassin had shot him first, and then the other man had—stood? Tried to run? Tried to escape?—before the assassin shot him as well.

Runge would ask the head waiter for the sequence of events, but Runge didn't trust eyewitnesses. They often had conflicting views of a crime. Instead, Runge wanted to see what the crime scene told him.

And this one was telling him a lot.

Behind him, voices rose. More police. He sighed again, not pleased. But he said nothing. He couldn't stop his colleagues from doing what they thought was their duty. He had tried innumerable times before.

Runge ignored the others. He crouched over the first body.

The man wore an expensive woolen suit. The sleeves were frayed, but he had tried to fix that. His tie was perfectly knotted, his collar starched, his goatee well trimmed.

The victim may not have had money, but he had pride.

Runge patted the body. His fingers found blood on the vest, blood he hadn't noticed when he first looked.

The victim had been shot twice—once in the chest and once in the head. The head wound had toppled him on his side, making the chest shot impossible. The chest shot had to have come first, with the assassin facing the victim.

Had the victim looked up? Had he known his killer? If so, why had he kept his grip on the chess piece, as if he were still in play? No good chess player touched a piece unless he intended to move it. And no good chess player knocked a queen off the board unless she had been in his hand.

Of course, Runge was assuming the man was a good chess player. But men quickly learned not to play chess in places like Café Central unless they were already good players.

Runge continued to search the corpse, looking for papers. Finally he found them inside the right breast pocket of the suit coat. Before pulling them out, Runge wiped his fingers on the clean side of the victim's jacket. Runge didn't want to get bloodstains on the papers, afraid he would obliterate important information.

Runge leaned back on his haunches as he pulled the papers open. They listed this victim as Lev Davidovich Bronstein, a Russian émigré.

Runge tucked the papers in his own breast pocket for later examination. He would take the briefcase as well, wondering what other surprises he would find.

He went through the body's other pockets but found nothing else, not even money. He wondered if this Bronstein had been robbed, but it looked—from the scene, at least—like the killer hadn't had time.

This sounded like an assassination, which Europe had seen too much of in the last few decades. But Runge had no idea who this Bronstein was or why anyone would want to assassinate him.

Maybe Runge's first assumption was wrong. Maybe the other man had been the target after all.

Runge stepped over the newspapers and stopped beside the second body. This man had been shot several times, and without great accuracy.

Runge crouched and searched this body for papers. He found them in the breast pocket also, already stained with blood. He couldn't read the address, but he did see that the man was Viennese.

The name stopped him.

Viktor Adler, one of Vienna's many trained psychiatrists and leader of Austria's Social Democratic Party.

Runge looked up at the face once again. Adler had been a lively man, filled with righteous anger at the empire, the conditions of the workers, at the rich. He had started Vienna's May Day parades, and he led them every year.

Adler looked older in death. His face sank in on itself, showing a flab that had not been obvious when he was alive. His gray hair spread around his head like a lion's mane, and his skin had turned a sallow white. Only the mustache seemed familiar, the large stylish mustache, and the blood-spattered glasses, still resting on the edge of his nose.

This changed everything. Runge's assumption that the other man might have been the target was probably wrong.

Few people in Vienna had as many enemies as Viktor Adler.

2005

AFTER HER SHOWER, SOFIE sat at her desk in her bathrobe, her hair wrapped in a towel. She wanted to confirm some things she had seen back when she started her investigation.

Sofie's office was her safe place, her hideaway. No one else ever came inside this area, which encompassed the entire third floor. She had knocked out several walls, leaving only the arches, so that she could move from area to area in the large room.

Each area housed books, running shelves from floor to ceiling. Near the shelves, she had comfortable reading chairs, so that she could just grab a book, sit, and read. She also had a library table in each area, so that she could make notes if she wanted to.

She kept the office spotless. It smelled faintly of lemon polish and old paper, scents that she loved. This floor was her favorite one in the house, perhaps her favorite place in all of Vienna.

She had wanted to live in a library, and now she did.

Still, she took a lot of precautions. She kept the office door locked, and her most valuable notes—the things impossible to find in any store—locked in her safe behind one of the bookcases.

She did not go to that safe now. The book she wanted was the best-selling, definitive book on the Carnival Sniper—the book that some say started it all.

Her first edition of the book was in a glass cabinet with her other prized books, away from light and dust and at a controlled temperature so that they wouldn't get ruined.

Her researcher's copy of *Death at Fasching* was the forty-third printing, with a lurid cover and the title in blood-dripping red. The photographs inside, grainy and indistinct, were lurid also, mostly of the victims, taken after death.

She had first read a copy just like this, sneaking it at intervals in the dormitory at boarding school, deathly afraid the school officials would find it and confiscate it.

They never did find it, but they had always considered Sofie a good girl—*almost too good*, one of her reviews had said, *given her history.*

She sighed and tightened the towel turban around her hair. She needed the book, and she needed the police reports. She had made three copies of those, and two were in her safe, with her personal notes.

The third rested inside her mahogany desk, in the very center of the room.

The police notes took up three thick accordion files. It took nearly ten minutes of searching before she found what she was looking for: the evidence list.

Johann Runge had drawn up the list and initialed it. Most of the items were typed, but a few were written in the same impatient scrawl that had made the initials.

The list went on for five pages, single-spaced, and included each item bagged and stored for the case. Runge was one of those detectives for whom the word "thorough" wasn't exact enough.

For example, he didn't just list Adler's clothes as one big unit, which was customary for the time. Instead, he listed each item, from the ruined suit coat to the watch fob, splattered with blood.

Sofie bent over the evidence list, feeling herself grow slightly dizzy. She was holding her breath. She exhaled, then forced herself to inhale, counting the breaths until she felt better again.

She did that every time she looked at this list, overwhelmed by the amount of material on it, and stunned that somehow police archives had let those files go missing.

Runge did not list the items alphabetically. Instead, he listed them by incident. Sofie had always believed the man had categorized them as he placed them in their original boxes—clothing, chess pieces, walking stick, papers. She imagined him adding to the list each time someone new died, his fingers hitting the old manual keys with increasing strength as his anger grew.

She ran her finger down the pages, searching. On page two, she found the notations she remembered:

-Three bullets, unknown origin, removed from west wall, Café Central.
-Two bullets, unknown origin, removed from ice patch on sidewalk near Café Central [see diagram].
-One bullet, unknown origin, removed from façade of Liechtenstein Palace, across the street from Café Central.

She turned the page, examining the list from the second shooting until she found the notation again.

-One bullet, unknown origin, removed from door at 19 Berggasse.

And from the third site:

-One bullet, unknown origin, removed from wall in Mannerheim apartment.

There were, she knew, no recovered bullets at the site of the Sniper's last known victim, but she checked anyway. And found something else that startled her, because her gaze had passed over it countless times before.

-Gun, abandoned by suspect.

Gun. But not what kind of gun. And the precise Runge, who listed the make of the watch Adler had been wearing when he died, had not listed the make or model of the gun, recovered at Wein Nord, the Vienna North train station.

Sofie's towel slipped over her eyes. Her hair was drying crunched up inside the terrycloth.

She left her papers out and went down to the second floor to get dressed for the evening. All the while, she marveled at her own misunderstanding of the bits of evidence she had.

Bullet, unknown origin. She had always assumed that meant that Runge hadn't known for certain that the bullets had come from the Sniper's gun or even from the same shooting.

But what if it meant an unknown bullet? A green bullet, made of an unusually tough alloy, with a slick coating that Runge had never seen before?

Sofie felt a trickle of excitement run through her. She had made the mistake she had been worrying about. She had made an assumption that could have stalled her investigation.

She had assumed that Runge hadn't been as good at his job as he had thought he was. But that might not be the case. Runge had the bullets and he had the gun.

Ballistics, as a science, was in its infancy in 1913, but Runge had a passing knowledge of it. In one of Runge's other cases, he had hired a German lab to use comparison photomicrographs to examine bullets. He had also suggested, long before it was practiced, shooting another bullet from the same gun to see if the bullet matched one used in a murder.

Sofie had known that, and had ignored it, preferring to believe what so many others asserted: that the Sniper had gotten away because Runge hadn't done his job.

Runge had been ahead of his time. He had made many mistakes by modern standards, but he had made fewer than most detectives of his day. And he had an intuitive knowledge of the importance of trace evidence in a murder case.

When Johann Runge wrote *bullet, unknown origin*, he meant a bullet that he had never seen before.

Sofie pulled on a silk short-sleeved blouse and a pair of tan trousers. She combed out her shoulder-length hair and pulled it back with a scarf.

Then she went back to her office.

It was time to reread *Death at Fasching*, time to examine it with a whole new eye.

Time to remember that Johann Runge was considered one of the best detectives of his day even after the Sniper escaped.

Time to reexamine all that she knew of the case, and assume that nothing was quite as it seemed.

1913

THE ASSASSIN REACHED Number 19 Berggasse quicker than he expected to. Berggasse was empty, which surprised him. The other streets had been full.

Number 19 was an elegant white brick building with an arched doorway and large windows. The brick was whiter now than it had been in the assassin's original time period, but other than that, the building looked surprisingly the same.

The velvet rope that stood outside the door and the signs indicating that Number 19 was the Sigmund Freud Museum were, of course, gone—or, to be more accurate, not yet there. But other than that, the building was exactly what the assassin had expected.

He leaned against a wall across from the six-story apartment building, hoping that no one saw him and thought his behavior unusual. He tucked his hand inside his coat, resting his palm on the butt of his Glock.

The front door opened and out stepped a small woman. She was young—probably not even twenty—and moved with the ease of youth. Her light hair was in braids woven around the base of her skull. She had a pleasant face that became beautiful as she turned and smiled at someone behind her. She wore a heavy woolen cape over long, wide skirts. Her hands were not stuck in a muff the way some of the other women's had been. She also did not cover her head.

Sweat ran down the assassin's back. He was no longer hot, just nervous. The histories had been right. Freud took his afternoon walk with his daughter Anna every day at the same time.

That also gave the assassin hope. So far, his timetable had been accurate. Bronstein had been in the Café Central, and now Anna Freud walked out of Number 19 Berggasse precisely when she was supposed to.

Then Anna extended her hand, and the famous man stepped into the thin sunlight. He was short and thin, except for a pot belly, looking frailer than someone of fifty-seven years should look. He carried a cane in his right hand, a pipe in his left, and he crooked his arm so that Anna could take it.

Freud's coat was the same dark black that the other Viennese men wore, but his hat was small and looked well made. His face was both familiar and unfamiliar. The nose was wide, the eyes narrow, the white beard well-trimmed.

But the assassin had never seen Freud's face in motion—had only seen it frozen in old-fashioned photographs, peering uncomfortably at the lens.

Hard to believe that this man would live another twenty-six years without the assassin's intervention. Twenty-six years in which he would pick destructive fights with his colleagues and students; twenty-six years in which he would invent new "truths"; twenty-six years in which he would revise his theories, making them worse.

His theories were simply that: theories, with no basis in fact. They always blamed women for the problems of the world, and claimed that sons of strong women were "weak" or "hysterical," again with no evidence.

Sons of strong women could be strong. The assassin was proving that.

Most people of the assassin's time would say that Freud was not as bad as Bronstein or the others, but in some ways, Freud was the most insidious. He influenced how people thought, how they looked at each other, how they treated each other. The subtlety of his work, its twisted nature, was lost on almost everyone who knew of it.

Freud looked up at the pale sun, squinted, and then said something to his daughter. She smiled fondly and slipped her hand in the crook of his arm.

They were going to walk away from him. The assassin realized he was so fascinated by the living, breathing man in front of him that he nearly forgot his mission.

The assassin yanked the Glock from inside his coat as he stepped out of the shadows. He used the laser sight for the first time, noting that the little red dot hit Freud squarely in the chest.

Then the assassin pulled the trigger.

The shot hit Freud, sending him careening into the white building, his hat falling away and drifting down the street.

Anna Freud looked around, but she didn't seem to see the assassin. She appeared more concerned for her father. She fell to her knees on the icy sidewalk and clutched his hand, screaming for help.

Freud's lips moved, but Anna didn't appear to hear him. Freud raised his head slightly, and his gaze found the assassin's. Freud's lips stopped moving and the two men stared at each other for a long moment.

The assassin could sense Freud's pain and confusion, his great curiosity as to who the assassin was and why he did what he had.

Anna's gaze followed her father's. Somewhere along the way, she had stopped screaming.

She half-stood, not relinquishing her father's hand.

"You!" she called. "You shot my father."

People were coming out of nearby buildings onto the street. They looked first at Freud propped up against the door, and then at Anna.

In a moment, they would look at the assassin.

He shoved the gun under his coat and turned, heading back the way he came. He needed to go north, not southwest, but for the moment, he had to get out of there.

The wind had come up. Freud's hat still rolled down the street as if it had a life of its own. The hat kept pace with the assassin, guarding him, reminding him.

Behind him, Anna Freud let out a wail. *Noooo! Noooo!*

Her voice followed him down the street, back toward the Ring, on the path that Sigmund Freud had taken every afternoon.

Until this one.

2005

UNFORTUNATELY, JOHANN RUNGE was not a writer.

Death at Fasching was a good read because of its subject matter, and because of the fact that Runge focused on the chronological sequence of events—not because of his deathless prose.

Every time Sofie read the book, she skimmed. She had probably done so the first time, back in boarding school. Unlike Runge, Sofie was a writer. Her ability to turn history into stories that people worldwide wanted to read had made her an international bestseller, much to the dismay of her academic colleagues.

They accused her of turning her back on academia when her first book hit the bestseller list. Then when her first royalty check came in, she really did turn her back, deciding to abandon petty politics for the silence of pure research.

So what if the academics were jealous of her success? She used her research abilities and her writing talents to bring history to people who had always thought the subject dry and uninteresting. The fact that she had readers seemed to her to be a victory.

She hadn't really minded, then, when the academic press eviscerated her for writing the Carnival Sniper book. The fact that she had sold the book—and for so much money—seemed to prove to the academics that she had never been a real historian in the first place.

Sofie had been prepared for those arguments, and they didn't sting as much as they would have when she was a newly minted Ph.D. who actually believed universities were places of ideas, not politics.

What disturbed her was that other historians whom she respected took up the argument, ignoring the scholarly articles that had been published on the Sniper. He was more than a curiosity, an anomaly in the march of history.

Like England's Jack the Ripper, the Sniper presaged trends to come. Many scholars believed the Ripper was the Western world's first serial killer, starting a course that would continue until this day.

But the Carnival Sniper symbolized something greater than Jack the Ripper did. Rather than picking isolated victims, the dregs of society, the Sniper proved that all men—great and small—were possible targets.

And that wasn't all he did.

The Sniper brought attention to a killing method that had already become common. By 1913, the United States had already lost two presidents to assassination. The Austro-Hungarian Empire had lost a queen, and Greece had lost its king.

All over the world, important leaders were dying at the hands of unknowns.

What the Sniper did was equalize the killing field. He murdered famous men and unknowns—all during the same period in 1913. He wasn't killing at random, or more people would have died in the Café Central or the Mannerheim.

He had chosen his victims in advance, for perverse reasons of his own.

Some writers had tried to find reasons. In the past, writers had tried to tie the Sniper to other famous murders of the era.

Some actually claimed that the Sniper was a member of the Black Hand and, as such, trained Gavrilo Princip to shoot Archduke Franz Ferdinand. The Sniper, the argument went, was too smart to have done the killing himself, but knew that the result would lead to the destruction of the Austro-Hungarian Empire and ignite the fire that was the Great War.

Runge had addressed all of those arguments in *Death at Fasching*. He did not believe that the Sniper was involved in the Archduke's assassination because Runge had gone to Sarajevo and examined the evidence himself.

The weapons were different, Runge had concluded; the method of killing was different; and the actual assassin too young and stupid to be the Sniper.

Sofie had always assumed that last assumption to be merely that— an assumption—but once again, her incautious reading of Runge's book had led her astray.

Runge had actually seen the Sniper that last afternoon in Wein Nord. Of course, Runge would know that Princip wasn't the Carnival Sniper. Runge had known because he had seen both men.

Sofie sat at her desk and read with as much attention as she could muster. She reviewed the facts of the case, grew annoyed (yet again) that Runge withheld so much information, and this time, studied his final chapters in which he outlined why famous assassins who operated after 1913 were not the Carnival Sniper.

His arguments at the end were meticulous, his attention to detail greater than it was in the earlier sections, partly because he was dealing with cases that were closed.

But the section that caught Sofie's attention, and held it, the one she now examined word by word, was the final confrontation in Wein Nord.

Runge skipped over many facts. He mentioned that he shot the Sniper, and as a result, the Sniper dropped his gun, but Runge did not mention how the Sniper escaped.

Sofie read that section over and over again, and could not figure out what happened to the Sniper.

She got up, went to her other books, and examined the interviews that journalists had done with the surviving witnesses from the train station. The witnesses, many of whom were elderly at the time of the interviews, also could not say how the Sniper escaped, only that he managed to slip through the police's grasp at the very last minute.

The Sniper had slipped away, just like the evidence had slipped away, leaving only questions.

Johann Runge had spent the rest of his life trying to catch the Carnival Sniper. Runge had kept his commission with the Vienna Police, finally retiring in 1940 to write his book.

Fifteen years later, *Death at Fasching* became a runaway bestseller.

Fifteen years.

Sofie set her copy on her lap and leaned back in her desk chair. The chair squeaked, something she had been meaning to fix but hadn't found the time. She put her hands behind her head, and did some mental calculations.

It usually took one year from completion to publication of a book—sometimes more if the publisher felt that the book had the potential to sell well. By the early 1950s, everyone knew about the Carnival Sniper. The Germans, always fascinated with things Viennese, had made a documentary about the case.

Every January, newspapers ran retrospectives on the mysterious, unsolved shootings.

The public had been primed for *Death at Fasching* for more than a generation.

So, factor in two years to get the book ready for publication. Another year to put words on paper which, for Sofie, was the easy part. But say it was the hard part for Runge, and extend that year to three.

It still meant that he would have been writing the book from 1951 to 1954. What did he do for the first eleven years of his retirement? He had already researched the case. He knew more about it than anyone but the Sniper himself.

Or had he? Runge had worked on other cases in the meantime. He had traveled all over the world as an expert on sniper shootings and assassinations. At the requests of several governments, he investigated cases and proved that they were not tied to the Vienna case.

Runge was an expert, but he was also haunted by the Sniper shootings. They were the only blot on a long and illustrious career.

Had Runge tried to solve them one last time? Had that been his initial plan for *Death at Fasching*? And if so, then when had he decided that a solution was impossible?

Or had he decided that at all?

What was the line from the book?

For me, the case will never be closed.

Sofie thumbed through the book until she found it, at the end of Chapter 20, just after the Sniper escaped, just before Runge started his search all over the world.

She closed the book over her thumb. In the archives, she had realized that Runge had been the only author to see the evidence. He had been sixty when he left the force. In 1940, men didn't retire at sixty. They continued working for another decade.

When had Runge gotten his book contract? She thumbed back to the introduction, and frowned. Runge, according to the introduction, had sold the book after he had written it. So he hadn't retired to fulfill a contract.

What if he had stepped down from his position as chief of the detectives to devote his personal resources to solving the Sniper case?

She leaned back in her chair. The case was famous, and he hadn't solved it. Besides, he was traveling a great deal at that point, using his expertise for other police departments. Maybe he was no longer considered a day-to-day asset to the Vienna Police Department. Maybe they felt it was better to have him work on this one particular case, travel, and consult.

That would have been an enlightened attitude for the time, but Runge had been an unusual man. One that Sofie just realized she understood not at all.

She had to divide her attention in this case. In addition to her other work, she had to focus on Runge, find out what kind of man he had actually been, and figure out what he had done with those missing eleven years.

She also had to trace the evidence boxes. She hoped that somehow searching into Runge's past would help her with that.

And she had to keep her own Sniper investigation moving forward. She needed expert help understanding the bullet evidence that Kolisko had just given her. She also needed a full report from Morgan-thau on Adler.

So much to do. The upcoming eighteen months felt like they were only days long. She would need at least three months to write the book—maybe more like six. Which only gave her a year to resolve all the issues she'd found.

The bullet was something new. But she couldn't write about it—not yet, not without knowing what it meant.

Bullet, unknown origin.

Unknown origin. Somewhere, somehow, there had to be a record of all the bullet types in the world.

She would have to find that too.

Sofie curled her feet under her legs and closed her eyes. She had expected this project to be a challenge. She just hadn't expected it to be so overwhelming.

So much information, and from such varied sources. Her agent would tell her to hire a research assistant—after all, the publisher was paying.

But even if Sofie could find a way around the confidentiality concerns, she had another problem.

She hated having anyone in the middle of her life. She had always been a loner. Her friends used to joke that they'd worry about her when they hadn't heard from her in six months.

She wasn't a typical Viennese, a woman who liked to sit in coffee shops, gossip and debate the issues of the day. She liked being alone, safe with her ideas and her thoughts. Only the Sniper case wasn't as safe as she had thought.

It was taking her on detours she hadn't expected, places she hadn't prepared for, people she hadn't thought clearly about.

People like Runge.

1913

WILLIAM PALMED THE REMOTE. He had the detonation code pre-programmed into it. All he had to do was set the timer, and then the nuke would explode.

He eased the remote back into his pocket, clinging to the nuke with his right hand. The nuke was harmless without the remote. There was no way to detonate it otherwise.

He had made certain of that.

He had found another seat, this one even further back. No one seemed to notice how nervous he was or how out of place, just like no one had noticed in Krakow.

When he got home, he'd tell his colleagues about this, how they'd been wrong about so much, how it was important to actually visit the past, to see what it had been like.

To change it.

He wondered how many of them would use him as inspiration. Perhaps he would become a hero to them. Perhaps he would be seen as an innovator, someone important—not just to his present, but to history.

William leaned forward and rocked ever so slightly. How many times had he had the historian's conversation—What Might Have Been?—which evolved into What Would You Change? when MIT announced that its scientists had invented a time-travel device.

The device had seemed worthless in those days. It didn't have enough power to take anyone more than five minutes into his own past.

But years later, when William was working on his Ph.D. at Harvard, he lived off-campus with some MIT post-docs. They confided that the time-travel device had become more sophisticated. The lab had developed several types of devices, some that took the time traveler decades—not minutes—into the past.

It had taken William two more years to get his hands on one of those devices. And even more time to make the connections that got him his nuke.

He'd been doing his own post-doc by them. He'd even told his colleagues at Harvard what he planned. He had found a central event, one that fell within his device's time range, an event that would change the history of the world for the better.

Of course, when William had outlined his event, not everyone agreed with his conclusions. At first William got angry, and then he remembered: Historians always argued, and always assumed they were right.

Only he'd prove it. William would prove he was right.

A simple, clean action, and the entire bloody history of the twentieth century would vanish as if it had never been.

It would all seem like a dream, if it weren't for the clacking of the train's wheels on the track, the growing chill in the car, and the bomb, still tightly clutched in his right hand.

2005

JOHANN RUNGE'S PERSONNEL FILES were in the police archives, albeit in a different branch. Sofie had never been to the personnel section before. It was in the Sühnhaus as well, but on an upper floor in the back—tastefully redone in whites and golds, with bright lights so that the employees felt comfortable.

The personnel files took up a lot less space than the evidence boxes. One entire room, filled with floor-to-ceiling file cabinets, was all that the archives needed.

The cabinets that involved detectives who had worked for the force before 1900 were on one wall. Cabinets that went from 1900 to 1960 were on another.

The archivist told Sofie that everything was filed alphabetically in the year of the subject's retirement, and there was a master list.

Of course, Runge hadn't been on it, confirming Sofie's suspicion.

The man had never retired.

So when Sofie mentioned that to the archivist, the woman took Sofie to a different room. It was older, danker, and hadn't been remodeled. The cabinets there were made of expensive wood, but covered with dust.

The archivist left Sofie alone to read. Any copies she wanted made had to be approved through official channels, but the archivist didn't mind if Sofie made notes.

"Even if I quote those notes in a book?" Sofie asked, making certain she understood the boundaries.

"That's fine," the archivist said, "so long as your quotes are accurate."

If Sofie's quotes weren't accurate, she knew from that comment, then the police department would sue.

These files were considered open, even if the subject had died. They were, Sofie soon realized, files for difficult officers, personnel troubles, and non-standard employees.

Probably somewhere in this room were files on officers still with the force. But Sofie wasn't interested in those. Only in Johann Runge. The archivist had pulled all the files relating to him, then pointed to a camera mounted on the ceiling.

"You're not to look at other files without my permission," the archivist said. "You're on your own, but we do monitor the room and keep the tapes. If you publish material pertaining to another officer, we will use the tape to show that you've violated your agreement with us. Is that clear?"

"Very." Sofie paid attention, even though she knew that the regulations wouldn't apply to her. She didn't like to get blindsided by rules she had only pretended to understand.

Then the archivist left Sofie alone with Runge's personnel file.

It was a revelation. The early material was written by hand, in dark ink. Runge's résumé—he was a university graduate, rare for police at the time—his initial write-ups, and his hiring report were all there.

From the beginning, he had been slated for detective work. The officer who hired Runge had believed that the man's obvious intelligence plus his love of detail would take him far in the job.

It had. But Runge's rise had come with a lot of struggle.

His co-workers resented him, feeling that he was arrogant and uncompromising. He was also contradictory—telling someone to perform one task, then assigning him another without canceling the first.

But those complaints seemed common enough to Sofie. The ones that interested her were the ones about crime scenes.

Apparently Runge was a terror at them. He had a procedure that he insisted upon, and anyone who violated that procedure faced his wrath.

It took Sofie a while to find the procedure in the file. The list, carefully typed, dated from 1911. It presaged current crime scene procedures—forcing police to be careful of the evidence, allowing only one or two officers inside a scene, closing the scene to the public, and making certain that the scene was photographed in great detail.

A lot of now-standard procedures were missing—such as wearing gloves to handle evidence, the idea that shoes and garments could pick up trace so that a scene had to be worked with precision—but those discoveries would come.

Sofie was actually surprised that Runge had taken his procedure list as far as he had. No wonder the other police officers at the scene resented him. At the time of these procedures, Runge was just a detective—and the procedure list itself merely typed up as suggestions for the squad.

But Runge apparently acted as if the procedures were written in stone. The procedures did allow him to close more cases than the other detectives on the force at the time, but they also made him the least liked detective in Vienna.

Some of the complaints in the file hinted that Runge's attitude actually made people work less hard for him. Runge's response, also recorded, was that other people didn't matter: He solved his own cases, and generally did a better job when he was alone.

That comment made Sofie sit back and smile. She had made similar statements herself. She might have liked Runge—provided she agreed with him. She had a hunch he was a formidable political enemy; after all, he survived on the force when a lot of the complainants (as Runge noted in yet another response to accusations) hadn't.

Apparently Runge was at the peak of his powers during the Sniper investigation—and at the peak of departmental hatred. A notation in the file from the chief detective stated the detective's hope that Runge's failure would take the arrogance out of him.

But it didn't. And Runge's fame only grew, supplemented by his desire to become an expert on snipers and assassins. He went to Sarajevo and helped locate Princip's accomplices, including the mysterious Apis whom Princip had said inspired him.

Runge also worked on the Stürgkh murder case, leading Runge to one of his life's many ironies: He arrested Friedrich Adler, Viktor Adler's son, as the murderer.

Runge had worked hard during the war, mostly on local cases. It was only after Europe settled into the quiet that it held from 1925 on that Runge became an international expert on snipers and assassins.

Sofie read the files with interest, discovering that Runge's life was complicated and fascinating. She found it amazing that he hadn't become more of a subject; amazing he was so often vilified for his one major failure as a detective.

By the time she finished the files, she understood how Runge's reputation had gotten tarnished. He became more difficult to work with over time, not less. Even though he was promoted to chief detective in 1931, the promotion had not been a political move. He had lobbied for it so that he could instate his procedures throughout the department, procedures that encompassed most of the existing forensic knowledge at the time.

Runge had not acted like a chief detective, either. He still took cases—often the plum cases—and toward the end of his tenure, traveled more than he worked in Vienna. His assistant, a man named Preeze, became the acting chief, and often detectives when to Preeze even when Runge was in town.

In 1940, Runge's lack of political savvy brought the department to a crisis. Detectives walked off the job, followed by other police officers at all ranks. The demands were simple: fire Runge, and bring in someone who actually understood police work.

The demands made Runge angry—they made Sofie angry, just reading them. But of course, she had the value of hindsight, knowing that the changes Runge was trying to instate in the department would become *de rigueur* in twenty more years.

Runge refused to give in. Then the chief of Vienna's police force called Runge into his office. Times had changed. Vienna's police had multiple duties—not just local duties, but also federal duties, reflecting Vienna's post-war status as a city-state.

The chief, with the power of the state and the city behind him, told Runge that he either had to step down from his position as chief of detectives or be very publicly fired. Runge, not intimidated by his boss, argued for nearly an hour.

Finally the two of them came to an agreement. Runge would step down, become a detective-at-large who consulted on various cases, but did not come into the office, in exchange for keeping his salary for as long as he chose to work for the department. A notation showed that Runge would also get his pension, even if he were still drawing a salary, starting at age seventy-five.

The files did not list which cases Runge consulted on nor were there any notations about Runge, other than a stop-salary form filed after Runge's death in 1960.

Sofie closed the file. She would have to get permission to copy it. The file, like the bullet, contained information never before presented in the Sniper case. And, like the bullet, the file raised more questions than answers.

Runge had not receive a reprimand for losing the Sniper in Wein Nord, as some claimed. Nor was there any analysis of Runge's supposedly controversial behavior of the case.

Sofie was certain after reading this that Runge's colleagues, most of whom had hated him, had spread the incompetency rumor when *Death at Fasching* came out. Since a lot of those colleagues were younger than Runge, they out-lived him, as did the incompetency story.

But the reason Sofie had come to the file—to find out what Runge had done from 1940 to 1951—was nowhere inside. She would have to do more digging.

She did take copious notes, actually copying several documents meticulously by hand, in case she wouldn't get the permission she wanted to photocopy the file. She also took down Runge's last known address, and the names of his wife and children.

The children would be old now—in their late eighties and early nineties—but they might still be alive. It would be intriguing to discover what they remembered about their father, his take on the Sniper case, and the book, *Death at Fasching*.

It took Sofie most of the day to go through Runge's personnel file. She forgot to eat lunch. She bought a bottle of water and a candy bar in the vending machines outside the police museum, sat on a bench, and ate them quickly, before going back to the evidence archive.

She spent the next hour looking through the evidence logs, covering each line meticulously, looking for familiar names or any reference to the Sniper case—either by name or case number.

And there she finally struck gold: A notation that had meant nothing to her six months before had new meaning after that morning's research.

The last person to view the Sniper evidence files had been Johann Runge—on the day he agreed to step down as chief detective.

1913

JOHANN RUNGE HAD BEEN going over the crime scene at the Café Central when someone finally thought to summon him to the scene of the Sigmund Freud murder.

Runge, for a brief moment, had rocked back on his heels and stared at the body before him. He had assumed that Viktor Adler had been shot for his membership in the Social Democratic Party.

Now Runge had to assume that the link between these murders was psychoanalysis itself.

Before Runge left the Café, he had dispatched another police officer to the Insane Asylum at Steinhof. Perhaps an inmate had escaped, gotten a gun, and was somehow seeking revenge on his doctors.

Runge had been inside that place more than once. If he had escaped from there, he would have gone after anyone responsible for imprisoning him in that place. It was a wretched, frightening spot that smelled of feces, urine, and human fear.

It took him only a few minutes to reach the crime scene at Berggasse. As he ran, he realized it would only have taken the killer a few minutes to traverse this distance as well.

They might even have passed each other—Runge on his way to the Café Central, the killer on the way to Berggasse.

Runge shuddered, then forced himself to concentrate on the scene before him.

People crowded in a semi-circle around the doorway to a white building. The crowd was unusually silent, so silent that Runge could hear a woman sobbing as if her heart would break.

He pushed his way through, excusing himself, and stopped at the edge of the circle. Several police officers ringed the inside, staring at the doorway as if they didn't know what to do. Runge looked too.

An elderly man leaned against the building, eyes closed, face slack in death. A streak of blood ran down the door, and more blood had sprayed on the white brick that formed the archway. A large pool of blood had gathered on the sidewalk around the dead man's legs.

Runge had seen the famous Doctor Freud a few times, but had never seen the old man without his hat. Freud's white hair was thinning, and his pink scalp, visible through the strands, made him seem even more fragile.

Runge approached the body, careful not to step in the blood. He crouched and started to search Freud's suit coat for his papers, to make certain that the dead man was indeed who he said he was.

The moment Runge touched the body, someone pushed him aside. He looked up to find a young woman, her hair in disarray around her narrow face, looking at him in anger.

"Don't touch him," she said.

Runge held up his hands, and realized a moment too late that they were dotted with Adler's dried blood. "I'm a police officer, miss."

"Leave him alone," she said again. "You don't have the right to touch him."

"Miss, it's my job—"

"Don't touch him!" she screamed, and another woman, older, her face haggard, pulled the younger one away.

The crowd whispered, and he caught the words *daughter* and *poor thing*. The young woman started to sob, and Runge realized that it had been her cries he had heard as he approached the scene.

The girl was devastated.

"What happened here?" he asked a police officer near the edge of the crowd.

"Couldn't get much out of the girl, sir," the police officer said. "She said the street was deserted, then a man in a black overcoat appeared and shot her father before walking away down the street."

"As if he didn't care," the man next to the officer said. "Anna said that the man seemed like he didn't care."

Insane, Runge thought, and shuddered. The air had grown colder, despite the bodies pushing forward. *Only an insane man would walk away from the scene of a shooting as if he didn't care.*

"Did anyone chase this man?" he asked.

"The young lady was alone with her father," the police officer said. "She was tending him, and begging for help. When it arrived, a few men hurried after the shooter, but it was too late."

Much too late. Freud was dead, and the killer was gone.

Runge would have to send officers to the homes and businesses of all the famous psychoanalysts in town. Which would deplete the numbers of men on the street, but he saw no choice.

One way or another, he had to prevent the killer from killing again.

2005

THREE DAYS AFTER HER EPIPHANY in the archive, Sofie found herself walking down a tree-lined street on the opposite side of the Ring from her apartment. Here the homes were stately and old. They didn't stand alone the way houses did farther out of the city, but had linked walls with individual entries.

The British called them row houses, but Vienna's version was too elegant for that name—the stately white brick, the well-manicured boulevard, the very proper courtyard shared by all in the back.

Sofie couldn't believe that Johann Runge had bought his home on this block with a policeman's salary, but he had, back in 1927. Perhaps the extra money had come from his consulting work. She didn't want to think that it had come from somewhere else.

She smiled at herself. Two months ago, she had been willing to believe that Johann Runge was an incompetent man who had let the Carnival Sniper escape. Then, she would have considered the theory that he had taken bribes. Now, after a week of intensive research, she identified with Runge; she didn't want to learn that he had done anything bad.

Historians called that Biographer's Syndrome—the tendency for someone to get so involved in their subject that the subject became as close to them as a friend or, worse, became an extension of themselves.

Sofie hadn't gotten that bad yet—she knew that Runge had his flaws—but she saw the tendency, and worked to shake it off.

She would have to investigate his finances as well, and all the legends about him. The amount of work that this side trip was giving her was beginning to make her wish for the days when all she had to worry about was researching the lives of little-known men like Lev Bronstein.

Some of her reports had come in. The DNA lab in Switzerland confirmed that the remains in Viktor Adler's grave were, in fact, Viktor Adler, putting to rest at least one conspiracy theory.

That report had pleased Sofie, and she had locked it in her safe immediately. One more new thing for her book. She still needed others.

Karl Morganthau's report also came in. The report was a treat—an in-depth analysis of the bones, clothing, and partial remains, as well as the trace evidence found in the coffin itself. Morganthau, bless him, had devoted two whole pages to the bullet and its removal. If anyone questioned the authenticity of that bullet given its unusual materials, they would have to go after not only Sofie, but the well-respected Karl Morganthau as well.

Kolisko's preliminary report on the bullet had shown up the night before. It was clearer than the phone conversation Sofie had had with Kolisko, but not by much. The report was mostly filled with promises: Kolisko would track the bullet; his chemist would figure out what the coating was made of; they would figure out what that type of bullet was intended for, since it clearly wasn't standard.

The only interesting part of that report was the section that dovetailed with Morganthau's. Kolisko had mentioned in passing that he didn't know how effective the bullet would be for a sniper, considering that the extra-hard core meant that the bullet would most likely go *through* its victim rather than lodge inside.

Which meant, in Kolisko's words, that the bullet would wound before it would kill.

Morganthau's report cited the unusual number of bullet holes in Adler's skeleton. Morganthau said he had never seen so many clean penetrations of bone, not from a single weapon, and not in a highly explosive situation.

Morganthau guessed that Adler had died from the preponderance of wounds, rather than from a single wound.

That corresponded with the eyewitness accounts of Adler's death. Adler had charged the Sniper, attempting, apparently, to disarm the man, or stop the man from shooting Bronstein.

The Sniper, according to the witnesses, had looked frightened, and had shot at Adler repeatedly, until Adler had finally collapsed.

The bullets pulled from the walls of the Café Central, then, had probably gone through Adler before they penetrated the plaster and lathe.

Sofie shuddered. What an awful day that must have been. She could imagine it too easily—all the regular customers of Café Central suddenly hitting the ground, trying to avoid being shot by what the press and police initially thought was a random crazy man.

She remembered the feelings, the dizziness, the way that the world seemed like it had tilted and become an unrecognizable place.

It had happened to her.

She had only been five, walking hand-in-hand with her mother through Palace Park. They had gone to a wild part, near water. She had a vague memory of trees and gleaming water, but no memory of the bathhouse or any of the other buildings hidden along the paths. Sofie couldn't even remember why her family had come to the park that day, if there was a party or if they were just going to enjoy a day in the sunshine.

In fact, Sofie's memory started with the gunshots. She had thought they were firecrackers. She had laughed and clapped, and then her mother grabbed her and shoved her underneath a green bench, telling her not to move, never to move, no matter what she saw or heard.

Her mother called to Sofie's father. Sofie had peered out from under the bench, seen him turn with a smile on his face, and watched him fall forward as a hail of bullets had hit him in the back.

Her mother had run to him. If she hadn't, the police later said, she might have lived. But she had run, screaming his name, and the bullets hit her, too.

Sofie buried her face in the gravel, putting her hands over her head. The shouts and sobs all around her, the sound of bodies thudding against the ground, and the gunshots, like firecrackers, coming from everywhere and nowhere seemed to go on forever.

She thought she had died. She wished she had died. But she hadn't. She lay there for hours, until the police found her, soaked in the blood of nearby victims.

She had pressed her face against the ground so hard that gravel had embedded in her cheek. At first, the police ignored her, thinking she was dead. And then she moved, ever so slightly, and they realized they had a survivor.

Oh, yes. She knew how it felt to have the world change in an instant, to find herself in a life-and-death situation, all because of a single shooter with a powerful gun.

Sofie stopped and made herself take a deep breath. The memory of her parents' death wasn't usually so close to the surface. But it was no surprise.

Her parents might still be alive if the Carnival Sniper hadn't become so famous. Some other sniper, that person who had entered Munich's Palace Park, climbed to the top of the Badenburg bathhouse, and picked off the happy people he had seen around him, shooting at them until no one alive remained in his view scope, and then, somehow, had gotten away—the police said he had probably taken the Carnival Sniper as his model.

They all did, the police had told Sofie's grandfather. *We've had so many snipers since that one in Vienna. We're not sure how to fight them.*

And that, she knew, was the connection. If she couldn't find her parents' killer—and she couldn't; no one could—then she would find the other person responsible. The Carnival Sniper. She would end the mystery of his identity and take away his power once and for all.

Sofie made herself look at the neighborhood around her—the tall trees, the beautiful homes. She was in Vienna now, not Munich. And she was an adult, not a child. An adult who studied snipers, hoping to find one and finally understand him.

She kept walking until she reached the corner townhouse at the end of the block. The house seemed no different from the others. It had no extra land, since it was flanked on its side by another sidewalk and boulevard. Still, the building was beautiful, and beautifully kept up.

Sofie had used her publisher to find out where the Runge heirs lived. She figured it would be easier for someone from SPPW to call Mayer Verlag in Berlin—the current publisher of *Death at Fasching*—to find out how to contact the heirs of the Runge estate. Let Mayer Verlag think that SPPW was trying to poach on their cash cow; it would keep Sofie's inquiries down, and make her research harder to trace.

A curtain moved in an upstairs window. Someone had noticed Sofie standing on the sidewalk outside the house.

She sighed. Time to make the contact.

She was nervous about this, more nervous than she had expected to be. She had no idea how Runge's heirs would receive her. They hadn't contacted her when news of her book contract broke, although some of the heirs of the victims had, hoping to split compensation.

The Runges didn't need compensation. The sales of *Death at Fasching* last year alone ran into the hundreds of thousands worldwide.

She climbed the brick steps and grabbed the old-fashioned brass door knocker. She pounded three times, hard, then stood back, and waited.

For a moment, she thought she had imagined the curtain movement. Then she heard a lock turn, and the door opened barely enough to reveal a black-fringed blue eye, a well-arched brow, and a wavy lock of black hair over a pale forehead.

"What?" The voice was male, unusually deep, and decidedly unfriendly.

Sofie made herself smile. "Hi," she said with as much warmth as she could muster. "I'm Sofie Branstadter. I'm looking for the heirs of Johann Runge."

"So you can offer them a share in the profits of your scandal-mongering book?" The voice seemed even chillier. The eye kept staring at her, making her feel very uncomfortable.

She had to work to keep the smile on her face. "I'm sure that'll be part of the discussion. Would you like to have it on the stoop for all the neighbors to hear?"

The door opened wider, revealing a wood-paneled entry. The owner of the voice receded in the unlit darkness, probably trying to unnerve Sofie.

So far, he was doing a good job.

Still she nodded at him, thanked him, and stepped inside.

The house smelled faintly of lemon polish and baked bread. Around the corner from the entry was the main room. It had no furniture except a grand piano, with its lid up and propped.

The piano looked like it was used. Music was scattered along the floor around it, on the bench, and on the windowsills behind.

Bookshelves lined the only wall without windows. One shelf contained piles of music books, but the others had thick volumes, some of which she recognized from her own shelves.

The door closed behind her.

"This way," the man said.

He was tall and slender. He wore a clean white T-shirt and blue jeans. His feet were bare and his hair was still damp on the sides. He smelled faintly of soap.

Up close, his angular face had a strength that she hadn't expected. In it, she saw a slight resemblance to Johann Runge—probably in the heavily lashed eyes, filled with intelligence.

"I take it," she said, "you're one of the Runge heirs."

"I am *the* Runge heir," he said. "My name is Anton, but I suppose you already know that."

She hadn't, actually, although she probably could have gotten that information through her publisher if she had insisted. Anton Runge was a familiar name, and it took her a moment to place it outside of the context of the Carnival Sniper project.

Anton Runge had won the Chopin Competition fifteen years before, and became, in the eyes of the press and the music world, Vienna's newest and most important pianist, someone who would rival the great performers of the nineteenth century in his brilliance.

Of course he hadn't. Like so many competition winners, he had made a few albums, then vanished.

"You're the musician," she said, and then felt her cheeks heat. That he was a musician was obvious from the piano.

Her question seemed to make him even tenser. "I dabble sometimes."

"That's not what I meant," she said. "I have some of your albums. I've been waiting for the next, but it seems late in appearing."

His frown grew deeper. She felt her face grow even warmer. She didn't know how to get out of this verbal tangle.

"After the Chopin," she said, "it seemed like you were going to have a solo career—"

"So you did check up on me." His blue eyes seemed even colder. "You don't have to flatter me to get information from me, Miss Branstadter."

"I'm not—I didn't—oh, hell." Sofie shook her head. This was why she dealt in books and old papers and people long dead, so that she wouldn't have to talk to the living. "Can we start over?"

"Sure," he said. "Do you want to go back outside and ring the bell again?"

She looked down. It took all of her strength to speak.

"I had no idea who you were," she said. "I got the address of the Runge heirs from my publishers. They apparently got it from Mayer Verlag, who gave them this address. I had no idea that Anton Runge the pianist was Johann Runge's grandson—"

"Great-grandson," he said.

"—until just a few minutes ago." She looked up. "I didn't mean to offend. Really."

"What did you expect?" he asked. "The heirs of Johann Runge, the much-maligned man who let the Carnival Sniper go free, to welcome you with open arms?"

Sofie shook her head. "No. I didn't expect that either. I just want to talk to you."

"I don't know why," Runge said. "I wasn't even born when my great-grandfather died."

"But perhaps your father—?"

"My father died three years ago."

"I'm sorry." Sofie glanced at the door. She had handled this introduction poorly. She had no idea how to begin again, or even if she could approach Runge in the way that she wanted to.

He had his arms crossed, revealing corded muscles. Of course he had strong arms, from all that piano playing. His hands were probably strong as well, his fingers powerful.

"Look," she said, knowing that her face had to be the color of a ripe tomato. "I've been doing a lot of research, and I think your great-grandfather is a key to this case."

"You and the rest of the world," Runge said.

"No," Sofie said. "Not because he screwed up. He didn't. We know all we know about the Sniper because of Johann Runge. It's just—I think he was holding back a lot of information."

Runge's eyebrows went up. "So, you can read. Bravo. Considering he mentioned that he wasn't telling all in his book."

Sofie shook her head. She had to look down again. Her eyes were burning, and she blinked hard, feeling unwanted moisture.

She was so bad with people. She had no idea why she had even put herself in this spot. She should have written a letter, or telephoned first, or maybe figured out some other way.

"I'm sorry," she said, taking a step back toward the door. "I didn't mean to offend you. Really. I just thought—well, it doesn't matter. I'm so sorry."

She pulled the door open and escaped outside. Her cheeks were on fire. She walked down the steps, making herself use the sidewalk and not run, knowing that part of her reaction was an old one.

It had taken her nearly three years to learn to trust people after her parents died. Finally, when her grandparents sent her to school, years later than the other children, she had often come home in tears.

She had had so many problems then that simply couldn't be hidden. She had to sit with her back to a wall. She had to see all the people in the room at all times.

And she hadn't wanted to talk to anyone, not even the teachers, not even to answer questions.

If it hadn't been for Miss Halder, who realized that Sofie was extremely bright underneath all her fears, Sofie would never have made it through those first years of school. Miss Halder had let Sofie read and then answer questions on paper rather than aloud. Miss Halder had tutored Sofie, not just in the mathematics she had missed, but also in basic social etiquette—survival skills for a crowded world.

Sofie stopped on the sidewalk. Usually she managed to avoid moments like that. She rarely went into a situation where she didn't know someone—or if she did go into that situation, she had already run through various scenarios in her mind.

She had planned on a hostile reaction from the Runge heirs. She just hadn't expected to know of one of them, to enjoy his music.

To respect him.

She put her hands to her cheeks. They were still hot. Her own fault. She should have been more prepared. She shouldn't have let her surprise at his profession blindside her.

Or his mockery sink in, past her defenses.

But she had, and worse, she had set herself up for it. She would go home, go through her research and figure out another way, one without Anton Runge's assistance.

And if she discovered that she needed something from him, she might get someone else to approach him. Someone tougher. Someone used to making demands.

She had friends like that. Even her agent might assist.

Now she knew what she was up against. She wouldn't be blind-sided again.

2005

ANTON RUNGE STARED at his closed door. He ran a hand through his thick hair, still damp from his shower, and shook his head.

What had he been thinking? He was never that deliberately rude. Or cruel. He had actually been cruel.

He knew better than that. Unnecessary cruelty was one of the many reasons he had stopped being a solo performing artist. The competition among musicians was so fierce that most of them tried to get ahead by bringing someone else down. It got worse at the competition level, and unbearable at the international level. All the others, the ones who hadn't succeeded, did whatever they could to make the successful performer feel small.

Anton had vowed that he would never do that—not again. For a while, he had been sucked into the horrible misanthropic lifestyle, and then he had realized he didn't need it. He couldn't be that person.

But he had just resurrected that person in front of Sofie Branstadter.

He supposed it wasn't a surprise. He had resented her from the moment he had heard she was writing a book on the Sniper. He hated the sensational treatment the case got, usually because it had consequences for him as well.

Reporters at the door, people wanting interviews—not about Anton or his music—but about the one failure that his family was known for, committed by a man he had never even met.

But that wasn't Sofie Branstadter's fault. She was the first of all the authors, all the documentarians, all the so-called Sniper experts, to ever approach him for an interview. Not a reaction to the recently published book, but actually wanting to talk to him about his great-grandfather.

We know all we know about the Sniper because of Johann Runge, she had said. And she had said it with respect.

Anton sighed. He peered through the vertical window beside the door.

She was standing where his walk met the city sidewalk, holding her cheeks. They had turned the brightest red Anton had ever seen.

He hadn't expected that from her. He hadn't expected to fluster her or upset her.

He hadn't expected her to be shy.

She certainly hadn't been on television, when she was being interviewed about the book after she had gotten that ungodly contract. There she had looked poised and brilliant, her eyes glittering, her expression smug.

Maybe she hadn't been smug. Maybe she had been nervous.

Just like she had been in his entry.

"Oh, hell," he muttered and pulled the door open.

At the sound, her hands fell from her cheeks and she turned left on the main sidewalk, as if she hadn't stopped at all.

"Miss Branstadter," he said.

She stopped, but didn't look at him. She was a tiny thing, but she did have poise.

Then he realized she could see him out of the corner of her eye. His grandfather used to use that trick—a way of seeming to look in one direction but actually watching something to the side. He used to say it was a policeman's way of staying out of danger.

Anton wondered where the intellectual Sofie Branstadter had learned it.

"I was rude," he said, "and there was no call for it. Can we take your suggestion and start over? You won't even have to knock on the door a second time."

Her entire body stiffened. She was thin, the kind of thin that came from too few meals rather than from too much exercise.

"I promise I'll be on my best behavior," he said.

This time, she looked at him, and he registered surprise in those dark eyes of hers. Surprise and wariness, like a wild animal that smelled food but suspected a trap.

"It's all right," she said. "My office can contact you. I shouldn't have bothered you."

"Well, you did bother me, and then I bothered me," he said, with as much self-deprecation as he could manage. "And then I realized that I'm curious about your visit. So come on in. I have some coffee and I haven't had breakfast yet, so there's still some pastries in the kitchen. Let's talk."

For a moment, he thought she'd say no. Then she smiled at him. The expression made her seem much younger.

"All right," she said, and walked back to the house.

1913

THE ASSASSIN HAD DOUBLED BACK and was now heading toward the Danube Canal. He had managed to avoid the Ring, but he was following streets so changed that he barely knew where he was.

Red Vienna hadn't been built yet. The buildings built for workers after World War I, when Vienna had been Socialist, had altered the face of the city. The assassin should have been able to see some of the larger, more famous ones in the distance as he headed toward the canal, but he didn't. Instead, he saw smaller buildings that leaned against each other as if they were exhausted.

He was exhausted, and hungry. His nausea was gone, replaced by a feeling of emptiness.

He shivered and pulled his coat closer. Two shootings had to put the entire city on alert, even in this day before mass media. The police had to be looking for a solitary man in a black overcoat, carrying a gun.

Fortunately the gun wasn't easy to see, and there were a hundred solitary men in black overcoats at any given time on the streets in Vienna. The assassin had to stop moving, had to find a place to spend the evening, maybe even the night.

The searching would slow, perhaps stop, and he would be able to continue with his plan. No one would look for him near the Mannerheim. No one would think that any person, living in what passed for public housing in Vienna at this time, would be in danger from an assassin.

They would search for him near the cafés and the apartments for the wealthy, the famous, and the middle class. They would try to find logic in the two shooting incidents, and when they realized there was none, they would make something up.

He hoped that would protect him, at least for the next twenty-four hours. It had to.

He had to finish what he started.

2005

ALL THE WAY UP THE SIDEWALK, Sofie berated herself. Anton Runge had made her feel small and foolish just moments before, and now she was going back for more of the same.

But at least this time, she was prepared, and she did have her questions to ask. Perhaps now he would answer them.

Even if he didn't, she might get a sense of how the family felt about Johann Runge.

This time, Anton held the door open for her like a butler. She had a fleeting fear that he might bow, but he didn't. Instead, he smiled at her, and his smile was devastating.

That was something she hadn't wanted to see.

The kitchen was through the door at the end of the entryway. The room was yellow, with eastern light that made it seem even brighter, and very warm. The smell of coffee hadn't permeated the rest of the house, but it lingered here, as if the walls had absorbed it long ago.

Anton wasn't kidding about the pastries, either. It looked like he had purchased an entire bakery full of them.

Sofie gave him a sideways glance when she saw them. He shrugged.

"My favorite vice," he said. "I run every day to make sure I don't end up like my mother's family—three hundred pounds of very happy Germans."

Sofie felt her smile widening. She didn't want to like him, not after the sharp, bitter side of him she had seen a few moments ago, but she did. She even understood where his bitterness came from, which was probably one of the reasons she had retreated.

"You look like you need a pastry," he said. "Take one. You won't rob me of anything."

She approached the counter as if it held gold. Tortes sat in the back, covered with crème and powdered sugar. They had to be for later. Up front, she saw croissants, several types of kuchen, and some small crumb cakes, which looked oddly out of place.

She took a slice of apple kuchen, set it on a nearby napkin, and carried it to table. Anton opened one of the tall cupboards, stood on his toes, and removed a plate. He rinsed the plate off, dried it, and set it in front of her.

"I'm usually alone, so I'm not very formal," he said.

Neither was she.

"How do you take your coffee?" he asked.

He was working very hard to charm her, where moments ago he had tried to alienate her. She felt off-balance.

"It's espresso," he added.

"With sweet cream," she said, just like she would at a café. Then she felt her cheeks heat again. Most people didn't keep sweet cream around unless they favored it themselves.

He opened the refrigerator, took out some cream and dolloped it into a cup. Then he poured the espresso over it, giving her the cup and a spoon to stir it up. But the liquid was already light brown. His method worked very well.

He made himself the same drink, took two crumb cakes, and sat across from her.

"All right," he said, "since we're starting over, to what do I owe this visit?"

Her flush deepened. She felt like she had when she was a teenager, forever embarrassed simply by having someone pay attention to her.

"I…." She bit her lower lip, looked down, and willed the flush to disappear. It wouldn't—she knew that from long and painful experience—

so she took a deep breath, and forced herself to go on. "I have been doing a lot of research, and I found some things that are pretty unusual. I think your grandfather—great-grandfather—found them too, but he never said anything about them, at least that I can find. So I was wondering if there's any family lore about them or about him, something that might shed some light on things."

She was taking a risk bringing this to Anton Runge, and the risk felt even greater after their initial encounter. But she had evaluated the situation before she came to Anton's house, and knew that the risk was necessary.

Besides, if he went to the press with some of the things she brought to him, she might gain a benefit from it. Because of the Runge name, some other details might come out of the woodwork, from other people who didn't even know they had important information.

"What kind of things?" Anton asked.

He sat across from her and took a large bite from one of the crumb cakes.

It was a trade, and she knew it. He had trusted her enough to let her in the house. Now she had to trust him with important information.

"In the police reports," she said, "he has an evidence list. There are items on it that I'm not clear about. At first, I thought he wasn't either, but now I'm not so sure."

"You read the police reports?" Anton asked.

She nodded.

"Maybe you are going to take this more seriously than some of the others have." Then he got an exasperated look on his face. "Sorry. You have no idea what it's like to be the only surviving member of a family that's supposed to specialize in the crime of the century. No one even cares that it's the last century."

His words sent a chill through her. She had been the only surviving member of her family for a long time.

She cleared her throat, forcing the past aside. "I am taking this seriously. My training is as a historian. I think the Carnival Sniper shootings have larger import than just their impact on Vienna. Just because it became a media event doesn't mean it lacks historical value."

Now she sounded defensive. She hadn't meant to.

Anton set his crumb cake down. He studied her. She had a sense nothing got past those long-lashed eyes.

"My turn to be nosy," he said. "I've seen your books. They're usually about real things, right? Like that first one on the Franco-Prussian War."

"The Sniper was real," Sofie said.

He shook his head. "That's not what I mean. You take something we all studied in school, like the war, and make it interesting. We get our history and our entertainment all in one dose. Like showing people the impact of the Great War on the twentieth century's various art forms—how it wasn't just the light that made the south of France the center of the cinematic world, but the fact that the artists had flocked there after the Great War ended. And sometimes you take an angle, like the women book—"

"*Vienna's Women*," Sofie said, surprised that he knew her work.

"—and make us understand what our teachers left out. Kind of a way of making history live. So I don't get the Sniper. It feels like you're selling out."

Was selling out something that he feared? Was that why he stopped being a solo pianist?

"The Sniper has interested me from the moment I found your father's book," Sofie said. "I think I was fourteen. I became a historian because of the Sniper. I wanted to know everything I could. So the other books were just training for this one. I had to make certain I was ready to write it before I even started."

She had never been that honest with anyone, certainly not someone she had just met. She had a giddy, airless feeling, and then she realized that she had been holding her breath.

She exhaled, swallowed, and tried to hide her nervousness by taking a sip of coffee.

"The Sniper," he said. "As a historian would look at him."

"More than that." Sofie set her cup down. "I want to see if modern police techniques can find him, can figure out who he was. I think your great-grandfather was close—"

"Hell, he touched the man," Anton said.

Sofie looked at him.

"Didn't know that, huh?" Anton said. "That's right. It's not in the book."

"There are a lot of things not in the book," Sofie said, "and a lot not in the police report."

"And you want to know what my great-grandfather was hiding," Anton said dryly.

Sofie shook her head. "I don't think he was deliberately hiding anything, at least not in the police report, not that I could tell. The book is different. He was honest about hiding information in that. I think he believed he would eventually solve this case, and all would come out. But he didn't solve it, did he?"

"To my family's eternal consternation, no," Anton said.

Sofie sighed. She looked down at the kuchen. "May I have a fork?"

Anton smiled, and shook his head. "I try to be polite and fail even at that."

He stood, opened a drawer, and pulled out a gleaming fork, handing it to Sofie. She used it to cut a small piece of kuchen. Her stomach growled. All she'd had for breakfast was an apple. She had been too nervous to eat.

Strange that she was not nervous now.

"I am curious," she said, pausing before eating the small piece she cut. "From 1940, after your great-grandfather stepped down from the force, to 1951, I can't find any trace of what he did. Do you know?"

Anton raised his eyebrows. "You're tracking my great-grandfather?"

"As I said, I think he was on to something."

"You sound like my father." Anton sipped his coffee. "My father always defended the old man."

"Against whom?" Sofie asked.

"My grandfather. He hated Johann Runge, said the man never paid attention to his family, was always running somewhere being important, when really all he did was prove how inadequate he was yet again."

Very bitter words. Sofie ate that bite of kuchen so she could think about them. The cake was spongy, the apples covered with a sweet mixture of sugar and cinnamon.

"I don't think he was inadequate," Sofie said as she cut another piece. "He solved a lot of cases, helped some foreign governments with high-profile assassins, and became a well-known man in his own right. It's only after he retired that his reputation suffered."

"His reputation suffered because he was an arrogant son-of-a-bitch who cared about no one but himself." Anton drained his coffee cup, stood up, and poured himself some more.

"You sound like you know him."

"That was my father's opinion, and my father *liked* him."

Sofie's breath caught. She had gleaned that from the personnel file, but it was nice to have familial confirmation.

"Did you know he was so successful?" she asked gently.

Anton shook his head. "Material success wasn't what mattered in this family. My great-grandfather's absence and his obsession with the Carnival Sniper—that was all that mattered."

"Even after his book did so well?" Sofie asked.

"Filthy lucre, from a project that my grandfather hated." Anton came back to the table, straddled his chair and sat down. "After my great-grandfather died, my grandfather refused to touch the money. He put the royalties in a trust for his children, and my father did the same for his. Both of them had only one child, so it's all come down to me."

"And you have maintained the trust?" Sofie asked.

"Hell, no. I don't have children." Anton sipped. "Besides, despite our earlier conversation, I'm not nearly as caught up in the whole family drama as my father and grandfather were. I didn't know the old bastard, so my grudge is merely second-hand. Or third-hand. And it's an inconvenience. I always wanted to focus on my music. Interviews always wanted to focus on Johann Runge's failure."

Sofie nodded. She wasn't going to go near the topic of Anton's career again. For all she could tell, that was the thing that had set him off in the first place.

Anton leaned back in his chair. "You think you have me figured out now, don't you? Tortured artist who gave it all up because he didn't get the attention he needed?"

Sofie shook her head. "I learned long ago not to make assumptions."

"Well, to answer your earlier question from the conversation we're pretending we didn't have, I stopped performing because I hated it. All of it, right down to the stage fright." He wiped his hands on his jeans, as if just the memories made his palms sweat. "I had the worst stage fright of any of my peers. My tutors all said it made me perform better, but I was miserable. And not sleeping, not eating, always too stressed. So I gave it up."

She didn't know how to respond to that.

He stood and walked over to the counter. "Another pastry?"

He hadn't finished his crumb cakes, and she hadn't finished her kuchen. But they both knew that he hadn't left the table because of that.

Sofie moved the conversation back to Johann Runge.

"So," she said. "Those missing years. Do you know anything about them?"

Anton shook his head. He was still looking at the pastries, his long fingers hovering over a croissant. After a moment, he came back to the table without taking any food at all.

"My grandfather didn't talk much about his father. My father only knew the old man, and spent most of his time defending him. I think it was pretty classic. They say affinities skip a generation—that grandparents and grandchildren always get along better than parents and children."

Sofie had heard that before too, but she had no idea if it were true. Her paternal grandparents had taken her in only briefly, unable to deal with her every day. Then they gave her to her maternal grandparents, who raised her. They claimed she was difficult, but, she knew, they also saw her only as a reminder of her parents' awful death.

"Was that true for you?" Sofie asked.

"Did I get along with my grandfather?" Anton smiled. "He bought me my first piano. Cleared out the living room to put it here. This was his house then. My father refused to have a piano in our house. Said he didn't want me to spend my time plunking around when there were more important things to do in life."

"Important like what?" Sofie asked.

Anton looked at her. "I thought you knew. You'd researched my great-grandfather so well. My father worked for the force. My grandfather would have too, only they weren't ready to take another Runge in those days. By the time my father came along, the Runges were famous again—thanks to that damn book—and he was able to capitalize on it. He wanted me to follow in the family business as well, but I didn't. I couldn't stomach it, which made things even uglier around my father."

Sofie nodded.

Anton smiled that self-deprecating smile again. "And this isn't what you came for, is it?"

"A historian is always interested in how events play out over decades," Sofie said, and felt her blush come back. The words sounded so clinical, and she hadn't meant them that way.

"Well," Anton said, as if he wanted to move the topic along. "I wish I could be more helpful on those missing years. My father and grandfather would have known. But no one ever asked them."

"More's the pity," Sofie said. "I actually came to ask a few other questions as well. The information that your great-grandfather might have had—did you ever read the book?"

"God, yes," Anton said. "Almost in self-defense. If something's controversial in the family, it's always safest to know as much about it as possible."

"Your great-grandfather mentioned that he had found several bullets and the gun. But he never said what kind of gun it was, not even in the police files, and he listed the bullets as being of 'unknown origin.' I used to think that meant he was never sure the bullets came from the Sniper's gun, but I think that interpretation is wrong now."

Anton's gaze focused on her. She seemed to have all of his attention now. "You do? Why?"

This was where she had to trust him. Sofie took a deep breath. "Because we found another bullet," she said.

His mouth opened slightly, then closed, and he nodded, as if he understood.

"In Adler's grave," he said.

Sofie's breath caught. "You knew about that?"

"The disinterment? I think all of Vienna knew about that." Then he shrugged. "I follow what you're doing pretty closely."

Sofie's mouth was dry, but she didn't want to ask for any water. "You do?"

"Yeah," he said. "I—hell, I don't know. I was pretty offended by the whole deal."

"Even though the first person to benefit was you?" Sofie felt her face heating up again.

"Me?"

"*Death at Fasching* has sold four times more copies since the announcement than it has in the past four years combined. You're making your money." She didn't recognize the voice that came out of her. She almost never berated anyone. She often fantasized about it, but she never did it.

"It's not the money," he said.

"No, it's that you don't want to answer family questions." Sofie stood. She was no longer comfortable sitting across from him. The polite man had been a mask for the bitter man underneath. "I'm sorry. I thought maybe I could trust you—"

"And you can," he said. "I was just being honest with you. I knew it was from Adler's disinterment because that's logical. But I don't know what you found."

His tone was soft, his expression conciliatory. This time, it had been Sofie who overreacted.

Only she wasn't going to apologize. She had felt off balance since she came into this house.

"We don't know, either," she said as she sank back into her chair. "Your great-grandfather's description is accurate. Bullet of unknown origin."

"Surely there's got to be a specialist you can hire who can figure out the origin," Anton said.

"They're not even sure what the bullet's made of, let alone who made it," Sofie said.

Anton frowned. He picked up his second crumb cake, took a bite, and chewed, apparently deep in thought.

"My grandfather," he said slowly, "used to say his father was crazy."

Sofie sat very still. Maybe this was what she had come for.

"He used to say that his father believed impossible things—that there were parts of this world no one understood, and no one could understand."

Sofie frowned.

Anton set the cake down. He shook his head. "I never knew what that meant, but it always seemed to be about the Sniper. My father would argue with my grandfather, and then they'd start yelling at each other, and I'd always leave."

He glanced over his shoulder, at the door leading to the entry.

"That piano saved me more than once. I'd sit there and pick at notes and pretend my family got along."

Fighting about a man who had already been long dead. It was a kind of history that Sofie had never experienced.

"Your grandfather lived here," Sofie said.

Anton looked at the door for another moment, then his gaze came back to her.

"Yes," he said.

"And his father before him," Sofie said.

"Yes. My great-grandfather left the house to my grandfather, who left it to my father, who didn't want it, so he gave it to me." Anton ran a hand through his hair. It was thick and dark, and fell back into place as if it had been trained to do so.

"Is it very different?" Sofie asked.

He blinked. "Is what different?"

"The house. From your great-grandfather's time."

He looked at the stove, which was obviously new, and then shook his head slightly. But he didn't answer her directly, at least not aloud.

"Why do you ask?"

Here was the critical moment, then. The one she had really come for.

"Because," she said, "I was wondering if your great-grandfather's personal items were still here."

"Personal items? You mean clothes and chairs and pipes?"

Sofie didn't want to tip her hand completely. "He was a well-known man who consulted on a lot of cases. He never really retired from the force, but they don't have any record of what he did to earn his salary the last two decades of his life. I thought maybe those records were here."

"What he did from 1940 to 1951." Anton's tone was dry. He seemed to have returned from whatever memory had held him sway, and he didn't seem pleased to be back.

She nodded.

"Maybe a few things about the Sniper," Anton said.

She shrugged.

"Something that the other writers missed, something to make you really famous."

Sofie bit her lower lip. "I've offended you again. I'm sorry. I'm not trying to make a fortune off your family."

"No, of course not," Anton said, "because you already have. That was a hefty advance."

"Yes, it was." Sofie spoke softly. "Is that your way of asking me to pay you for access to his papers?"

"Christ, no!" Anton pushed away from the table and stood up. "I don't need your money. Like you said, I make more than enough off my great-grandfather's royalties. It wouldn't matter to anyone if I ever worked again. Anyone except me, of course."

He took a deep breath, ran his hand through his hair again, and shook his head.

Sofie waited. He seemed to be calming down. She was finally getting a sense of him, realizing that some of his reactions to her questions had nothing to do with her, but with this family history that she didn't entirely understand, a history that seemed to have centered around Johann Runge.

"I never heard of any papers," Anton said after a moment.

"How about boxes?" Sofie asked.

"Boxes?" He looked at her. "What kind of boxes?"

"I don't know, exactly."

"Why would you think he had boxes that pertained to the Sniper investigation?"

"Because," she said, "if he didn't take them, then I'm afraid they're gone forever."

"The police don't keep evidence from open cases?"

"Sure they do," Sofie said. "But not in this case."

Anton sighed. "You came here looking for the evidence, hoping we had it."

"Yes," Sofie said. "Because if you don't, then either it's been lost or stolen."

"It was probably stolen." He rubbed a hand over his face. "You have no idea how crazy some of these Sniper fanatics are."

Sofie smiled. "I'm getting an inkling."

He looked at her, tilted his head, and finally smiled, too. "I bet you are."

He returned to his chair, stretched out in it, and extended his long legs.

"I haven't changed much in this house," he said. "There's a lot of stuff in the attic and the basement, stuff that I have meant to go through and have never gotten around to."

Sofie's heart started pounding. There was actually a chance that the evidence was here.

"If I find things that pertain to the Sniper case," Anton said slowly, "why should I give them to you?"

"You don't have to give them to me," she said. "I don't want them. I was just hoping to have access to them, maybe to photograph them, and use them for my book."

"And if I find this stuff, and decide to write my own book?" he asked.

"It's your family, your belongings," she said. "You can do whatever you like."

"But I should trust you," he said.

She shook her head. "I never said that."

"You should have."

"I can try to convince you," she said. "But ultimately, it's got to be your decision. I want to write the definitive book on this case. I want to put the case in its proper historical context, and I think I have the skills to do it. I certainly have the money to do so—the publisher's backing, the laboratory facilities, the cooperation of a bunch of world-class experts. But it's my vision, my book, my choice. And I won't change that. So you can't give me things and demand that I take your interpretation. You can't withhold things and expect me to cave in until I agree to your terms, whatever they might be. So the decision here is one-hundred-percent yours."

"If I find anything," he said.

"If you find anything." She had a hunch that he knew where to look, that her questions had brought up a memory. But she had meant what she said; she didn't want him to become part of her investigation, to control it or to change it in any way.

He stood.

Sofie stood too.

"How do I reach you?" he asked.

She gave him her business card.

He stared at it for a moment.

"If you write the definitive book," he said, "will people finally let go? Will they finally stop caring about the Sniper?"

"Probably not," she said.

He sighed. "I was afraid you'd say that," he said.

1913

WILLIAM LEANED HIS FACE against the grimy leather seat. A young man had gotten up about an hour before, and headed to the back of the train car. He went through the doors, stepping across the dangerous coupling as if it meant nothing to him, and vanished in the car beyond.

Most of the travelers seemed weary, as if this trip were a burden to them—not in the way it was to him—but as if it were something to be endured, taking them from one bad place to another.

It was a burden to him because he had believed that getting on the train would be the end of his mission. He had been wrong.

He hadn't expected the difficulties in approaching Papadopoulos, nor the way that Papadopoulos would guard his wooden box.

The box served as Papadopoulos's suitcase. Papadopoulos was too poor to own a real leather suitcase, so he tied a rope around the wooden box, added a handle, and carried it. He wasn't the only person on the train who had done so. In fact, in these filthy seats so far from the dining car, wooden boxes seemed to be the suitcase of choice.

William stared at the box, willing Papadopoulos to set it down. The man hadn't moved since he looked around the train car. Perhaps he was asleep sitting up.

Still, William didn't know why Papadopoulos guarded the box so tightly. According to the histories, all that he had inside besides a change of clothing were papers, letters of introduction, and notes for an essay he planned to research and write in Vienna.

Nothing important except the letters of introduction. Nothing of great value to anyone else on the train.

Perhaps Papadopoulos was already paranoid. Or perhaps he had always been cautious by nature.

William wouldn't know now. All he could do was stare at the back of Papadopoulos's head, and hope for a chance to get to the box before the train arrived in the station.

If not, he would have to do it in the station, just for the sake of the symbolism. Wein Nord was centrally located. Papadopoulos's new home in the Hietzing District was not.

No matter what he did, William had to plant the nuke in that box, type the activation code into the remote detonator, and then disappear before the bomb went off.

William didn't want to die for his cause.

He wanted to see the effects of his work by the time he got home.

2005

SOFIE LEFT HIM ALONE in this house, filled with the ghosts of men who were greater than he was.

Anton Runge stood next to his piano for nearly an hour, staring at the composition paper he'd left on the music stand. He'd been hired to write a piece in five parts for the Vienna Boys Choir. They wanted something original for their Christmas concert, something that showed off Vienna's musical tradition, something that was both modern and yet had hints of the past.

So far, he had thrown away more than fifty false starts.

He hadn't had the guts to tell Sofie Branstadter that he had given up performance so that he could write. Because his writing, while it wasn't as well-known as his solo career, had become his passion. He was beginning to make a name for himself as a composer, and that meant more to him than all the applause in the world.

But even if he succeeded, he would never be as large a personality as the other men in his family: his great-grandfather, a man who still haunted not just Vienna, but the entire world; his grandfather, one of Vienna's most influential politicians both in front of and behind the scenes; and his father, whose arrest and conviction record made Johann Runge's seem like child's play.

These were men who had embraced life. Who had beliefs and followed them. Men who had made a difference, not just to themselves, but to the world around them.

All Anton did was give people a little easy listening, some musical pleasure now and then.

He sat on the bench and ran his fingers lightly over the keys. He didn't depress any of them, just felt the ivory beneath his fingertips, the slight breaks between each key.

He knew the piano better than he knew himself. It was his escape, his refuge, and once, his nightmare. That was why he had quit performing. Because he used to dread going to the keyboard, dread the very thing that had once given him solace.

And that, he knew, had been wrong.

It had been such a relief when his father died. No longer did Anton have to leave Vienna to escape his family's presence. Even the house seemed lighter, as if the arguments died with his father.

But Sofie Branstadter had brought them all back. She had, and so had the reporters who wanted yet another interview about the past, and all those interminable documentaries, revived because the interest in the Sniper had rekindled again.

There were boxes everywhere in this house, boxes he'd never opened, even as child when he'd secretly explored every nook and cranny. Somehow he had known that opening the boxes would be the worst thing he could ever do.

Sofie hadn't lied to him. If he did find Sniper material here, buried underneath his grandmother's wedding dress and his father's childhood drawings, then the hype would get even worse.

He admired that: the fact that she refused to lie.

He had liked her in spite of himself. The nickname he had given her, Miss High-and-Mighty Branstadter, didn't fit. Like most shy people, she seemed aloof in public. In person, she was overly smart and sensitive and much stronger than anyone would initially expect.

She had handled his anger, after all, and much of it she hadn't deserved. Much of it had remained hidden in this house, submerged in the music, in his lack of courage.

He didn't have to face other people because there weren't any around. He didn't even have to face his memories, because he had set up his life so that they wouldn't get triggered.

Until interest renewed in the Sniper, and because no one knew who the Sniper had been and everyone knew who had chased him, Anton's family became important yet again.

And the ghosts rose.

Maybe they rose because they hadn't been properly buried. Maybe, if someone wrote the right book—with all the correct research—maybe then the focus in the Sniper case would change.

After all, if the Sniper were unmasked, then maybe Anton's great-grandfather would cease being the whipping boy of Viennese history and might actually become a historical figure in his own right.

There were boxes all over this house. Boxes Anton had never looked at.

Anton was the only member of his family left.

Perhaps it was time to see what kind of inheritance he had actually received.

1913

THE ASSASSIN SAT in the corner of the café, his gloved hands wrapped around his hot coffee glass. His back was to the wall; from his seat, he could see the door.

This café wasn't as elegant or as warm as the Café Central. Which made sense, since he had crossed the Danube Canal and was now in the working-class districts. People here did not have the time or the money to spend all day in cafés.

He had been lucky to find this one, and even luckier that it remained open late.

He had no idea what he would do when it closed.

This café was crammed into an old brick building that appeared to be crumbling. The ceiling was low, the floor filthy. Round tables were shoved together with barely enough room for two men to sit back to back in the aisles.

A woman ruled over this system, just like she ruled over the wait staff near the counter. She was a rounded, middle-aged matron who wore her silvering hair in braids around the top of her head. Her black dress was worn at the collar, and covered with stains; it was probably the only weekday dress she had.

From her conversation, the assassin got the sense that she was the wife of the owner, and contrary to Viennese custom, she remained in the café even though the men would have preferred her to leave.

She watched the assassin with suspicion from the moment he entered the café, and for a while, he feared that she knew who he was and what he had done.

Then another man came inside, a man who obviously didn't belong either, and the woman gave that man the same look she had given the assassin.

At that moment, the assassin's shoulders relaxed. He was in a neighborhood café, frequented by regular customers, and because of it, the woman viewed him with suspicion. She would remember him after he completed his mission, he knew that much, but right now, he was just a stranger taking up space in her café, space she would rather use for a customer she saw every day.

Several of those customers sat at the round tables, eating croissants as if they were dinner. The other stranger sat a few tables away, reading a badly printed broadsheet he had brought in himself. The broadsheet looked familiar; when the assassin recognized it, he smiled.

Pravda. The strange man in the corner was reading *Pravda.*

"Sir?" The woman stood over him, her arms crossed over her large bosom, her Germanic face twisted in a frown. "We are closing."

The assassin blinked.

"I'm sorry," he said, not willing to stand while she was so close. Even though she seemed to have no idea who he was, he didn't want her to catch a glimpse of his Glock. "I had no idea of the time."

She nodded, as if she had expected that response, then she moved to another table to tell its patrons to leave.

The assassin took one last sip of his coffee and shoved his half-eaten croissant in his pocket. Then he stood, careful to keep the Glock covered, and walked out of the café.

The *Pravda* reader stood outside, lighting a cigarette. He wore dirty pants and a torn overcoat. He looked like he didn't have much money, either.

The assassin stepped outside, and waited until the other patrons left before turning to the *Pravda* reader.

"Is there some other place open at this time of the night?" the assassin asked.

The *Pravda* reader took a long drag from his cigarette. The smoke he exhaled was so blue that the assassin wanted to cough.

"You have no room for the night?" the *Pravda* reader asked.

The assassin wasn't willing to give the *Pravda* reader that much information.

"I'm a stranger here, and I'm hungry," the assassin said. "I did not order enough to eat, and now I'm wondering where I can get a good meal."

The *Pravda* reader's gaze ran up and down the assassin. The assassin resisted the urge to pull his Glock closer, to make certain that it was hidden. The *Pravda* reader's gaze lingered on the assassin's shoes.

They weren't covered with blood; the assassin had made certain of that. Still, he tensed.

After a moment, the *Pravda* reader raised his head. His eyes shone, and the assassin got a sense that the man knew that the assassin had just murdered *Pravda*'s editor.

"Go to the Ring," the *Pravda* reader said. "I'm sure you will find an open restaurant there—one you can afford."

That last was spoken with contempt. Perhaps the *Pravda* reader hadn't figured out who the assassin was after all. Perhaps the *Pravda* reader had looked at the assassin's clothing and assumed he was a man of money, the kind who did not belong in the Brigittenau district.

"Thank you," the assassin said, but he did not move. After a moment, the *Pravda* reader made a sound of disgust and headed down the street.

The assassin watched him go. The *Pravda* reader was walking toward the Augarten. If it weren't so cold, the assassin would have gone there, too. A lot of transients had slept in that park throughout history. The assassin doubted it would be much different now.

Initially, he had planned to stay in one of the many inns around Vienna, but his long-ago research led him to believe that an inn-stay would call attention to him. The assassin had to find a place to sleep without getting too cold, without freezing to death, without calling attention to himself. He had to stay in this part of town, and he had to be prepared for his hit the next morning.

He had to stick with the plan, and that meant finding someplace to spend the night.

2005

IT WASN'T FAIR to call the space behind the eaves an attic. The roof slanted in the front and back of the house, paralleling the street so that the block of row houses shared not just their walls but their roof as well.

The slanted area cut off the rooms on the upper floor and someone, long before Anton's family had owned the house, had built walls there, adding storage areas.

As a child, he had loved those spaces. They smelled of mothballs and dust and secrets. In the back corner of one room, he caught the hint of his mother's perfume—an almost forgotten scent.

She had died in a car accident when he was three, and his father, heartbroken, had never remarried. Anton had better memories of his grandmother, a regal woman who had presided over most of the city's grandest occasions. She had always been too dressed up to coddle her only grandson, but she had given him sweets and books and, when he reached four, she used her rainy-day fund to pay for the piano lessons that had eventually become his life.

When she died, he hadn't missed her the way he later missed her husband. Her lack of warmth had hurt the bond between them.

But Anton had always missed his mother.

His memories of her were fleeting—a heavyset woman who had a warm lap and a soft voice. She smelled of perfume and baking bread. He always thought of her when he came into a house that smelled of baking.

He never knew why he associated her with baking; he had meant to ask his father about it, but the time had never seemed right. And now his father, like the rest of them, was gone.

Still, the rules the family had given Anton in childhood stayed with him. *Don't play in the attic. We store treasures there and treasures are precious, and easily broken. Leave the boxes alone. There could be spiders in the dark. Horrible, ugly spiders that killed with a single bite.*

It had been the spiders—his father's warning—that had worked, of course. Anton's father had always known what scared him most. Even now, now that Anton was a full-grown adult who knew that there were very few lethal spiders, and almost none in Europe, he still carried a flashlight into the attic. A flashlight, and a can of bug spray, just in case.

He hadn't been in the attic rooms since his father died. Then Anton had taken the possessions he had wanted to keep from his parents' home, and left them in their own boxes in the center of the front attic room.

The boxes were there, looking newer than all the rest, but still covered with a fine layer of dust. Cobwebs grew around the single bulb hanging from the ceiling and, as Anton flashed his light throughout the room, he saw even more cobwebs hanging down from the beams providing the roof's support.

He left long enough to grab a hat, a duster, and some gloves. Then he tackled the cobwebs first, feeling the dirt fall from the ceiling like rain. Twice he stopped to brush himself off, and once he thought he actually saw a spider only to realize he had mistaken a ruined piece of lace for a black widow.

When he'd finished giving in to his phobia, he brought in two lamps and plugged them into the sockets on the inside wall. Then he dusted off the floor, sat down, and started to dig through his family's past.

The amount of stuff amazed him—love letters between his parents, poetry written to his grandmother from someone Anton had never heard of, photographs of people he didn't recognize—many of them identified in his grandfather's cramped handwriting.

In one corner, he found books, most of them lurid novels, written in English—a language he was only passingly familiar with. Most of the novels had partially naked women on the cover, and subtitles that made little sense: *She was bad, and murder made her worse!* was his favorite of the ones he could understand.

Beneath some beautiful handmade pillowcases and table linens, he found some Russian pornographic magazines, all of which dated from his father's teenage years. That made Anton smile—the image of his young father, sitting up here alone, looking at dirty pictures and worrying about getting caught.

By the middle of the afternoon, Anton took a break. He went to the kitchen, ate a sandwich standing up so that he wouldn't get dust on his favorite chair, and then he tackled the second attic room, under the back eaves.

There the boxes looked even older. Many were made of wood. Behind them, he found old furniture—rocking chairs, tables, and some dishes that were so delicate he was almost afraid to touch them.

The furniture intrigued him, and he decided when he got a chance, he would clean it up, replacing some of the bulky items he had grown up with, with the older, more stately items he found here.

But he didn't find any evidence boxes. In fact, he didn't find much from his great-grandfather at all. It was as if Johann Runge had been banished from the upper rooms—only his wife, his son, and his son's family had any claim to this place.

Which only left the basement, an area that had not been forbidden at all while Anton was growing up, but a place he'd never had much interest in. The basement always smelled of overripe apples and mold, a scent it still held even though his grandfather, who had insisted on making homemade cider, had stopped doing so years ago.

Anton left the attic rooms but didn't go to the basement—at least not yet. He was tired and dirty, but less discouraged than he had thought he would be.

He almost felt victorious, as if he had entered a forbidden place and survived: no spider bites, no ancient secrets discovered, no memories that should have remained hidden.

He went to the main floor to take a shower, and found himself humming for first time that day.

2005

EVEN THOUGH SOFIE was shaken from her meeting with Anton Runge, she still had one more appointment, one she didn't dare miss. The Crime Research Lab was located in Leopoldstadt, the working-class district between the Danube Canal and the Danube. Sofie took a tram to the lab and walked the few blocks from the stop to the old district.

She loved this part of Vienna. She had spent part of her childhood here, under the shadow of Vienna's famous Ferris wheel, the Riesenrad, living with her favorite set of foster parents. She had been placed in foster care after her maternal grandmother had died. Her grandfather, old and senile, hadn't been able to take care of a child.

This set of foster parents—her third—had taken her all over this neighborhood, trying to draw her out, telling her about the history, explaining the various religions.

She had loved the synagogues the most, the old buildings that looked so different from their Christian counterparts. They had a peace to them, and an air of study, that she appreciated, even though she had to cover her head the few times she entered.

Her foster mother, a non-practicing Jew, had spoken to the rabbis about Sofie, asking for advice on how to care for this terrified child, who clung in crowds and preferred to sit under tables rather than at them.

The rabbis had no good advice, at least that was what Sofie had overheard her foster mother tell her foster father. After that, Sofie knew she wouldn't stay in the house much longer. That had already become the pattern—the frightened child, who woke screaming from nightmares, and the foster parents too overburdened with their other responsibilities to care for her.

One set of parents had actually begged a doctor to treat her, but he said that medicine had no real cures for diseases of the mind. There was only psychoanalysis, a quack science, held in as much esteem as séances or phrenology, something people did once they had given up hope.

It had been Miss Halder who had insisted that Sofie have a consistent home life, Miss Halder who told Sofie that anyone would still be scared after what she had been through, Miss Halder who taught Sofie that all answers could be found in books.

Sofie smiled as she walked. She did not blame her foster parents for their inability to deal with her. Her experiences were so different from most children's that she was surprised anyone could deal with her.

She was still surprised, at times, that she had become a functional adult.

The Crime Research Laboratory was in an old stone building that looked as if it had housed a series of disreputable businesses. The CRL wasn't disreputable—it was one of the most respected private forensic labs in Europe—but CRL had initially started on a small budget, preferring the low rents of the Leopoldstadt district.

As the CRL grew, they found large offices, but decided to stay here, away from the main part of Vienna's political and legal culture. The CRL management and employees felt that the symbolic distance helped maintain an actual distance between the various organizations, and kept CRL's work pure.

Sofie stopped before walking inside. The Riesenrad still towered over this neighborhood. She could see the giant Ferris wheel rising above the trees, moving slowly as fairgoers spent their weekday afternoon in small cars, looking at the city of Vienna.

In all the years she'd lived in Vienna, she still hadn't gone to the Prater, had never walked through Vienna's most famous park. As a child, she could hear the laughter from the Fun Fair, and the music rising from the various tents, and she wished she could go. She would resolve to go.

But she would never tell anyone of that resolve, and even though she saved up her money so that she could walk through the gates of the Prater alone, she never did.

She couldn't bring herself to walk in a park for entertainment. She had walked *through* parks in recent years, but never ambled in them, enjoying the greenery and the trees, and the concession stands near the sidewalks.

Every time she saw a park bench, her stomach twisted, and she had to hurry on.

The Riesenrad continued its slow turn, the ancient gears glistening in the sunlight. Sofie gave the old wheel one last look—promising herself that she would one day sit in it—and then she went inside the labs.

CRL smelled faintly of formaldehyde, chemical cleaners, and processed air. The temperature inside was cooler than outside—the air conditioning was probably on in preparation for summer's heat—and the lights were dim enough that Sofie had to blink to force her eyes to adjust.

Once they did, she saw the familiar reception area, with its plush chairs and end tables covered with science magazines. A woman sat behind a glass desk, a headset on her ears, her hands handling the call board in front of her.

"May I help you?" she asked Sofie.

Sofie identified herself and gave her appointment time. Then she grabbed a copy of the morning's paper and sat down to wait.

She didn't have to wait long. A thin man wearing a long white lab coat came out of a side door, grinned at her, and beckoned as if they were old friends. As she walked toward him, the man stuck out his hand and introduced himself.

He was Max Kolisko, the enthusiastic ballistics expert she had spoken to on the phone.

"Did you find me another bullet?" he asked as they walked through the immaculate halls leading to the meeting room.

"I'm still looking," she said.

He shoved his hands in the pockets of his lab coat, pulling it down, and making his lanky frame seem even longer.

"I hope you find one," he said, "and I hope it's just like this one."

She looked at him in surprise.

He shrugged a single shoulder. "Right now, we have a cool mystery, and I, for one, don't want it spoiled by the facts. It makes me feel like a kid again. You remember those *Asimov Readers?* The ones that had all the neat science stories?"

Sofie nodded. She did remember the translated Russian books and their little orange covers, designed for various grade levels, with suggestions about reading skills. She had skipped right over those suggestions, reading the books out of order, until she realized that Asimov was not her favorite writer. His characters, so dogmatic and Russian, always struck her as flat.

"I loved the ones about time travel," Kolisko said. "And this bullet, this inexplicable bullet, makes me feel for the first time since I've become a scientist as if I'm encountering the Asimovian universe."

She wasn't sure what he meant by the Asimovian universe, and she wasn't sure she wanted to know. But she did appreciate his enthusiasm.

"You still can't find out where the bullet came from?" she asked.

"Or the material it's made of." Kolisko held open the glass door leading into the conference room. The conference room had been added to the building sometime in the last forty years. The room's main wall was made of glass, and its furniture, which probably hadn't been replaced since the room was built, was a blond wood that seemed more Scandinavian than Viennese. The light blue carpet was worn from too many feet and not enough cleanings.

Two other scientists, both wearing lab coats, sat at the table, as well as CRL's manager, whom Sofie had dealt with before.

The manager, Talia Vaitmann, was a solid woman with steel-gray hair and stunningly blue eyes. Her skin was the color of old parchment, and she looked like she had been indoors all of her life. She wore a steel-gray suit that matched her hair, but did nothing for her looks.

She stood as Sofie entered. The scientists remained seated. One was a red-haired woman who appeared to be in her mid-thirties. The other a young man with thick glasses and hair so short that Sofie couldn't discern its color. They sat at opposite ends of the table, but looked equally uncomfortable.

Kolisko introduced them. The woman, Ledora Gutterman, specialized in metallurgy at CRL. The young man, Franz Axel, was the chemist Kolisko had spoken of. Both had other duties, but apparently those duties weren't relevant to this meeting.

Sofie's stomach clenched, and she regretted the salad she had had for lunch. Something was wrong here. Only Kolisko seemed happy to see her.

Still, Sofie smiled and eased into the chair farthest from the door. She refused to sit with her back to a glass wall.

She glanced at the clean tabletop. No one had brought her reports. The two scientists had their hands folded on the tabletop, and a half-full glass of water sat in front of Talia Vaitmann's chair.

"I take it we're not going to review the various pieces of evidence I've brought you," Sofie said, deciding to take control of this meeting right away.

She didn't want them to see her nervousness. Apparently everything was lining up against her this day—first Anton Runge, and now this.

"We've had an interesting investigation," Vaitmann said. "And before we proceed farther, we need to know the origin of your bullet."

Sofie felt the muscles in her neck tighten. If she wasn't careful, she would get a headache by evening. "That's what I hired you to find out."

"No, no," Vaitmann said. "Where you got it."

Sofie glanced at Kolisko. He hadn't sat down. He still looked like an innocent who read Russian science fiction novels, not someone who tested bullets for a living.

"Why do you need that information?" Sofie asked.

"Because we have run into a bit of a problem," Vaitmann said. "Dr. Axel contacted an American scientist about the coating on your bullet, and within two hours, we are getting phone calls and warnings from the American government."

"What?" Sofie hadn't expected that. She didn't even know the Americans had interest in foreign affairs, let alone foreign sciences. "From who in the American government?"

"From their Department of State, but it is clear that the inquiry truly comes from their Department of War. It seems we have worried them." Vaitmann seemed worried herself. She touched the mass of gray hair curled like a helmet on her head.

"I don't understand," Sofie said. "How could we have interested the Americans?"

"We were told," Vaitmann said, "that this material is patented to a United States company, although they would not tell us which one, and that knowledge of the material outside of the United States is limited."

"How long has this stuff been around?" Sofie asked.

"My source tells me that it's new," Axel said. "It's a coating, a polythylene coating that acts like a tough shield. No one has heard of it before this year."

"This is the source that reported you to their government?" Sofie asked.

Axel's acne-scarred cheeks grew red. "After I spoke with him, yes, their government contacted us. But that was my error. I contacted him directly, knowing that the United States Federal Bureau of Investigation keeps an eye on him."

"Why?" Sofie asked.

"Because he once headed their chemical weapons branch." Gutterman, the other scientist, spoke with undisguised loathing. It seemed that she was angry at Axel for reasons Sofie didn't exactly understand.

"You think this is a chemical weapon of some kind?" Sofie asked, feeling as odd as she had when Kolisko had spoken of the fiction he read as a boy.

"It's clearly a new technology," Axel said. "I've never seen the compound before. Neither have any German or Russian scientists I spoke to. When you talk chemicals, you go to the Germans and Russians first, then the Chinese if you can, then the Americans. I have no Chinese contacts, so I went to my American friend, and didn't do it through back channels because I didn't feel it was important. I mean, all we're talking about is some kind of plastic here."

"Plastic coating a bullet," Gutterman said.

"Dr. Gutterman was to trace the tungsten we found inside the bullet," Vaitmann said, "but she says it's not traceable. We have people trying to track this bullet down, but no one has heard of anything like this. Dr. Kolisko says he thinks you got this bullet during your work on the Sniper case, but I can hardly believe that."

Sofie's entire back ached now from her rigid posture. "Why not?"

"Because," Axel said, "my American source was very clear with me. This compound has only been developed in the last five years. This bullet could not have come from any of the Sniper's shootings."

"But it did," Sofie said softly. She glanced at Vaitmann. "You will hold to our confidentiality agreement?"

"One hundred percent," Vaitmann said. "It's one of the guarantees of our business."

Sofie didn't like the discussion with the outside scientists, although she knew it had to be necessary. "I watched Karl Morganthau take the bullet from the body of Viktor Adler, one of the Sniper's victims. We disinterred Dr. Adler a few days ago, and immediately went to the autopsy room, where we opened the coffin and examined the corpse. The bullet came from the corpse itself. It had clearly been there since 1913."

All the scientists looked at each other. Talia Vaitmann raised her eyebrows, and leaned back in her chair.

"That's not possible," Gutterman said. "A bullet like that should have bored through flesh. It shouldn't have remained in a body."

"Bullets don't always act the way we expect them to," Kolisko said softly. "Maybe the velocity was different or the angle was off. Maybe the bullet hit something that left it intact but that it couldn't pierce."

"That bullet can pierce almost anything," Gutterman said. "It's one of the hardest things I've ever seen."

"You're saying some company was onto this compound one hundred years ago?" Axel asked.

Sofie shrugged. "I'm not saying anything. The Americans are the ones who are making preposterous claims. Maybe they've had these things in development for a hundred years and didn't want anyone to know."

Vaitmann looked at the chemist as if she wanted him to approve of the idea. "Dr. Axel?"

He shook his head. "That presupposes too many discoveries. We'd know about them. Putting polymers together like this takes a sophistication that no lab had before the Great War. I doubt any lab had it afterwards, either. No one was developing weapons, not after the Treaty of Versailles and the punishments mentioned."

"Not even in secret?" Kolisko asked.

"Maybe the Chinese," Axel said. "We never know what they're doing. But their level of scientific advancement parallels ours. I simply do not believe that anyone could have developed this bullet before 1950."

Sofie bit her lower lip. "I saw the bullet come out of Dr. Adler's body, and I know that body has been underground since January of 1913."

"Perhaps Dr. Morganthau planted the bullet?" Gutterman asked.

"To what end?" Sofie snapped. "He's the most widely respected man in his profession. Why would he plant a bullet like that?"

"To sabotage your investigation," Gutterman said. "Some people do not believe we should use current resources to investigate the past, not when there are so many other crimes that need solving."

It seemed, from the way she spoke, that Dr. Gutterman was one of those people.

"Dr. Morganthau isn't like that," Sofie said. "He's a forensic anthropologist. He believes in studying the past."

Her anger must have been apparent to the room. They looked at her in silence.

Vaitmann gave Gutterman a sideways glance. Sofie saw disapproval in it.

"We've worked with Dr. Morganthau," Vaitmann said, "and we didn't mean to imply that his methods were anything but professional."

She emphasized the last statement, then looked at Gutterman again. Gutterman studied her hands.

"It's just this bullet is very unusual, and we will continue to study it, of course. We may need to outsource the historical material—perhaps someone knows of a small plant that made bullets like this at the turn of the last century, and we are just unaware of it."

"I doubt that," Axel said. "That material—"

"Scientists should never discount the improbable," Vaitmann said.

"Miss Branstadter is going to see if she can get another bullet for us," Kolisko said, as if Sofie weren't there. "If it's like this one, then we know that the bullets came from this time period."

"If the Americans are doing secret research on this material, what's to say they're telling you the truth about when they started?" Sofie stood. She was tired of their arguing. If she did find another bullet, she'd take it to a different lab and see what they came up with. Maybe they would come up with a more plausible scenario.

"Leonardo da Vinci did design the first tank," Kolisko said.

"But never made it," Axel countered, as if he had done so before.

"The point is that ideas can be ahead of their time," Kolisko said.

Sofie sighed. "Look, what's so special about this material that it has to be kept secret?"

"Nothing, really," Axel said. "Its best use is as a coating. For example, if I used it to coat a pan, and cooked meat at a high temperature over an electric burner on that pan, then nothing would stick to the pan's surface, even if I didn't use a cooking oil."

"So?" Sofie said.

"From what I can gather, this material is useful in high-velocity weapons. If you shoot that bullet at a high velocity, then Dr. Gutterman is right, it should be able to pierce anything. The coating just makes the piercing easier."

"Actually," Kolisko said. "The coating protects the barrel of the gun so that it doesn't get damaged."

"The important thing is," Axel said, "that the Americans developed this material in a lab working on weaponry, which is not something they discuss much. So the patent is held by the government itself, and they tend to keep things secret."

"Especially the Americans," Vaitmann said. "They're notoriously uncooperative on scientific issues."

"And paranoid," Gutterman said.

"So the fact that we even have this material has set off flags all through their system, and they're going to want to know how we got it," Vaitmann said.

"You can't tell them," Sofie said.

"And we won't," Vaitmann said. "But I have to admit that their curiosity has raised mine as well. I want to know where this bullet originated."

"Me, too," Sofie said. "And that's why I hired you. If you're not up to the task, then I'll find another lab."

Vaitmann's lips thinned. "We'll find it. Don't you worry about that. We'll find it somehow."

But, as Sofie left the meeting room, she realized she did worry. She worried about the information leaking. She worried about the lab's attitude; that they were willing to believe she or someone in her team had brought the bullet into the investigation to throw it off. She worried about the potential media problems, not just now, but once the book came out.

If she quoted Crime Research Labs, and they acted like they had here—quarrelsome, paranoid, worried—then they could undercut the work she did.

She would need a second opinion on that bullet. She would have to take it to another lab. And this lab had better have credentials as good or better than Crime Research Labs, which was known as the best private lab in Europe for traditional forensic work. But maybe she didn't need the best private lab.

Maybe she needed the opinion of the best public lab.

She needed the British. She needed Scotland Yard.

1913

RUNGE RETURNED TO THE RING long after dark. His stomach growled, and he was shocked that he was hungry. Crouching over three dead bodies in one day should have left him without an appetite.

But life ultimately won out, and he knew, before the night was over, he would have to eat something.

For the moment, however, he stood outside police headquarters, his own head throbbing. The cold had become bitter—the wind off the Danube even icier than it had been the night before.

Still, people paraded past him in costume, adding to the air of unreality. Women, their faces hidden by feathered masks, held up their skirts, revealing tiny booted shoes that couldn't protect their feet against the cold. Men had their hands possessively against the women's backs, apparently ready to catch their companions should they slip on the ice.

Carriages went by, their occupants covered in fur-lined blankets, the tops of their costumes visible in the clear night.

Fasching. Carnival season in Vienna. Crazy season, made worse by this killer who had appeared out of nowhere.

Runge reached into his pockets and removed a pack of cigarettes. He pulled a cigarette out with his teeth, then put the pack back into his pocket. Then he struck a match, cupping it between his hands as he lit the end of the cigarette.

In the distance, a woman's laughter sounded as brittle as the wind.

Carnival. How he hated it. Those days between New Year's Eve and Shrove Tuesday, where even the poorest man had a ball to attend. In the mornings, Runge often saw uniformed attendants carrying bags holding their costumes, heading to work with confetti in their hair because an extra tram ride home would cost too much money.

Runge never attended the balls, although he used to. His wife always chided him—reminding him that the balls, filled with gaiety and life, gave Vienna its reputation. She loved to waltz, and she liked to pretend, even if just for an evening, that she was part of Vienna's elite, able to go from sumptuous meal to fantastic party to sumptuous meal without a thought to money or wasted time.

But since Runge's promotion within the detective bureau, he had not attended another ball. Not that he hadn't been invited. The police had their own, as did two of his favorite pubs. And, as a young police officer, he learned that he could attend almost any ball he wanted so long as he was willing to provide protection.

Over the years he'd been to everything from the Opera Ball to the Public Bath Attendants Ball in Stahlehner Hall.

He'd been to everything—except the balls held by the Hapsburgs, which, of course, had been the only ones his Lettie had wanted to attend. He had tried to please her with the others, but she never had the good time she had always planned.

Lettie, in Carnival, was as crazy as Vienna.

Runge took a long drag from his cigarette, trying to shake the disapproval he felt. The city shouldn't still be celebrating. Three men had died that afternoon—murdered in the coldest blood—and still revelers were on the streets, concerned with their own good time before Lent made them give it up.

Runge took one final drag from the cigarette, then tossed it onto the ice-covered street. He ground the butt with his heel. The cigarette tamed some of his hungry, but fed his anger.

The killer could be any one of the costumed people walking past him. Right now, the man who had murdered two psychoanalysts and an expatriate Russian could be laughing with a beautiful woman, sipping Cognac and tapping his feet to the romantic music of a Strauss waltz.

The killer could have been a guest at any of the three hundred or more balls held in the city during this season, including last night's Lunatics Gala, held at the Insane Asylum at Steinhof. Sigmund Freud had not attended that gathering, Runge had learned this afternoon, preferring to stay home and write on his latest book.

So far as Runge could tell, nothing Freud had done in the last week had angered anyone. His enemies lived outside the city, in France, Switzerland, and Germany. Only a few, like Alfred Adler (who was no relation to Viktor) lived inside Vienna. And Alfred Adler, for all his squabbles with Sigmund Freud, was not a man who would carry a gun into the streets of Vienna and shoot from a distance.

But Runge had sent one of his men to check anyway, and he had found that Alfred Adler had an alibi. There wasn't even a convenient lunatic who had newly escaped from the asylum. And those who had been recently released—pronounced "cured," if such a thing were possible—had no connection to Freud or Viktor Adler, at least none that Runge had discovered so far.

All he knew was that the killer's shots were not random. The man had entered Café Central and had walked toward Viktor Adler with great purpose. Then the killer had fled and, with the precision of a military general, arrived at 19 Berggasse as Sigmund Freud and his daughter Anna left for their daily walk.

The shootings had been planned, and there would be more. Runge knew that much. But aside from warning Vienna's other psychoanalysts to be cautious, Runge did not know what to do.

The killer was a ghost, a masked man, a cipher. Seen and unseen, as common as the average man on the street.

And that worried Runge the most.

2005

THE LIGHTS IN THE BASEMENT were so old that the bulbs were a yellowish color no longer manufactured in Europe. As Anton walked down into the strange light, he felt like he was walking into his own childhood.

He used to come down to the basement every fall with his grandfather. His grandfather, who had spent part of every summer on a farm that belonged to the maternal side of the family, learned how to make cider when he was just a boy. That was a tradition he insisted on passing along, and Anton was going to be the person who learned it.

All Anton remembered from the experience was the mess and the frustration. It seemed to be a lot of work for very little payoff, particularly when cider was available every fall at the market already made, the work done.

But when Anton smelled that faint scent of apples mixed with mold that seemed to come from the very walls, he got a vivid memory of his grandfather's large frame and booming voice, talking about the way that some traditions should not be lost.

The basement was a series of badly constructed rooms, shored up with wooden beams. The foundation had originally been laid with brick, but the mortar had come loose in a lot of places, falling to the floor like sand.

Anton had never looked at the walls before, not as a homeowner, and he wondered if their seeming weakness truly was, and if it was something that he should have dealt with a long time ago.

Probably something to deal with now. If nothing else, Sofie Branstadter had gotten him to visit his past and think about his future.

Anton smiled ruefully and stepped over the threshold of yet another door. The boxes in the basement were stored near the north wall, as far away from the steps as possible. This room was the last, filled nearly to the brim with items stored years ago and forgotten.

Much of what Anton found were bits of furniture in need of repair. Several three-legged chairs bowed their way around boxes of dishes and silverware that seemed to come from various generations. A couple of broken tables, a ruined feather mattress (which stank of mildew and looked like it had suffered from a mice infestation), and several quilts swollen with moisture were his major finds.

Most of the stuff down here should be recycled or tossed out. He sorted as he went—items he might someday repair, items beyond hope, and items to give away. So far, the items to give away pile was the largest.

He methodically worked his way to the back, opening box after box of linens and baby clothes and toys that predated even his great-grandfather. Some of this stuff must have come from the home his great-grandfather had lived in before he bought this one.

Anton felt like he was digging through the layers of his family's existence, discovering entire strata of the past that he hadn't even known about.

Finally, around dinnertime, he stood, rubbing his sore back and wondering where the time had gone.

And that was when he saw the additional light.

It startled him, that light. He knew all the overhead bulbs were on a single wire—the basement's electrical system dated from the 1920s and had not been redone when Anton's grandfather remodeled the upstairs. Redoing the ancient wiring in the basement had been something Anton had planned to do for years now.

The light seemed to come from a crack in the wall. The crack appeared behind some boxes that were still in place, but he wouldn't have seen it if he hadn't moved the boxes nearby.

Forgetting how tired and hungry he was, he started in again, moving boxes until he had placed an entire stack of them on the far wall.

Then he stopped. Dust motes as large as flies swirled in the breeze he had made. His skin was sweat-covered and filthy, and he was breathing harder than he did when he ran.

The light still taunted him through a crack in the wood, only the crack wasn't a flaw. It was designed there. Along the edge of the crack, he found rusted hinges.

Behind all the boxes, and all the unrepaired furniture, and all the unwanted junk from his family's history, Anton Runge had found a door.

It only took him a few minutes to move the other stack of boxes. Then he stood in front of an old, rotted wooden door that was locked on the outside.

Someone had added a metal bar above the doorknob. The bar was also on hinges, and was thin—an old-fashioned way of double-locking a door, long before deadbolts. The bar had a slit in the center that exactly fit the ring on the nearby doorframe. Someone had stuck a padlock into the ring and locked it tight.

Anton lifted the lock, felt rust flake on his fingertips, and sighed. There were no extra keys around—he had discarded the ones that seemed to go nowhere shortly after he had inherited the house.

But the rust wasn't coming from the padlock. It was coming from the metal stand holding the ring in place. Anton grabbed his flashlight and peered closely at the doorframe.

The wood was splitting where the metal stand had been drilled in. The screws were coming loose, flaking rust on the lock itself.

Anton grabbed the metal and pulled, then stopped, thinking of his precious fingers. If he broke one or sliced it on the wood, he wouldn't be able to play the piano for weeks. He had to be more careful.

He cast around the room for something that would act as a pry bar. He finally found a screwdriver that looked as old as the door itself.

He used the screwdriver to force the metal off the doorframe, and then he pushed on the bar.

The door swung open, sending the dust motes swirling again. A waft of fetid air reached him, and Anton coughed, thinking that none of this could be good for him.

Still, he stepped closer to the room. A single bulb covered with cobwebs so old they were coated with dust hung from the unfinished ceiling. A desk had been shoved against the far wall, with a chair pushed up tight against it.

The desktop was clean except for an old manual typewriter and a stack of paper beside it.

Anton's breath caught. The walls were lined with old wooden file cabinets, the kind that a *fin de siècle* office would have, and in front of the cabinets were stacks of boxes that ran at least waist high.

He stepped inside, leaving fresh footprints on the dust. No one had been in this room in a very long time.

Anton leaned over the boxes, stretched, and grabbed the top drawer on the nearest filing cabinet. The drawer slid as if it had been oiled just the day before.

Inside, he saw row after row of files, all labeled in a neat hand. He pulled out the first file, and let out a small breath when he saw the label.

Freud, Anna.

He thumbed through the file, looking at an ancient photograph of a young woman with heavy hair and a pleasant demeanor. Incident reports, a hand-scrawled semi-biography, and a genealogical chart.

Anton's heart was beating hard. Sweat ran down the side of his face and dripped onto his arm. The little room had no ventilation, but he didn't care.

The file also contained a typewritten transcription of an interview, given at police headquarters on January 15, 1913. Anna Freud was being interviewed by Johann Runge in the presence of a police transcriptionist. The topic was the death of Anna Freud's father.

One of the Sniper's victims.

Anton wiped his forehead with the back of his hand. Could he be so lucky? Could these be Johann Runge's files? All of them, hidden back here as if they didn't exist?

Why had his great-grandfather done that?

Or had he?

Anton leaned back and peered into the main room. The debris had to have come after his great-grandfather's death. Maybe no one knew what was in the room. Maybe they had been forbidden to enter it, just like Anton had been forbidden to go to the attic.

Or maybe Johann Runge had locked the room himself, meaning to come back one day, pulled some boxes in front of it, and then never returned.

How the room got locked and forgotten didn't matter as much as what it held inside.

Anton grabbed the flaps of a nearby box and pulled it open. Inside, he saw more files, these carefully labeled and marked 1925. He opened one before he realized that these were all connected to the assassination attempt at the Peace Conference—an attempt that Johann Runge had investigated and helped solve, an attempt he made a point of mentioning in *Death at Fasching* as having nothing to do with the Carnival Sniper.

Anton pulled the chair away from the desk and sat down, suddenly overwhelmed.

The files existed, just like Sofie Branstadter had said they did.

The question was, what should Anton do with them?

2005

KOLISKO'S COMMENT BOTHERED HER.

Sofie sat cross-legged on the floor in the far corner of her library, digging through her history-of-science books. It was too late to call Scotland Yard; she would have to do so in the morning. But the day had disturbed her enough so that she couldn't rest. She had to work.

But before she started on her own research, she had to look up something—something that Kolisko's comment had triggered.

She had a book on top-secret experiments, rumors, and lies, a book that had been banned by the governments of six nations. She finally found her copy, shoved behind a stack of papers she had copied from the masters and doctoral thesis room of the University of Vienna. She had kept those for one of the history projects she planned to start after she finished with the Sniper.

The book, *Buried Discoveries*, contended that the state—be that state Russia, Britain or China—considered some scientific discoveries so dangerous that it confiscated all the research, refused to allow the scientists to continue working on the material, and conducted a disinformation campaign on the ideas that were already out among the public.

Some of the ideas weren't easily buried. Sofie had double-checked the author's research on the idea that had interested her—the use of nuclear energy to make bombs. Apparently, when the atom had been harnessed in the early 1940s, the German scientists realized that the energy they had discovered had great destructive powers.

These men had opted to bury those powers and the knowledge of their use, as they worked to find a cleaner, cheaper, and more reliable form of energy than coal- and oil-burning. And they had succeeded, although the rumors of nuclear energy's destructive power remained, like a cautionary tale.

What Sofie had learned through her research was that it would take a great deal of work and a unique delivery system to create an atomic bomb. Without a large source of financing (which no one confessed to), the scientists didn't have the inclination or the resources to create such a weapon.

Which didn't, as one scientist said, stop governments from doing so. There was just no evidence that anyone had found that any government had pursued this research.

For which Sofie was quite relieved. The Cold War between Russia and China hovered over all of Europe like an unanswered threat. The last thing the world needed was for one side to gain a tactical advantage and turn the war hot.

Sofie had initially bought *Buried Discoveries* because she had been toying with writing a book about weaponry and war, and she had double-checked the research as a start for that project.

When the project hadn't happened, she put the book away and turned to other things.

But she had read through *Buried Discoveries* first, and had been intrigued by its many notions. One of its more preposterous notions concerned time travel. Initially, she had scanned that section, but she had remembered it.

Now she read it with fascination.

The book's author, Conrad Linz, claimed that in the 1950s, Russian scientists began to experiment with time travel. First they managed to send a clock backwards one minute in time. Then they found ways to send objects back five minutes in time.

For many years, the Russians stalled at that point. They built a small novelty device—a prototype for a toy that would allow people to go back only a minute or two in time—but never sold it on the market.

Because the graduate students working on the project had fiddled with the machine, they made it possible to travel months, then years, into the past. The changes happened too quickly. Some of the graduate students were lost; they never returned. Others came back shaken, claiming that the past could easily be changed.

The problem was that changing the past did not change the future. In other words, the scientists did not suddenly find themselves in a whole new present.

Changing the past created alternate timelines. The Changed Past led to a New Future, one that was never as the changer had imagined.

The scientists postulated that the people who had changed their past had used their time travel devices to return to the present—only to find themselves traveling along the new timeline rather than the old. It was impossible for the Changers ever to return to their own world.

Sofie read and reread this section several times. In it, Linz interviewed the science fiction writer Isaac Asimov, whose novels often focused on alternate timelines as a cautionary tale.

Even so, Asimov was quoted as saying, *people still wanted to travel in the past.*

The scientific research had been conducted at several state-run universities and according to the agreements the scientists had with those universities, the discoveries belonged to the universities themselves (although the scientist could write about it). A lot of university research was monitored by the state, even in Austria, but particularly in Russia which, despite its conversion to a parliamentary democracy after the Great War, still held onto some of its tzarist, autocratic roots.

When the prototype time-travel model got out of hand, the government shut down all time-travel-related research, claiming it was too dangerous. Anyone with a machine and a passion for the past could make terrifying changes in someone else's present.

Linz theorized that the government was protecting itself—not wanting to lose power in any timeline—but Sofie wondered if it wasn't simply the threat of losing control over history itself that stopped the research.

Sofie set the book down and reached for her other science texts, wishing she knew more about physics. She remembered learning in her Physics for Poets class that time travel was theoretically possible, just not practical, and she found a reference in her fifteen-year-old textbook.

She could find other references as well, all of them claiming that time travel would some day become a reality so long as certain problems were overcome. *However,* one of the books stated, *since science now seems certain that time travel will, by its very nature, create alternate timelines, no one can seem to find a practical use for it. Perhaps, if observers can be sent back without creating alternate timelines, things could be learned from the past. Until then, time travel is a creative dead-end.*

Sofie closed that book and hugged it to herself. She wasn't sure what any of her findings meant, if anything.

As Kolisko had said, the idea itself was intriguing.

But she had been a researcher long enough to know that interesting ideas were usually just that—ideas. Intellectual games that students played, with no real consequences and no real value.

Much as she liked the fanciful idea that some time traveler had assassinated people in the past, she could never look at that as a realistic option.

Chances were that the bullet came from some obscure company, experimenting with a concept that went nowhere, and that the Sniper had somehow been connected to that.

Sofie set the book down and frowned. If she could isolate who made the bullets and where they were distributed—and if her assumption that it was a little-known company was right—then she might actually be close to discovering who the Sniper had been.

She smiled softly to herself. Scotland Yard had rooms and rooms filled with expensive giant computers and super-large databases on all sorts of things from fingerprints to DNA to ballistics.

She would need to figure out a way to get access. That had been her problem in the first place. The Yard had wanted to know exactly what kind of evidence she had, how long she had access to it, and what types of tests they had to perform.

When she had contacted them, she had had none of that information, so the Yard made it clear that they couldn't help her.

She had turned to private labs, which had led her to Crime Research Labs for fingerprints, ballistics, and a few other types of evidence, and two different labs in Switzerland—one for fabric analysis and another that specialized in old DNA.

But she had wanted the Yard, and this afternoon, CRL had given her an excuse to contact them.

She doubted that any researcher at Scotland Yard would suggest time travel as the cause for an unusual item.

Sofie put the books back on her shelf. She had wasted enough of her day on this idea, intriguing as it was. She had real research to do, and she had to get to it.

1913

BY THE TIME RUNGE REALIZED he needed to go to Huetteldorf, the trams had stopped running.

He sat at his desk in police headquarters, the gas lamps turned on low, studying Bronstein's papers. A large smear blocked important information, but Runge had waited for the blood to dry. Then he carefully flaked it off, using a straight razor and a delicate touch.

When he could finally read the words, he leaned back in his chair.

Bronstein had had a family, a wife and two young children, who probably did not know that their husband and father would not be coming home.

Runge ran a hand over his face. He had not expected this. Somehow he had thought that a man who whiled away his afternoons in a café had no job and no home. Indeed, Runge could find no employment listed, but that was not unusual for recent expatriates.

The problem was that Bronstein had been in Vienna for six years. He should have found employment. He should have had a way to support his family.

Runge leaned beside his desk and reached into the briefcase that he had found near the body. Lots of newspapers, some clearly unread, and many handwritten papers, most of them in Russian.

Runge did not read Russian, but some of his colleagues did. He would get them to translate for him.

Unfortunately, none of those colleagues were here this late, either.

Runge sighed and rubbed his eyes. He was afraid to return to his apartment, worried that he would be called out again. There was no reason the killer had to be just a daylight shooter. He had committed his first known murders indoors. There was nothing to stop him from shooting people at night.

Runge stood, feeling restless. Perhaps he was approaching this wrong. Perhaps Adler was with Bronstein because they both had ties to the socialists. Bronstein was an expatriate, after all. Most of Russia's expatriates in the last decade had been exiled for political reasons.

Perhaps there was a side to the famous Freud that Runge knew nothing about. Perhaps the man had socialist leanings.

The family would know.

And until that evening, Runge had not thought to find out.

2005

BY MIDNIGHT, ANTON HAD MADE A DECISION.

He climbed out of the basement, dirty, disheveled, and curiously elated. Over the past five hours, he had read excerpts from dozens of cases, all of them either committed by snipers or assassins, and many of them happening in Eastern Europe, although not all of them.

Johann Runge had traveled all over the world, and studied killers—killers who shot people they apparently had no tie to, killers who used a gun.

So far as Anton could ascertain, the boxes held the files from other cases. The wooden filing cabinets held the materials from the Sniper investigation.

There were six large cabinets that he could see, maybe one or two more behind the boxes, and each cabinet had to hold hundreds of files.

Anton could go through it all, or maybe even hire someone to transcribe it, but he couldn't put it all in perspective. That wasn't his training or his inclination. As elated as he felt for discovering the material, he didn't react that same way when he thought of letting the world know about it.

Either some stranger would come into his house and co-opt the material or Anton would be hounded for the rest of his days for the files.

He could probably donate them all to the History Museum of the City of Vienna, but that almost felt like a betrayal of his family.

His great-grandfather had kept all of this for a reason. Maybe Sofie Branstadter had been right. Maybe Johann Runge had thought he would discover who the Sniper was before his own death.

But he hadn't. He had tried, and failed.

Unless the answer was somewhere in those files.

Maybe his great-grandfather had died before he had been able to complete the second book.

The only way Anton would know the answers was to read through the files. And then he would want someone to put them in some kind of order, to vindicate his great-grandfather if such a vindication was possible.

Anton already knew that Sofie Branstadter had the training to go through this material and make sense of it. She would also be able to bring it to a larger audience.

The question was, would she make an agreement with him that allowed him to keep control of the material—and what she published from it? Or would she insist on complete control?

By the time he finally turned on the shower, he had the answer to those last questions as well. He would propose some kind of collaboration with Sofie Branstadter over these materials, and make her access to them contingent on his conditions.

He could offer her an informal agreement, or they could see his family's attorney and draw up the agreement there.

Either way, both would benefit. Sofie would have fresh material for her Sniper book, and Anton would maintain control of his great-grandfather's legacy.

Anton stripped and let the hot water wash the dirt of generations off his skin. In the morning, he would call Sofie Branstadter and tell her he had made a discovery, but not what it was.

Then he would show her the room.

He wanted to see her surprise.

1913

THE ASSASSIN CREPT into the Augarten. Snow covered the paths and decorated the trees. The statues looked like ice sculptures. Aside from the footprints from people who had visited earlier in the day, he saw no signs of human life.

And why should there be? It was past midnight, dark and bitterly cold. No gaslights illuminated the paths through this park, and the moon was a simple sliver. He felt, not for the first time that day, as if he had stepped into a made-up world.

The Augarten was huge and old. The park had been founded in the sixteenth century—for the royals, of course—and then opened to the public in the eighteenth.

The assassin was stumbling through, staying in the footprints, trying to recognize landmarks. The trees were the wrong height, and the paths—if, indeed, that's what the footprints followed—seemed to be in the wrong place.

He looked for the Flakturm, and couldn't find it. The large concrete tower, painted with murals and decorated with flags from Austria's long history, didn't seem to be part of the Augarten now. He wasn't sure how that could be. The Flakturm, he knew, dated from the twentieth century—he'd seen that porous concrete shell often enough to recognize the terrible yet somehow permanent construction.

The park just didn't seem the same without it.

The assassin had been wandering through Brigittenau for hours now, looking for an empty building or a place to sleep. His feet felt like ice and his fingertips were numb. He was trying to keep them warm inside his coat, but even that was no longer working.

A few of the local pubs were open, but he'd found, when he'd gone in them, that he was horribly out of place. Not because he was out of time—the patrons didn't seem to notice he was from the future any more than any of the other Viennese had—but because of his clean woolen coat, his woolen pants, and his expensive shoes.

He was not wearing the costume of a working man, and that immediately made him suspicious in this part of Vienna.

He felt vaguely desperate, not wanting his entire trip to be ruined because he couldn't find shelter for the night. And yet, he knew if he got much colder, he wouldn't be worth anything. He might as well go back because he wouldn't be able to shoot straight at all.

If he went back, he would not return.

This was definitely his last trip to the past.

Then he stumbled out of the trees and saw a familiar building shading the night sky. The Brigittakappelle—the Chapel of St. Bridget—which marked the north side of the Augarten.

He stopped in front of it, saw lights flickering inside. His heart seemed to catch in his throat and for a moment, he couldn't take a breath.

He hadn't been in a church in ages—not since he first came up with this scheme. He used to find comfort in churches—in their age, their gravity, their sense of timelessness.

But he stopped feeling the comfort when he realized there was no such thing as timelessness—that time, like anything else in the world, could be changed, manipulated through the actions of man.

The assassin sighed and shoved his fists deeper into his coat. The wind rose and played with the hair on the nape of his neck, sending a shiver through him.

He didn't exactly make a decision to walk up the stone steps. Instead, he found himself pushing against the door, stepping inside to the familiar damp scent of ancient stone walls mingling with the vaguely plastic smell of beeswax candles.

And candles were everywhere, burning in their small votive cups, flickering in the wind blowing through the open door. He let the door close behind him, then stepped deeper inside, his shoes scraping against the stone floor.

At least it was warm in here, out of the wind, the heat of a thousand tiny candles taking the chill out of the chapel.

No one greeted him. No one stepped out of the back to see who had arrived. Not even the statues faced him. The Virgin looked at the babe in her arms, the expression on her Renaissance-designed face both tender and worried. And the crucified Jesus, hanging on his cross in mute agony, seemed more concerned with his own pain than the assassin's.

The assassin stayed by the door, his hands still tucked in his pockets. The shivering hadn't stopped.

He swallowed, and slipped inside, finding a pew away from the candlelight. The pews were hard; no one had covered them with cloth or cushions as he had found in countless other churches.

But he didn't care. A few hours out of the wind was all he needed.

He set the timer on his pocket watch for six a.m., stretched out, and fell asleep.

2005

SOFIE MADE WIDE, circling doodles on the pad beside her phone as she listened to the series of clicks that let her know she was still on hold with England's Scotland Yard. Its forensic arm was buried deep in cases that had to go to trial; doing outside work for a "lark," as the head of the unit had characterized her book, was not something the Yard normally did.

They hadn't told her that when she had contacted them a year ago. When she mentioned that on this call, the head of the unit had laughed.

"We find any way possible to discourage these private cases."

He didn't even seem swayed by the fact that she could and would pay. Apparently, it wasn't good form to discuss money with the head of the forensics unit.

Sofie curled her feet under her legs and leaned forward on her desk. She should have gotten dressed before getting her coffee and climbing the stairs to her office. She was actually chilly in her robe and bare feet.

And she didn't feel very professional. It almost seemed like the man she'd been speaking to knew she was underdressed. Or perhaps the British treated everyone with that slight air of condescension.

The clicks continued. Sofie wondered if she should have started counting them. Maybe they happened every ten seconds. Then she would know how long she had been on hold.

Of course, she knew that anyway. The antique clock she had bought on impulse nearly a decade ago showed her that she had been listening to clicks for going on ten minutes now.

Sofie sipped her coffee and wondered if it was bad form to hang up on Scotland Yard. She wanted their help, but there were other places she could go for her backup lab.

Finally, the clicking stopped, and Sofie stopped doodling, barely breathing, as she waited. The last thing she wanted to have happen after ten minutes of being on hold at international rates was to lose the connection.

Then a hum in the line told her that the officer had returned. "I'm terribly sorry, Miss Branstadter," he said. "Regulations require that I speak to other members of the organization before I can commit us to anything like this. Can you tell me—?"

His question was interrupted by a soft beep. Her call waiting, notifying her that someone was on the other line.

"I have another call," Sofie said. "May I call you back?"

"In a week or so," he said. "By then, I should know where we stand."

Sofie suppressed a sigh of irritation. She thanked him and hung up, doubting she would ever call him back. The Americans' Federal Bureau of Investigation didn't have as good an international reputation, but rumors were that their science was more up-to-date. Perhaps she would contact them before making any decisions about Scotland Yard.

She depressed the button in the phone's cradle, and then greeted the caller on her other line.

"Miss Branstadter?" It was Anton Runge. Sofie recognized the voice, even though she had only met him the day before.

His call made her set down her pen.

"After your visit yesterday," he said, "I searched some of the old storage areas in the house and I found a few things. Would you like to see them?"

Would she? She would give her right arm to do so. But she knew better than to sound that eager.

"I'd love to," she said. "Can you bring them to my office? I'm on the other side of the Ring from you."

She would meet him in the entry and look over what he found. If it was important, she could move it to the office herself.

"Um, actually, I think you'd better come here." He sounded surprised, as if he hadn't considered leaving the building.

Sofie paused, uncertain whether or not she wanted to return to that house. For the most part, Runge had been polite, but his anger had been very difficult for her. And that house seemed to bring up memories for him, memories that obviously weren't so pleasant.

"Is there a reason you can't bring the items here?" she asked.

"Yes," he said. "You'll understand when you arrive."

She hadn't expected that answer. She had expected him to say something about the possibility of reporters seeing him arrive with boxes at her apartment, or the fact that he didn't want the materials out of his house.

But this cryptic statement excited her even more. Maybe the boxes were too big. Maybe the evidence was there, and fragile, and he wasn't willing to touch it.

"I'll be there in an hour," Sofie said, and hung up.

Then she leaned back in her chair and pulled her robe together.

He found something.

She hoped it was the something that she needed.

2005

PRECISELY ONE HOUR LATER, someone knocked at the door.

Anton wiped his hands on his jeans, feeling more nervous than he felt before a performance. He pushed his hair out of his face, tugged his T-shirt down, and wished he had worn something else.

Then he wondered where that thought had come from.

His work boots clicked on the wooden floor as he walked through the entry. He had gloves stuck in his back pocket and a hat on the banister at the top of the basement stairs. He wasn't going to get quite as filthy as he had the day before.

He pulled open the door. Sofie Branstadter stood before him, looking beautiful and tailored, hair perfect and makeup lightly applied. She wore a white silk blouse and light brown pants along with low-slung heels that wouldn't make it two steps on the uneven basement floor.

He had forgotten to warn her to dress down.

Still, he smiled and swept his hand toward the interior. "Come on in."

She didn't smile back. Instead, she gave him a curious look as she stepped into the entry.

He closed the door.

"What did you find?" she asked.

Apparently she wasn't much for small talk. Neither was he, but he felt uncomfortable all the same without the usual formalities to start the conversation.

"I'm sorry," he said. "I should have warned you. The stuff is in the basement still, and it's really messy down there."

Sofie shrugged. "Everything can be cleaned."

"Let me at least get you a jacket to cover that blouse," he said.

But Sofie held up a hand. "I don't care if I get dirty. I want to see what you have."

"All right," he said.

If she was like other women he had known, she would care once she realized the blouse was ruined. But he'd learned long ago not to argue with someone who was determined.

"Follow me," he said, and led her down the stairs.

He had spent the hour while he waited for her moving the boxes around so that he had access to filing cabinets. He also put some extra lights in that small room—portable lights, so that he wouldn't tax the fragile electrical system already in place there.

He led the way, but he made sure Sofie followed closely behind him. She touched the railing lightly, more nimble in those shoes than he would have expected.

And she didn't grimace at the cobwebs still hanging beside the stairs, or at the piles of junk he had moved in his search the day before.

Instead, she came forward with her eyes wide, taking in all the material around her, and looking a bit like a child who was being led to someplace magical.

"I spent most of yesterday looking," Anton said, mostly because he couldn't stand the silence, "and I was about to give up when I saw this light...."

As he led her through the maze that the basement had become, he told her the story of finding the secret room. Occasionally, he would glance over his shoulder. Sofie's eyes sparkled, and that expression of anticipation seemed to be even stronger.

He felt an odd hopefulness, as if he were doing all of this to please her, and he tried to shake it off.

"No one ever spoke of this room?" Sofie asked when he'd finished.

"No one," he said. "Not my father, not my grandfather. I had no idea it was here."

Sofie kept pace with him, not seeming to care that a strip of dirt that might have once been flypaper brushed her cheek or that her lovely blouse already had dust smudges across the arms.

More than once he extended his hand to help her across small barriers, and each time she placed hers lightly in his, he felt as if she had given him her trust.

By the time they reached the room, his nervousness returned.

The room seemed to glow behind the pile of boxes and ruined furniture. All the lights he had left on in there overwhelmed the dim lights in the rest of the basement.

"It's so bright," Sofie said.

"I wanted us to be able to see," he said.

Then he helped her the last few steps. She stopped in the door of the room (which he was already starting to think of as his great-grandfather's room), and just stared.

"All of this you discovered yesterday?" She wasn't really asking a question. It sounded more like awe.

"Yes," he said anyway. "From what I can tell, the filing cabinets pertain to the Sniper, and the boxes are my great-grandfather's other cases."

But Sofie walked to the typewriter first. She extended her hand. It was shaking, almost as if this very place overwhelmed her.

It had certainly overwhelmed Anton. It still overwhelmed him, which was one of the many reasons he brought her down here.

She touched the keys of the typewriter lightly, as if she were touching a sacred object. "Do you think he wrote down here?"

"I have no idea," Anton said. "But it wouldn't surprise me."

His great-grandfather had been used to rooms without windows— the precinct in his great-grandfather's day had had a lot of windowless rooms—and he seemed to have been a fanatic for privacy. What could be more private than a room with its own padlock, in the basement, far away from the other business of the house?

"It would certainly have kept his wife and son out," Anton said, feeling awkward referring to his own grandfather that way. "And I have no idea what's in most of these boxes. They've probably got some gruesome stuff. I saw one or two photographs yesterday—one of Archduke Franz Ferdinand—that I wish I'd never seen."

"Your great-grandfather consulted on the Archduke's assassination," Sofie said, still looking at the typewriter. Her fingers still lightly touched the keys, as if she couldn't believe how close she was to a historical moment.

"He consulted on a lot of assassinations," Anton said. "I think there must be entire books' worth of material here."

He'd said it before he meant to—turning this moment to work, instead of the thrill of discovery. Still, Sofie didn't seem to pick up on it. Instead she examined the entire room.

"You're sure the Sniper stuff is in the files?" she asked.

"I'm not sure about anything. I know that Sniper material is in at least one of the cabinets and that some of the boxes have material on other cases. I also know that the boxes aren't of equal weight. Some are damn heavy."

His back ached in memory of a few of those boxes. He hadn't lifted them this morning, instead pushing them along with his feet until they were in their proper place.

"May I?" Sofie asked, indicating one of the cabinets.

"Be my guest," he said. And because they hadn't set rules yet about how she could use the material, he stayed close to the door.

She pulled open the nearest file drawer—the second drawer down, which was easier for her to see inside—and leaned over it like a vulture out of a nature show.

Her slender fingers moved the files, her cheeks flushed, and she shook her head almost constantly, as if part of her were denying what she saw.

"This entire drawer is filled with eyewitness reports, and diagrams, and the history of the Café Central." She sounded stunned. "He even has a list of all the patrons who were there, their families, friends, and acquaintances."

She pulled a file out of the drawer and thumbed through it. Anton watched her in fascination. She seemed to have forgotten he was there.

"He kept these up-to-date. When someone died, he clipped the obituary and put it in the file. He did follow-up interviews and wrote down their biographies." She was shaking her head again. "This is an unimaginable amount of work."

That had been Anton's sense. And he had never been good in school—at least not with research projects. Music, art, even mathematics—he had excelled in all of them with little work. But research made his skin crawl.

"Yeah, I know," he said. "There has to be enough material here for a dozen non-fiction books."

This time, Sofie looked up at him. She blinked, then frowned a little, and finally smiled.

"No," she said. "I didn't mean this was a lot of work for me or anyone compiling the material. I meant that your great-grandfather did a tremendous amount of work. I'd wager that now we know what he did those missing eleven years. He finished his research on the Sniper case, maybe expecting to catch him."

"And yet, he didn't," Anton said.

"At least not that we know of," Sofie said, her voice rising with excitement. "Who knows? Maybe the answer is in here, and your great-grandfather just didn't have time to write the book."

Her gaze met Anton's and held it for a moment. Then she flushed and set the file back in the drawer.

"You have quite a treasure trove here," she said.

Anton nodded.

"You didn't have to call me, you know."

Her words surprised him. He had been expecting her to negotiate, so when she said something different, it took a moment for the sentence to register.

"I know," he said softly.

"I mean, you could compile all this—hell, you could hire transcriptionists and just sell these as individual books. *Johann Runge's Files on the Franz Ferdinand Assassination. Johann Runge's Files on the Carnival Sniper Case, Volume One.* With the photographs and diagrams in the files, you'd have so much material, you could keep publishing until the day you died."

Sofie had folded her hands in front of her dust-covered brown pants. She seemed almost sad.

"You think a publisher would go for that?" Runge asked, intrigued more by her manner than her words.

"Yes," she said. "I think several publishers would go for it, and I think you'd get a bidding war. Especially over the Sniper material. The others would have to come out slowly, after you're done with the Sniper files."

He studied her for a moment. She wasn't trying to negotiate her own way in. She hadn't assumed that the files belonged to her or that she had the right to use them. She hadn't even asked permission to use them, at least not yet.

He would have asked by now.

"Are you advising me to do this?" he asked.

She shook her head again as she surveyed the room. She wasn't saying 'no' to him; clearly she was as overwhelmed by the material as he had been, but for a different reason. She seemed surprised that it existed, even though she had been the one to guess that it was here.

"You could do anything you want," she said, her hands still clasped like a demure schoolgirl's. "You could hire your own researcher. You could hire your own ghost writer for that matter—do a follow-up to *Death at Fasching*, based on your great-grandfather's notes, bill it as the book Johann Runge always meant to write."

"It seems like a lot of work," he said.

"You wouldn't have to do the work, though. The work is here. All you need is someone to organize it." She glanced at the files longingly.

"You're not interested?" he asked, thinking he knew the answer.

Her breath caught. "In being your ghost writer, no, I'm not."

Anton nodded. He had expected that.

"Organizing the material, maybe," she said, surprising him again. "But you could get someone so much cheaper than me."

"This is what you were looking for," he said.

She turned to him. Her expression was open, almost lost. "This is so much more than I was looking for. And it wouldn't be fair to take the surprises from you. It's your family's legacy."

"I'm not a historian," Anton said.

"I know," she said. "Which is why I'm telling you what you can do. You have a lot of options. You need to know that."

"Why?" he asked.

"Because," she said, and her voice was breathless, "once people know about this, they'll try to take advantage of you. You have to know what your options are before you make a deal with anyone."

"Including you," he said.

She nodded, and turned away, but not before he saw the disappointment in her gaze.

"Including me," she said.

Her honesty intrigued him for the second day in a row. He liked her—she was smart and prickly and ethical. He hadn't encountered a lot of ethical people who were interested in the Sniper.

"What kind of deal would you like?" he asked.

She shook her head, only this time it was in response to his question. "You're not ready to deal."

"I am," he said. "I've been giving this a lot of thought. I wouldn't have found this without you. I had no idea it was here."

"You would have found it. You would have remodeled or dug through the boxes, and you would have found it." She crossed her arms as if she were cold. But it was warm in the small room.

"All right." He was willing to try a different tack. "Let's say you knew I had all of this material, and you wanted it for your book. What kind of arrangement would we have?"

She shrugged. "It depends. Libraries and museums usually want the material to stay in the viewing rooms, under lock and key, and then they want credit. But you have a gold mine here—"

"Don't worry about me," he said. "What would you ask for?"

She bit her lower lip and continued to stare at the files. "If you were a library?"

"Private citizen with all this material," he said.

"Free access. Ability to quote it all. If there's evidence here, I'd like to test it."

"I haven't found the evidence," he said, "or at least, anything that I would recognize as evidence."

"Have you looked through all the boxes?"

"No," he said.

She was silent for a moment. "I'd ask for all of that, and maybe permission to come back if I decide to write a book about your great-grandfather. He seems even more fascinating than I thought."

"Yeah," Anton said. "Me, too."

Sofie gave him a soft smile.

"Why aren't you asking me for those things?" Anton said. "I know that you're writing the book."

"And you don't approve, at least you didn't yesterday."

"So?" he said. "Libraries rarely have approval over what people do with their material."

"True enough. It's just…." Sofie shrugged, turned away, hugged her arms around her chest even tighter. "This is your legacy. Your family's history. I value that."

"Then let's draw up an agreement for access," Anton said.

She shivered, ever so slightly.

"That's what you want, isn't it?" he asked into her silence.

She nodded. "But it's only fair that you know what happens to evidence when it gets tested. Some of it gets destroyed."

"We'll deal with that," he said.

"You might change your mind when you realize how much this is worth."

It was Anton's turn to smile. "I told you yesterday that I make enough royalties off my great-grandfather's book not to worry about that."

"Vast sums of money often make people change their minds," Sofie said.

"I won't change my mind," he said. "That's why I want to draw up a document."

"I have a standard one," she said. "It's in my purse. You'll want a lawyer to check it over before you sign it."

He nodded.

"And you might want to check with a literary agent, too."

He smiled again. "I can take care of myself, Sofie. I've been in the music industry for a long time now. It makes your business seem nice."

She flushed.

He held out his hand. "Come on. Let's look at your agreement, and see if we can come to an understanding."

2005

SOFIE TOOK ANTON'S HAND. His fingers were warm and dry and long, with the strength that she had imagined they would have. Her cheeks grew warmer, and she hoped he wouldn't notice.

She had already been unprofessional this morning. She hadn't realized she was attracted to him until she showed up at his door dressed as if they were going to lunch instead of rummaging through old boxes. He'd noticed that she wasn't appropriately dressed; she hoped he had no idea why.

He helped her out of the room, through the maze of broken furniture and boxes. He had conducted an all-out search, and he seemed very excited about it. Yet he was willing to hand over the secrets of the material—the surprises, the real value—to her, with no remuneration.

It made her uneasy.

She didn't like to take advantage of people, and she felt like she was taking advantage of him.

Maybe she would talk with her agent about him, see if they could set up the transcription deal. Then Sofie's conscience wouldn't bother her. Then she would get her surprises, and he would have something extra as well.

She would wait a few days and then talk to him.

The thing she had to get, though, was permission to take the evidence. Permission to test it. She would be hard-nosed about that. If she had to, she'd bring in the police department, who could probably claim—with the law on their side—that the evidence was theirs. If Anton didn't give her permission, the department would.

But she was getting ahead of herself. If she got him to sign the document, then she was clear. At least she had thought far enough ahead to bring it. She had learned on her very first book that such papers were necessary. People made promises all the time, and promptly forgot them when they were faced with success.

It seemed to take Sofie and Anton less time to get out of the basement than it had to go down there, perhaps because Sofie wasn't anticipating any more. Anton led her into the kitchen, which was messier than it had been the day before. The dishes piled near the sink confirmed the story of his search; he hadn't had time to clean up after himself. Although he had kept himself fueled on pastries. The large plate from the day before was nearly empty.

Sofie had left her purse in the entry. She fetched all four copies of the document—one for him, one for her, one for her agent, and one for the publisher—and gave Anton all of them.

He raised an eyebrow. "You came prepared."

"You told me you had found something," she said, feeling awkward. "It's a formality—"

"I understand," Anton said.

He grabbed a pen off his counter, paused to read the papers, and then signed. One by one, he slid them back to her. She signed them as well, and gave him his copy.

"Satisfied?" he asked.

She nodded. She was more than satisfied. She was elated. Never in all her years of doing historical research had she had a find like this morning's.

"Well, then," he said. "Let's get to work."

1913

RUNGE CALLED ON THE FREUDS FIRST because he did not have to take a tram to reach them. He went as early as he dared. A friend of the family let him in the arched doorway, and directed him to the study where Sigmund Freud had had his medical practice.

Runge thought the study a bad choice. He didn't want the family to be thinking about their loss while he was there; he wanted to talk with them—particularly Freud's wife—about Sigmund Freud's life.

The friend left Runge alone while rousing a member of the family. Runge used the moment to explore the business area of Freud's residence.

Three small rooms made up the famous man's practice. The rooms had overstuffed but tasteful furniture, most of it purchased before the turn of the century. The first room was the waiting room. It was dark, with only one small window overlooking the courtyard.

Runge couldn't imagine waiting there for whatever procedure the doctor did. Runge had heard horrible things about Freud's practice—discussion of private matters, sexual matters, and examination of patients in the most personal ways.

The entire place made Runge nervous, and not just because he was investigating a death.

The door to the consulting room was locked. Beyond the consulting room was the study, the place that the family friend had urged Runge to wait.

The study was also dark; no one had bothered to light any lamps. Apparently it was still too early in the day. The thin light from the single window, also overlooking the courtyard, illuminated the slightly messy desk.

It looked as if Freud had just left—which, in point of fact, he had. He had meant only to go out for a walk. He had not meant to die.

The study smelled faintly of pipe smoke, although Runge saw no evidence of a pipe. This room seemed more personal than the other. Floor-to-ceiling bookshelves ran the length of it, and on one wall, glassed-in cabinets housed pottery, sculpture, and knickknacks that seemed very old.

Runge had just stepped beside the desk to investigate them when the main door opened all the way.

"Detective Runge?" a woman's voice asked.

He turned, surprised to see the matron of the house. Martha Freud was a solid woman, dressed entirely in black. She had laugh lines near her eyes and a pleasant mouth. Her nose, long and wide, was the only thing that prevented her from having her daughter's beauty.

"I'm sorry to bother you, ma'am," Runge said, giving her a slight bow. "I have a few questions that can't wait."

She nodded gravely and walked into the room. She passed him, leaving a trail of sweet perfume, and sat behind her husband's desk. She seemed about to fold her hands over the papers, then stopped, as if she didn't want to disturb them.

Her eyes teared, but she blinked hard, and the tears did not fall. She put her hands in her lap instead, and sighed.

"I am willing to do anything I can to find this man," Mrs. Freud said. "I am given to understand that he attacked two others before he found my husband."

"Yes," Runge said. "That's what I wanted to discuss with you. Some of my colleagues believe the shootings were random. I am not so certain. I wanted to know if there was any connection between these men and your husband."

"I have not looked at the papers," Mrs. Freud said. "I am not—"

Her voice broke. She swallowed hard, then took a deep breath, as if she were trying to compose herself.

"I can discuss this with one of your children," Runge said gently, although he preferred to talk with her. She would know more about her husband's friends and associates than her children would.

"No." Mrs. Freud withdrew a handkerchief from her sleeve and dabbed her eyes. "It's better that I do this. My children are understandably shaken."

As was she. But Runge now understood the role she was determined to play. She would ignore her own pain for as long as she could while tending to her family. Perhaps later she would find time for herself.

"The men who died," Runge said, easing himself into the chair across from her, "were Lev Bronstein and Viktor Adler. Did your husband know them?"

"Viktor. He knew Viktor," she said. "They went to school together. Viktor studied psychoanalysis, although he did not practice. He is the one who found us this apartment. He lived here before we did."

Runge's breath caught. Those were the kinds of details he had been looking for. The tie between Adler and Freud in the killer's mind might have been as simple as their address.

Or buried deep within their history.

"You said he did not practice," Runge said. "His activities with the Social Democrats are well known. Was your husband involved with them?"

"My husband did not have time for local politics. His work was too important. He was finishing another book…." Her words trailed off as her fingers rose. This time, she touched the papers before her, cautiously, reverently, as if she were afraid she would damage them.

"Can you think of any reason someone would want them both dead?" Runge asked.

Mrs. Freud's smile was soft and sad. "There were many people who did not like what my husband did. Even more than did not like what Viktor Adler did. But those people who did not like my husband, most of them were not from Vienna. And Viktor, while he is known in the Empire, is not hated outside of the city."

Runge nodded. He had had that sense of Adler as well.

"What of Bronstein?" Runge asked. "He and Viktor Adler were playing chess when the killer arrived. The man killed them both."

"I don't know any Bronstein," Mrs. Freud said.

"He is a Russian, and a regular customer at Café Central. Other than that, I have been unable to learn much about him."

Mrs. Freud shrugged. "Perhaps he is one of Viktor's political friends."

"But you don't know," Runge said.

"Our association with Viktor Adler had become very casual when he left his practice," she said. "I did not know him well before that. My husband does. He's the one—"

It was her first slip, and she caught herself the moment she made it. She brought her fingers to her lips, blinked hard again, and sighed.

"I'm sorry," Runge said again. "I know this is difficult."

"Yes," she whispered.

"Would there be other connections, things you might not be privy to, things that someone else might be able to tell me?" Runge asked.

"My husband kept his patients' confidences," she said, squaring her back. "So there is much I don't know."

"Do you think this Bronstein could have been a patient?"

"I do not know," she said.

"Did your husband keep records?"

"He kept notes," she said. "But I am uncertain whether or not I can show them to you. I'd have to consult with his colleagues."

"Would you please?" Runge asked. "I will come back in a few days. And if there is any connection between these two men, however slight, I would like to hear about it."

Mrs. Freud nodded. Then she stood, regal as an empress, and extended her hand.

Runge took it and bent over it, as proper as if they were at a ball. "I thank you for your helpfulness, gracious lady."

"It gives me something else to think on," she said, "besides all the empty years ahead."

And her voice did not tremble as she said that, nor was it filled with self-pity. Just a dry acceptance of a fact, a fact that had not existed the morning before.

The killer had not thought of this: the way his actions devastated a family and perhaps, in Freud's case, an entire profession.

Runge thanked Mrs. Freud and let himself out. Then he stopped at the door where Sigmund Freud had died, and stared at the spot across the street.

Freud was not political.

Perhaps Runge's colleagues were right.

Perhaps the killer was shooting at random.

And if he was, God help them all.

2005

SOFIE NEVER EXPECTED ANTON to help her, but she was glad he was. For a few moments, she stood in front of the office door, feeling overwhelmed at the volume of material.

She wanted to read all of it, to catalogue it, to make it into a library all by itself—a useful one, for Sniper research, investigative research, research into all the other cases, and research into Viennese history. But she couldn't do everything. She still had her deadline to consider, and mountains of work on her own book.

Which meant that first, she had to find the evidence.

She started on one side of the office, and Anton on the other. They opened each box before moving it, labeling the general contents on the box top.

They spent most of the afternoon, labeling and moving, discovering more and more files, all of them to do with cases other than the Sniper. Sofie was covered with dust and sweat. She no longer felt like that woman who had dressed for a date.

Before they started, Anton had offered her a work shirt, and she hadn't taken it. She almost wished she had, not just because her favorite ivory blouse was probably ruined, but because it would have shown him the same kind of trust he had shown her.

He was helping her dig into his past.

The boxes were a treasure trove of crime history, political history, and European history. So far, she hadn't discovered anything to suggest that Johann Runge had traveled to the Americas, but she knew he had. In those missing years, Runge had traveled over much of the world.

Sofie was about to suggest a dinner break when she opened a box that had no files at all. Her breath caught, and she crouched, feeling her already aching legs complain.

Inside the box, she found carefully marked bags. The bags were made of a very old paper, and it crinkled at her touch.

"Anton," she said, "I think you might want to see this."

She wasn't just calling him over for curiosity's sake. She was calling him over as a witness, so that he would see if her touch did any damage.

Slowly she pulled out the first bag, and set it on the box beside her. Then she unrolled the top. A faint odor of rot rose, almost the ghost of an odor. Still, Sofie blinked, feeling the urge to sneeze rise with the smell.

Anton handed her a flashlight and Sofie used it to peer inside the bag. Clothing, neatly folded, lay on top, newsprint between the layers.

Each item of clothing had a piece of paper pinned to the upper right-hand corner.

Sofie looked at the first.

> Shirt worn by L. Bronstein at time of death
> Case Number 1913112236

Sofie swallowed hard, feeling that exhilaration that came from discovering something she had thought lost forever.

"What is it?" Anton asked.

"The evidence," she whispered.

It was poorly stored, and probably badly contaminated. Still, it was here—or at least one box of it was—and that meant the others probably were as well.

"If you don't mind, I'd like to call my photographer," Sofie said. "We need a record of all of this, some kind of documentation of the state in which we found it."

Anton was still staring inside the box. His expression was blank and a little frightening. For a moment, Sofie thought he would deny her.

Then he nodded. "Phone's upstairs," he said. "Let's go."

Sofie let out a small sigh. She hadn't wanted him to stay alone with the evidence, but she hadn't known a way to discourage him. She was relieved that he was coming with her.

Still, she could barely contain herself as she headed for the stairs.

She had the evidence, the missing evidence.

And with it, she would be able to discover more about the Sniper than anyone anywhere had ever known.

1913

THE TRAIN SLOWED NOTICEABLY.

William craned his neck toward the window, but could see nothing. His sleeping seatmate leaned against the filthy glass. William turned toward the other side of the train car, and could still see nothing.

Then someone behind him murmured, "Vienna," and the word was filled with love and relief.

Vienna. They were getting close.

Brakes squealed against the rails as the train's momentum eased.

William's companion woke, bumping William's arm. His fist tightened around the nuke. He lifted the small device out of his pocket and cradled it against his chest.

Around him, people stood. Conversations started as passengers reached for the boxes they had stowed above the seats.

Papadopoulos turned sharply to his right. His eyes were narrowed, his pockmarked skin flushed. Apparently his seatmate had jostled him, too.

But William could not hear the interaction if, indeed, there was any. The conversation around him, the squealing brakes, the laughter in anticipation of arrival, drowned out everything else.

Papadopoulos stood.

William did, too, as did his seatmate. The man stretched, then glared at William, who was blocking the aisle.

William had no choice. He stepped forward, catching the stench of sweat and wet wool from Papadopoulos's coat.

This was William's chance—maybe his only chance. In the confusion, a few moments before the train stopped at the station.

His heart was pounding. Now he would see what he was made of.

A few short movements, and he would prevent the death of millions—perhaps billions—of people.

William slammed into Papadopoulos's back, jostling the wooden case from Papadopoulos's left hand.

The case fell, its pointed edge catching William on the arch of his right foot.

He winced in pain, but followed the case down anyway—

—and banged shoulders with Papadopoulos himself.

2005

UNTIL THEY FOUND THE EVIDENCE, Anton hadn't actually believed it existed. He realized, as he helped Sofie move all the nearby boxes, that a part of him never believed the Sniper case had happened at all.

Not even when he found the filing cabinets filled with his great-grandfather's case notes. After all, a writer could make all of that up, just using the notes to help him create his fictional world.

But the evidence itself, ten boxes' worth and counting, was something else entirely. It was proof positive that at least five people had died, and his great-grandfather hadn't been able to prevent the last three deaths.

Proof positive that some madman had escaped justice and might have, as Anton's great-grandfather feared, continued to spread his terror all over Europe.

The photographer had shown up shortly after Sofie had called her. Greta Thaler was tall and slender, dressed in jeans and a T-shirt, her long hair pulled back, making her look somewhat plain. Three cameras hung around her neck, and she held another in her hand.

Unlike most women Anton knew, Greta Thaler did not carry a purse. She also did not talk much. When Sofie had introduced them, Thaler had nodded and then taken his picture.

She took another one almost immediately of Sofie, and Anton caught a sense of the photograph. Sofie looked like someone who had been going through a basement full of boxes. Her white shirt was gray and streaked with black, her hair had bits of something dark hanging from one of the strands, and a large streak of something crossed her face from her left cheekbone to the right side of her chin, as if she had wiped her face with the back of a very dirty hand.

Anton hadn't realized until Thaler arrived how important she was to the project. Sofie had been right; the contents of that office had to be officially documented—the search for the materials needed more than his and Sofie's word that everything occurred the way it had.

Thaler turned toward the piano. She got one shot of his workspace before Anton could reach her.

"Please don't," he said.

"I thought you wanted all of this documented," Thaler said as she continued to peer through her camera's viewfinder.

"I want the basement documented, not this," he said. "This is my home."

She took one more picture and then shrugged. Anton's calm vanished. He wanted to take the camera and pull the film out. It was this kind of lack of privacy—this sort of invasion—that had convinced him to quit performance in the first place.

"Greta," Sofie said, "let's go downstairs."

Sofie pointed the way, and Thaler headed toward the basement.

Sofie put her hand on Anton's arm. "I'll get those pictures for you."

"I would appreciate it," he said.

Then he hurried down the stairs. He wanted to control Thaler's access. No more pictures of his family's possessions. Only the room, its contents, and the discoveries.

He needn't have worried. Thaler was standing in the middle of the pile of junk, camera in hand, circling, as if she didn't know how to attack it.

"The room is this way," Anton said.

Sofie was right behind him. "You need to take a few wide shots of the room, and the stuff outside, all as a unit, and then we'll concentrate on the evidence boxes. Can you help us out for a few days?"

Thaler nodded as she walked, still concentrating on all the stuff. Anton could almost see her thoughts: She was composing shots as she moved.

He understood that. Even when he wasn't thinking about music, a tune ran through his head. He had learned to ignore most of them; every once in a while one became so insistent he had to go and write it down.

It didn't take Thaler long to take the exterior shots that Sofie wanted. By then, Sofie had pulled out two more boxes of evidence.

"There has to be at least ten of them," she said to Anton.

He nodded and helped her search.

As they moved, a flash occasionally illuminated their workspace. Anton was happy he wasn't facing the camera; if he were, he would be seeing only colored dots by now.

Then Thaler switched cameras. She asked Sofie which box they wanted to start with. Sofie pulled out a third box, one she had been looking in.

"First, take a picture of everything inside it before we touch any of it. Then a shot of us handling the materials." She reached into a pocket and removed two thin pairs of gloves. She tossed one pair to Anton.

He slipped the gloves on and felt powdered latex against his skin.

Sofie had also pulled her gloves on and was opening the box. Thaler was taking photograph after photograph, as if she had an infinite supply of film.

Sofie crouched beside the box. Anton knelt on the other side, feeling the hard floor against his knees. He was more tired than he had been willing to let on. He wasn't used to physical labor, and two days of this had exhausted him.

Still, he reached inside and removed a stationer's box. On the top, someone had written *Evidence* in a bold hand. Anton handed the box to Sofie.

She waved her hand at him, refusing it. "Let's have the first photographs be of you looking at this stuff."

For legitimacy, he supposed. And human interest. The great-grandson investigating his great-grandfather's work.

The box was hard to open because it had been closed for so long. Anton had to wedge his fingers between the top and the bottom before he could pull them apart.

Inside were hundreds of sheets of paper, all of them covered with Cyrillic script, a few of them covered with brown fingerprints.

Sofie leaned over those, touched them lightly, and murmured, "Blood."

Anton felt gooseflesh rise on his arms. He set the papers back inside the stationer's box, and moved it to the space of the floor where the contents of this large box would go. Instead, Sofie took it from him and inspected the upper right-hand corner.

"It is the same case," she said, pointing at more lettering there. "See?"

Anton looked, and saw the case number. Thaler took a picture of the wording.

Then Anton reached inside the large box again, this time removing a woolen suit jacket. It smelled of sweat and tobacco, and it was stiff to the touch.

Sofie took that from him, too. "More blood."

Anton shuddered. He was ready to be done with his part in this little performance for the camera.

"It's yours now," he said.

Sofie smiled at him, but the smile was an absent one. She reached inside the box, removed more bags, all of which contained clothing, and spread them out on the floor before she declared that box done.

Thaler had to change film. "This is amazing," she said to Sofie.

"I know." Sofie was carefully putting the materials back into the box. "I can't believe it."

Thaler gave Anton a sideways glance as if she couldn't believe it either, and somehow blamed him—as if he had created all of this for some unfathomable reason.

He turned his back on her and pulled out a fourth box. Inside, they found more clothing, a pipe, and a hat that had been crushed by its long time in the box.

Another box revealed even more clothing, some chess pieces, and a few brown-stained newspapers.

Anton was about to call it a night, when Sofie opened a box and made a strangling noise.

"What is it?" he asked.

"Bullets," she said. "An entire bag of bullets."

Her skin had turned pale.

"That's important?" Anton asked.

She held a hand over the top of the box as if she were afraid to touch its contents.

"It might be everything," she said.

2005

CALLING THIS A BAG OF BULLETS was incorrect. The bag was filled with small cardboard boxes, and in each, a single bullet rested on the bottom, as if it were more precious than gold.

Each box had a label—Café Central, west wall, #1; the Mannerheim, wall shot—and Sofie hoped—no, she actually found herself praying—that she would find a corresponding diagram somewhere in all of these papers.

A few of the bullets had been flattened by the impact. Some blossomed like flowers or stars. Sofie couldn't tell if they were the same bullets as the one Morganthau had found in Adler or not. But a few were different. Like the one found in the wall of the Mannerheim.

It seemed to have lost its tip, but the rest of the bullet was mostly intact.

And its outer shell was green.

"Is that some kind of oxidation?" Anton asked.

Sofie shook her head. She extended her hand with the cardboard box open, the bullet centered inside.

"Make sure you get several shots of these, Greta," Sofie said. "I want them in color."

"Already doing it," Greta said. "This is creepy stuff, Sof."

Sofie nodded absently. She didn't feel creeped out—not like she had at the Adler autopsy. She felt almost giddy.

More green bullets. The first had not been a fluke. The Sniper had used green bullets on his victims—green, unidentifiable bullets.

She doubted anything could make her happier, and indeed, nothing did.

Until Anton found a bloodstained box inside another box.

The first box filled with other miscellaneous items. On top, someone had placed a large box, made of rough wood. It had a large handprint on one side.

Anton seemed a bit squeamish about the blood, but Sofie was too excited to be. Even Greta seemed to be involved, because she used more film than Sofie had ever seen her use at any of their previous shoots.

Sofie opened the blood-stained box. It had fabric inside, as if someone planned to use it for a suitcase. The fabric was yellowed with age, but had no bloodstains on it.

Then Anton called her name. His lean face was paler than usual, and for a moment, she thought he seemed very tired.

Then she realized the emotion she saw wasn't exhaustion. It was shock.

"You have to see this," he said.

Sofie peered into the larger box. She saw more clothing, which had not been bagged: carefully folded white linen shirts and a single pair of pants. A long metal tube with writing in a foreign language—it appeared to be English—on the side rested on top of one of the shirts, and next to the tube was a silvery, shiny ball the size of her fist. The ball did not look like a toy; it had marks on the side and a small design in red at the bottom with the word *warning*—one of the few English words she recognized—written across it.

Sofie glanced at Anton. Greta hovered above them, taking more photographs. Anton reached inside, lifted up one of the shirts, and there, beneath it, was a gun.

But it was unlike any gun Sofie had ever seen. Its handle appeared to be made of rubber. The grip was formed to fit someone's hands. Something had been attached to the bottom of the barrel, right near the trigger.

Along the slide were three foreign words—again, they looked like English, but Sofie couldn't tell.

"Do you know what this says?" she asked Anton, pointing at the words.

He shook his head. "I'm a pianist, not an opera singer. I never had to learn all the various languages. I can tell you it's not French, Latin, or Russian."

Sofie smiled. "I could have told you that. It looks like English to me."

"Me, too," Greta said, and took another picture. "So, aren't you going to pick it up?"

Sofie bit her lower lip. She hated guns. She had never touched one. "Anton?"

"Go ahead." He had his hands folded around his knee. "It's your project."

"It's your great-grandfather's gun."

He shook his head. "I know that it's not my great-grandfather's. His service revolver is upstairs. It was one of my inheritances."

Sofie nodded, just once. She leaned over the box and touched the label taped to the gun's barrel.

Sniper's gun
Recovered at Wein Nord
Case Number 1913112236

She let the paper drop. Recovered at the Vienna North Station where the Sniper had gotten away after killing his last victim, where he had disappeared into the crowd.

She had always thought it amazing the Sniper hadn't shot anyone else in his escape attempt. Now she knew why.

Somehow Johann Runge had gotten the Sniper's gun.

"Your great-grandfather doesn't mention confiscating the gun in his book," Sofie said.

Anton shrugged. "I don't remember much about that last part of the book. I always wondered how the Sniper escaped."

"You and the whole world," Greta said as she leaned in closer to take pictures of the gun.

"I think people could have forgiven him for failing to solve the case if he hadn't been so close to the Sniper in the station," Anton said. "Random shootings are always hard to solve."

Sofie nodded. She didn't tell Anton that some of the police notes indicated that the shootings weren't random. Johann Runge had mentioned that in the book, too, but he had equivocated, stating at the end there was no obvious link between the last two victims and the first three.

"I'd like to take this box with me," Sofie said. "And the bullets. I need to have them tested."

"I suppose if you're going to be formal, I should be too," Anton said. "We'll need to make an inventory before you remove evidence from the basement."

"Good suggestion," Sofie said. "Do you have some paper?"

"I do." Greta pulled a notebook from her back pocket. "Inventory away."

She took photographs of them inventorying the boxes, photographs of the two of them signing the inventories, and photographs of Sofie, struggling with the box of evidence as she staggered out of the basement.

More documentation than any book would need, but plenty for the critics when they attacked her for lying about her sources.

Her heart was pounding as she carried this old box. She felt like she was stealing evidence, even though she knew she wasn't. It all felt so illicit, as if this material was never meant to be found. Now that it had been, it almost seemed as if testing it was violating an old code, as if she were taking something that had risen to mythic status and bringing it down to earth.

Greta followed her up the stairs. Anton stayed below to turn out the lights. After a moment, his flashlight beam showed on the floor below.

When she reached the main floor, Sofie rested her box against a kitchen chair. Her stomach rumbled. She couldn't remember the last time she'd eaten.

"Wow. I can't tell if you look victorious or like someone who was just hit by a truck," Greta said.

"She looks like someone who has put in a fantastic day's work," Anton said as he closed the basement door.

Sofie looked at him in surprise. He smiled at her. In one hand, he held his flashlight. In the other, he had a copy of the inventory. He looked as filthy as she felt, and just as pleased.

"Would you mind if we came back tomorrow?" she asked.

"And the next day and the next," he said. "You're obviously not going to finish up down there any time soon."

Sofie nodded. "I don't want to disturb your work."

"I don't think that can be helped," he said. "I think until we get that room sorted, you'll need my help."

And he would want to continue supervising her until he was certain she wasn't going to walk out with anything. At least, that was what Sofie assumed he was thinking. She had no real idea what his plans were. Every time she thought she had a sense of him, he changed.

"You need my help too, right?" Greta said.

"For a few days, at least," Sofie said. "I suspect when I get down to the documents, I won't need either of you. It'll be a matter of cataloguing everything and seeing how useful it all is."

"Well, when you called," Greta said, "I never expected anything like this. It's pretty amazing. I can't wait to get these photos developed."

Sofie smiled at her. Greta had been leery of the project at first, just like Morganthau had been, but they had both come around.

Sofie wiped a hand over her face. Her eyes burned from all the dust in them. "I guess we should call it a night, huh?"

Anton shoved his copy of the inventory in the pocket of his pants. He seemed so casual about all of this. Sofie hoped that would change. If it didn't, she was afraid it would hurt her later on.

"Let me carry the box to your car," he said.

Sofie put a hand on her forehead. She was so absentminded sometimes. "I took the tram. I'll have to call a cab."

"I'll give you a lift," Greta said. She reached into her pocket and grabbed her keys.

Anton looked like he had been about to say something, but instead he smiled. "Where're you parked?" he asked Greta.

She told him, and he picked up the box. He carried it while Sofie held the doors for him, feeling oddly out of control of her life.

Everything had changed in the last few hours—changed for the better. She was going to have answers where before there had only been questions.

She really was going to write the definitive book on the Carnival Sniper.

And Johann Runge was going to help her—reaching out from the past and influencing the future.

She shivered, feeling less alone than she ever had. She would have a collaborator, a man who had been dead for decades.

And she welcomed him.

1913

LEV DAVIDOVICH BRONSTEIN lived in the suburb of Huetteldorf. The address had surprised Runge when he found it the day before, but the dwelling that possessed the address startled him even more.

It was a villa, which rose against the sky like the palaces it tried to emulate. The building was ornate, the landscaping—barely visible beneath a coating of snow—expensive.

It wasn't until Runge stepped inside that he understood how Bronstein, a man with frayed cuffs and almost no money in his pockets, had afforded such an elaborate home.

The villa had no heat.

Runge saw his breath as Mrs. Bronstein led him toward the back of the villa. He shivered slightly. The chill was noticeable here, and the rooms mostly unused. The furniture was covered in sheets, and dust coated the floors.

Mrs. Bronstein was a small woman, with blond hair pulled into a heavy bun at the nape of her neck. Her long face still held a beauty that had faded with time and poverty, but Runge suspected it wasn't her beauty that had attracted Bronstein. It was the intelligence in her blue eyes.

Even though she had tried to act timid when she had answered the door, and even though her shoulders had stiffened when she realized

Runge was with the Viennese police, it was clear that she was a woman of great strength. The timidness vanished with her confident walk toward the back rooms, her chin raised with pride despite her poverty.

Her clothing was as well pressed as Bronstein's had been. It was also as old. The back of her collar had pilled and her dress had lost some stitching around the waist.

Mrs. Bronstein led him into the servant's kitchen, the only room filled with light and heat. Two little boys, about five and seven, sat at the table, eating plain bread and drinking tea.

The boys did not look up when Runge entered, as if they were used to strangers in their midst. No plate sat in front of Mrs. Bronstein's place, just another cup of tea, lightened with the barest touch of milk.

"May I offer you anything?" Mrs. Bronstein asked.

Runge was surprised she had any food to offer. "Thank you, no. I have had breakfast."

She sat in her chair and indicated that he should sit as well. He did, across from the boys. They made him nervous, such silent wide-eyed children, too thin and too intent on their food to pay him much attention.

Mrs. Bronstein watched Runge, as if she expected him to speak first. She was clear-eyed and wide awake. Not a woman in mourning. Mrs. Freud had seemed clear too, but she had had shadows beneath her eyes, and tears were always close to the surface.

There were no newspapers in this meager kitchen, and he doubted anyone had come all the way out here on the first tram to let Mrs. Bronstein know what happened at the Café Central.

Runge glanced at the children. "Perhaps there is somewhere else we can have this discussion."

Mrs. Bronstein's tense shoulders hunched into her neck. She was worried, but he didn't know what the cause of the worry was.

Then she turned to her boys, and spoke to them in Russian. The language was harsh to Runge's ears. The boys looked at him, the oldest with his eyes narrowed, and then stood.

The boys did not look happy, but they didn't argue. They left the kitchen together, the oldest looking over his thin shoulder at Runge as if warning him not to hurt his mother.

Runge waited until he heard a door slam. Mrs. Bronstein stared at him. He was surprised; any other woman would have asked what had become of her husband.

He had no idea how to give her the news. "Your husband did not come home last night—"

"He does not sometimes." Mrs. Bronstein's interruption revealed her nervousness. A flush colored her cheeks, accenting the high cheekbones and giving her an added beauty. "Occasionally he misses the last tram."

This news surprised Runge, and yet explained Mrs. Bronstein's acceptance of her husband's absence. Runge wondered if she was one of those women who did not mind when her husband failed to come home.

"What does he do in those cases?" Runge asked.

"He goes home with whomever he has been talking to," Mrs. Bronstein said. "Last week, it was Karl Renner. Last month, it was Otto Bauer."

Runge felt a thread of excitement build in his chest. Both Renner and Bauer were prominent Socialists. Perhaps Mrs. Freud had been wrong. Perhaps her husband had had a political involvement after all, one she had not known about.

"Does your husband spend time with Viktor Adler?" Runge asked.

Mrs. Bronstein tensed even more. "They enjoy a game of chess on occasion."

Runge nodded. He couldn't keep up the pretense any longer. "No one came to see you yesterday?"

Mrs. Bronstein's jaw trembled. "My husband is here legally. He has papers."

"I know," Runge said gently. "I have seen them."

She clamped her mouth shut and folded her hands together.

"There is no easy way to tell you this," Runge said. "Your husband and Viktor Adler were playing chess yesterday in the Café Central when a man approached them and shot them both to death."

Mrs. Bronstein let out a small gasp, almost like a sigh, and put a hand to her chest. Her eyes grew rounder, stricken, but she didn't say a word.

"I am sorry." Runge kept his hands on his knees, resisting the urge to reach to her. She looked very alone, suddenly, and very young.

She swallowed, frowned as if she were trying to understand what he had just said—really understand it, not just hear it—and then she asked, "Are you certain?"

He reached into his breast pocket and removed Bronstein's papers. They were smeared with blood, the stains now dried and brown.

He spread the papers on the table so that Mrs. Bronstein could see them. She slid one over to her—the main page, the one a man could not go without—and stared at it.

Her hand trembled. She looked up at Runge, and now her eyes were filled with tears. "Shot him?"

"Yes, ma'am," Runge said. "He was shot twice. The man killed both him and Adler. And not just them. An hour or so later, this man shot Sigmund Freud as well. Do you know him?"

She shook her head. "Was he at the café?"

"He was in front of his home, going to take a walk. His family says he's not political at all, but he is well known. He's a psychoanalyst, just like Viktor Adler. Was your husband in that profession?"

She touched the edge of the paper, tracing a blood smear with her finger. "Lyova, he is a writer. Was. He had a newspaper. In Russia. We left because he does not—did not—approve of the Tzar."

And beneath those words, Runge heard volumes. Many of the Russians who left because they "did not approve" of the Tzar had barely escaped the country with their lives.

"Lyova?" Runge asked.

"Lev," Mrs. Bronstein said. "Leon. My husband. We—there are many nicknames—he calls me Sedova, although my first given name is Natalya. It is just our way."

And not just theirs, Runge knew. Many Russians used a variety of pet names for each other. But he was glad to have asked, and he filed the other names away for further reference.

"What newspapers did he write for?" Runge asked.

"Mostly his own. You have seen it, no? *Pravda*. It means truth." She spoke with undisguised pride. She believed in her husband's work, whatever it was, whatever it had been.

Pravda had not been one of the newspapers found near the body, but Runge had seen it. To call *Pravda* a newspaper was the highest form of charity. It was a cheaply made broadsheet. Many of the Russians in the city read it, but did not discuss its content.

"It is a Socialist newspaper?" Runge asked.

"There are discussions of Socialism," she said with barely disguised caution.

"Mrs. Bronstein," he said. "My colleagues believe that your husband's death was a random shooting. I do not. But I cannot figure out what happened to him if I don't know who he was, who his friends were, what he has done."

She took the paper and clutched it in her trembling hands. "You come here," she said, voice shaking, "and tell me my husband is dead. You bring papers covered with blood. You expect me to believe you. How do I know this is the truth, that you are not doing this to harm my husband, to manufacture charges against him? I have heard from no one else of his death. Wouldn't someone tell me?"

Runge didn't know the answer to that. How many people knew this small family lived in a large and cold villa in Huetteldorf? How many people even knew that Bronstein had a wife?

"I am not so cruel to tell you that kind of lie," Runge said. "But if you want to wait to talk with me until you know for certain that I am telling the truth, I can come back."

A single tear ran down her cheek. She wiped at it angrily. She seemed to be debating with herself.

"My husband has lived in Vienna peacefully for nearly six years," she said. "We have had no trouble. We are good citizens."

Runge nodded, careful not to interrupt the flow of her words.

"He is focused on Russia. He loves her, but she does not welcome him. He has even fought for her. He helped her form the parliament—the Duma—to work with the Tzar, but it did not go the way that we had hoped. My husband, he still writes of this, of ways to make Russia a better land. He has done nothing wrong here."

"I understand," Runge said.

"You can see what he has done," she said, her voice growing hoarse. "It is there for all the world to see. He writes it down, all of it, in his paper. And uses the name they call him now."

"What name is that?" Runge asked.

"Trotsky," she said, as tears dripped on the paper she was holding. "He is Leon Trotsky. There. Now you know. Please do not hurt him."

This time, Runge reached for her hand. "I promise," he said. "No one can hurt him anymore."

2005

AT MIDNIGHT, ANTON found himself too wound up to go to sleep. He paced the main floor of his house, thinking of the events of the day.

Sofie's excitement had been electric—her face lit up as though from within. She had been so worried about him, about not cheating him and not putting herself in a position to get hurt later on. He saw all that clearly, and he wished that he could show her he had little interest in his great-grandfather's things.

That wasn't entirely true. Anton had a huge interest in his great-grandfather's things, just not in exploiting them for public consumption.

If Sofie or someone else wanted to do that, fine. At some point, he might hire someone to transcribe the documents, but that would happen years after Sofie's book came out.

This was a curiosity to him, a part of his past he knew nothing about, a puzzle that should have been solved long ago and never was.

And it inspired him.

He realized suddenly that he had been pacing to a tune he had never heard before. Music rarely came to him of a piece; usually he had to work at it.

But he wouldn't have to work at this one, not if he wrote it down now.

He walked to the piano, sat on the bench, and grabbed his composition paper. He shoved the previous sheets of unfinished work aside, took out a pencil, and scrawled the melody onto the page.

Then he put his fingers on the keys and began the difficult work of discovering the harmonies, motifs, and counterpoints the melody needed.

It was a march, he knew. A march filled with joy, and victory for a battle won, but uncertainty too. The march needed a darkness, to take it away from Sousa, to make it more than a simple rallying of the troops.

Anton wrote and played long into the night, knowing deep down that the march would not exist if it weren't for that open door in the basement, and the smile he had seen on Sofie Branstadter's pretty face.

1913

THE ASSASSIN'S EYES felt like they were filled with sand. If he were home, he would go back to bed for another hour's sleep—take the edge off, wake refreshed.

But he wasn't home. He was on Meldemannstrasse, half a block away from the Mannerheim. His stomach churned with anticipation, the thick rich whipped cream he'd let the café put on his morning pastry not sitting well at all.

He had to swallow hard to keep it all down—the pastry, the cream, the coffee. He had gotten up early, not that he'd slept much in Brigittakappelle. Even if the pew had been comfortable or the chapel warmer, he probably wouldn't have slept.

Every time he closed his eyes, he saw Freud, looking at him with confusion.

The assassin put a hand over his stomach, willing it to calm down. Two more victims. Only two more victims, and he could go home.

He shifted the shoulder holster under his coat. His shoes crunched on the ice-covered walk. The sun shone this morning as well, unusual for Vienna in January, but it made his task easier.

He crossed the street and stopped at the edge of the block, staring up at the Mannerheim. It had the sheen of new construction, but the institutional brick looked familiar, and the double-hung windows, spaced evenly on every floor, looked exactly like they had in the photographs. The main part of the building, with its impractical flat roof and unusually small entrance, looked like a freshly painted version of the place he had expected.

His throat was dry. History didn't help him this time. The assassin had known that Bronstein would spend his day in the Café Central, and that Freud would be leaving his apartment in the middle of the afternoon. The assassin also knew exactly what time the train would arrive in Wein Nord and where to line up the best shot.

What he didn't know was whether or not Adolf Hitler would leave the Mannerheim this morning.

No one kept track of the young Hitler's day-to-day routine, not even Hitler himself. There was no exact diary, no retelling of his movements moment by moment.

When Hitler had lived in the Mannerheim, he had passed himself off as an impoverished artist who could barely afford the two-kronen-per-week rent. He never told anyone of the inheritance that would have allowed him to easily rent a forty-kronen-per-month apartment.

He didn't tell people much of anything. No one knew that he was in Vienna, not just to apply to art school (which repeatedly turned him down), but also to avoid Germany's compulsory draft.

He had been a coward, even then.

Or even now, depending.

The assassin's stomach turned again, and he felt the beginnings of a headache. He couldn't quit now. Not with Hitler so close.

If Hitler died now, he would be a failure, a forgotten man, an artist without imagination who sold postcards on the street to make his meager rent.

But the key was getting to him. In *Mein Kampf*, written nearly a decade after he left Vienna, Hitler had outlined his average day at the Mannerheim. He would get up at nine, have a light breakfast, then go to the reading room for the morning papers. By ten, he was sketching his latest painting. If the weather cooperated, he would leave the Mannerheim before noon and sell his paintings outside.

The assassin raised his head, looking at the six stories of the dormitory sections towering above him. The windows were closed, and they had wooden cross sections, making it impossible to jump out of them. The hallways were narrow, the stairs narrower.

If he went to the reading room on the top floor and shot Hitler, escape would be impossible. If he went to Hitler's private room and used the silencer, he might get down the stairs before being caught.

Or he could go into the kitchen and pray that no one tackled him while he tried to get away.

That would mean more casualties, and the assassin already felt sick about the unknown man he'd shot in Café Central.

The assassin glanced at his watch. 8:45 a.m.

He had to make a decision. If he waited for Hitler to leave on his morning rounds and Hitler did not leave the building, then the assassin would have no choice. He would have to go to the reading room—and the final part of his mission, just as important as this date with Hitler, might not occur.

This mission the assassin had set for himself was all about risk.

Risk, courage, and luck.

He stepped into the shelter of a doorway, reached into his shoulder holster and removed the Glock. Then he slid his hand into the specially made pocket inside his coat. His fingers brushed the prototype, pushing aside a few other items until he felt the cylindrical form of the silencer.

His hand was shaking.

The assassin turned his body away from the street to attach the silencer to the muzzle of the Glock.

Then he slipped the Glock under his coat, holding it there, his right arm crossed in front of his stomach as if he were ill.

He hoped no one saw him. He would only get one chance at this.

He took a deep breath and reminded himself:

Risk, courage, and luck.

This part of the mission would take all three.

2005

SINCE SHE HAD IMPORTANT new evidence, Sofie tried Scotland Yard first thing the next morning. She got nowhere. Even though she spoke to someone else, he seemed to care even less than the first person she had talked with.

Finally, she was transferred to the right section of the Yard, only to learn that it was still trying to decide if it wanted to handle the case.

Sofie had no choice but to return to Crime Research Labs. She did empty a few items out of the box. She had to send the clothing, with its DNA samples, to Switzerland. She also kept some of the bullets back in case the Yard eventually decided to help. The gun, she knew, could be retested without doing damage to it, but she wasn't certain about the bullets. So she kept a few of the undamaged green ones just in case.

She put them in her wall safe, wondering if that was secure enough to hold them.

She hadn't been able to sleep all night. She knew this evidence would lead her to the Carnival Sniper. If the Sniper was in the system—or even if a relative of his was—then she would be able to find him. Most of Europe had donated DNA to the various government databases, which then shared the information; donating DNA had become a requirement in the early 1990s, not just for crime-solving, but for paternity tests and support payments and for tracking genetically inherited traits. One of the many reasons Sofie had decided to do the Sniper book now was that as of three years ago, all of Europe had its DNA on file.

She was amazed at how nervous she felt, though, driving the box of evidence to CRL. Not because of that last meeting—she knew that this box would make a great deal of difference to all of them—but because she didn't want the evidence out of her sight.

Because she was feeling slightly paranoid, she insisted that Kolisko meet her at the front desk and take the bullets and gun himself.

He wasn't at the front desk when Sofie got there. She leaned the box an end table and had the receptionist page him. She was surprised when the receptionist told her to take the box to the back.

Sofie balanced the box on her hip, using one arm to hold up the weight. Her other arm was tired from lifting, and she was struggling also with the weight of her purse.

At least she had dressed properly that morning. She wore a T-shirt and an old pair of pants, as well as sneakers and some light socks. She brought more gloves—they were in her purse—and a hair net, not so that her hair would stay out of the evidence, but so that anything crawling around in that dirt and dust wouldn't be able to get on her.

The backs of her calves ached from the high heels she had worn the day before, and her little toe was blistered. She couldn't favor her foot, though, not with the extra weight of the box.

The directions the receptionist had given her sent Sofie down another of those sterile corridors that smelled faintly of disinfectant. The walls were solid, and the doors had hatched windows, so peering inside wasn't an option.

Kolisko's door stood open, fortunately, and he was leaning against the jamb, waiting for her, arms crossed.

"It sounded like you have something good," he said.

"Very good." Sofie followed him inside. The room was filled with microscopes and pipettes and a whole bunch of equipment she didn't recognize. The chairs were made of metal and looked very uncomfortable. The three tables reminded her of the blonde-wood tables that had been in her sixth-form chemistry class.

"Set it here," Kolisko said, clearing some papers off a small desk. He turned on a desk light, and that was when Sofie realized how dim the large room had been.

She set the box down and let out a small sigh. Then she rubbed her back. She was going to be tired after this week was over.

"Heavy?" he asked.

She shook her head. "Just awkward."

"So what've you got?"

"First, I need the transfer forms," Sofie said. "We have to label all of this. I don't want any of it lost."

Kolisko made a face at her, but he got the forms. She filled them out quickly, had him sign off, and kept a copy for herself. Then she took out a pair of her thin latex gloves and slipped them on, preparing to show him some of the evidence.

"You're acting like this'll go to court," Kolisko said.

"Worse," Sofie said. "It'll go to the court of public opinion."

He winced. "You gonna show me this stuff or not?"

Sofie opened the box. She grabbed one of the small cardboard boxes, the label still attached, and handed it to him.

Kolisko read the label first, then opened the box. "Holy son of a bitch," he said. "You found me another one."

"More than one." She took out the remaining boxes and set them on the desk. "Be sure to keep them with their labeled boxes. I'm not sure of the reason the evidence was labeled this way, but if I find out why, I want to be able to reconstruct it."

"This is the evidence from the Sniper case?" Kolisko sounded awestruck.

"I have boxes and boxes of it," she said.

"Where'd you find it?" he asked.

"Exactly where I should have realized it was all along," she said, not willing to give him any more than that.

He opened the other boxes, peered in. "My God, they flower. I wonder what they hit to make them do that."

"It should say on the box," Sofie said. "Some of the bullets are pretty intact."

"No kidding." Kolisko looked like a child with a new toy. He grabbed a pair of gloves, slipped them on, and poked at one of the bullets.

"I have a few other things." Sofie took the round tube out of the box. The tube was light and hollow, with writing on the side, words she did not recognize, and some numbers as well. "Do you know what this is?"

Kolisko took it from her. "It looks like a silencer, but not like any I've ever seen."

He tapped it with the knuckle of his forefinger, then peered into the barrel.

"Without testing, I'm guessing that this is aluminum or some other light alloy." He frowned at it. "I wonder if it works dry."

"Hmm?" Sofie didn't understand.

"Silencers generally use water or oil, something that'll keep the gun's performance the same even though the sound is suppressed." He touched the mouth of the barrel. "This one doesn't seem to use anything like that, although I'm just guessing at this point."

"No guessing," Sofie said, not wanting him to get into too many technical discussions, at least not yet. "I'd rather you know."

"This is part of the Sniper evidence?" he asked, rubbing his fingers along the smooth edge.

"It all is," Sofie said.

"1913?" he said.

She nodded.

"Wow," he said, then set the silencer beside the bullets. "You have something else for me, don't you?"

"The *pièce de résistance*." Sofie reached inside the box and very carefully removed the gun. She did not touch the trigger nor did she let the barrel point at either of them. Still, she was shaking as she touched it.

She hated guns.

Kolisko's eyes lit up. "You have the gun? Where did you get the gun?"

"Apparently the police had it all along," Sofie said. "It was one of the pieces of information that they held back."

Kolisko reached for the weapon with both hands. Sofie recoiled.

He noticed, and let his hands drop. "I won't hurt it. I promise."

She wasn't afraid he was going to hurt the gun. She was actually afraid he wanted it too much. His desire to hold it made her heart pound.

Why did anyone like these things? They were designed to kill. And guns like this one—a pistol, a revolver, a *hand*gun—were designed to kill people.

Like her parents.

"Sofie?" Kolisko said. "You okay?"

She nodded. She extended her hands, the gun flat on them like an offering. "Here."

He watched her as he took the gun, as if he was worried that she was going to do something unpredictable.

Once he had his hands on the gun, Kolisko held it properly. He kept the muzzle pointed down, but he turned the gun from side to side.

"I've never seen anything like it," he said. "It doesn't even feel like a gun. It's too light. Did you check the chamber?"

"Huh?" Sofie asked.

"Jesus, Sofie, I'm going to have to teach you how to treat a weapon. The first thing you do is make sure the thing isn't loaded." Kolisko kept the gun pointed away from her, checked the chamber, and let out a small breath. "It's not loaded. You were lucky."

Her cheeks were warm. She hadn't even thought of the fact that the gun might be loaded. She tried to remember if she had pointed it at Anton, even accidentally, and she couldn't.

But it had sat beside her on the car seat, inside the box, wedged between items, probably pointing at her. She had touched it half a dozen times in the past twenty-four hours.

"I don't even see a safety," Kolisko said, "but there has to be one."

He set the gun on the table, and pointed to the small square box near the trigger.

"Look at this, Sofie," he said. "I don't even know what this is. I've never seen it before. And I can tell you already this gun is too light. No gun manufactured now weighs this little. And I've never seen this kind of grip before."

"What about the words?" Her voice didn't shake, even though she thought it might. His comment about the gun being loaded had unnerved her badly. "Here? On the slide?"

He looked at her, as if surprised she knew that part of the gun when she hadn't even known to check for bullets. Or maybe she had called it by an incorrect name.

"I've never seen that before, either," he said. "Some of the words are English. I don't know what the rest are. Maybe a product name. I'll have to check the database for that, too."

"English?" she asked. "You think the gun is British?"

"If I had to guess, I'd say it's American, especially after that response we got on the bullet. But this gun is awfully sophisticated—there are parts on it that might take me days to figure out—and the Americans at the beginning of the twentieth century weren't very sophisticated at all. They preferred weaponry that got the job done with a minimum of force. It wasn't until after the war when the soldiers came back with new needs and new desires for their weapons that American gun technology took a giant leap forward."

Sofie shook her head. "So I'm confused. Did you just tell me it can't be American?"

"Right now, I'd say it's out of time." Kolisko grinned at her. "But you could say that I'm holding onto my favorite fantasy."

Sofie felt herself shiver, but she smiled, pretending a lightheartedness she didn't feel. "If that's your favorite fantasy, you're in trouble, Max."

He grinned, too. "You got anything else in that box of tricks?"

"One more thing." She reached in and removed the solid silver ball. "Do you know what this is?"

She held it flat on her palm. The metal was cool to her touch.

Kolisko took it gingerly, holding the sphere between his thumb and forefinger. "I have no idea, but I'm guessing it's some kind of grenade. That word on the bottom, that's English for *danger*."

"I recognized that one," Sofie said.

"Sniper evidence?" he asked.

"I told you—"

"It all is, right." He took a deep breath. "They never said anything about this, either."

"I haven't looked through all the records," Sofie said, realizing she was making the understatement of her career, "but I doubt anyone knew what this was."

"Did it come from the Sniper?"

"I can't tell you that," Sofie said. Because she didn't know. But she wasn't going to confess to that, either. Let him think she was withholding information. It was always safer that way.

He carried the sphere carefully to another table, grabbed a metal box with his free hand, and opened it. Then he set the sphere inside, closing the box again.

"I may not be the person to handle that thing," he said as he turned around. His forehead was covered in sweat.

"You think it's dangerous?"

"It says it is," he said. "I tend to believe signs like that. Sofie, if you find more things like that, you call me. I'll take care of it, okay? You're not handling potential weapons well at all."

Her cheeks grew even more heated. She hadn't thought that digging through old evidence files could be dangerous, but now that Kolisko had pointed it out, she supposed it made sense.

She hadn't ever thought of research materials as something that could hurt her. But then, she'd never done primary research with evidence from a crime before, either.

"You've seen grenades like that?" she asked, deliberately taking the subject off of her.

Kolisko shook his head. "I've seen nothing like any of this stuff. And I gotta admit that's really odd. If it's all prototypes, I want to know where they came from and why a guy like the Sniper had them. And if it's something else—"

"Not time travel," Sofie said.

"I'm not going to rule anything out," Kolisko said. "You shouldn't, either."

Sofie didn't like how uncomfortable this topic made her. Did he know about the experiments that happened fifty years ago?

"Max, you're being silly."

"No, I'm not," he said. "I just know that the moment you close your mind to something is the moment you fail at whatever task you're doing."

Sofie looked at him. He seemed so normal, hands shoved in the pockets of his wrinkled lab coat. Once she had dismissed him as just a science guy. She hadn't really realized how much depth he had.

"Ruling out the improbable is not closing your mind," Sofie said.

Kolisko raised his eyebrows. "Really?" he asked softly. "Are you absolutely sure?"

Sofie didn't answer him. Instead, she shook the inventory at him. "I want a report as soon as possible."

"Yes, ma'am," he said.

"And see what you can get from Scotland Yard's database, without telling them about the project," she said. "I want as much information as I can get."

"I promise I'll be thorough," he said.

"And write the report for dummies," she said.

He nodded. "The scientifically illiterate will not have to worry about me."

"And I'm sure we all be very grateful." Sofie waved at him and left his office. She hurried down the corridor before she realized there was no reason to rush.

Except that he made her uncomfortable. Well, not him exactly, but the fact that he wanted her to think about uncomfortable things.

Sometimes she wished this entire project could be more straightforward.

But if it had been, someone else would have solved the Sniper shootings long ago. She was probably the first person to have the solution within her reach—and it was unnerving her.

She wanted to be as meticulous as possible, no matter how much Kolisko chided her.

She wanted everything to be lined up in a row, so that each sentence she wrote in her book would have entire documents' worth of proof behind it.

Such a thing probably wasn't possible. But she was going to do her damndest to make sure she came close—without flights of fancy getting in her way.

1913

THE CASE BURST OPEN, and papers slid across the dirty floor. The Cyrillic writing on a nearby page looked cramped. One of the other passengers stepped on a sheet, and Papadopoulos cursed, reaching for it.

"Let me," William said, then bit his lower lip, his cheeks heating. He had spoken in English.

Papadopoulos scrambled for the papers, reaching for them, not caring who he bumped into.

"I'm sorry," William said in Russian, knowing that Papadopoulos did not understand German. "Let me help you."

Papadopoulos growled at him, the words mangled by his fake Greek accent. William reached for the case, picked it up, felt the soft wood beneath his fingers.

There was supposed to be a compartment in the corner, a small bit of fabric nailed into the wood. His fingers found it before his eyes did, and he shoved the nuke inside, acting so quickly that for a moment, he was afraid he had dropped it.

Papadopoulos pushed against another passenger's legs, reaching for the papers. Papadopoulos was breathing heavily through his nose, as if he were trying to control his anger.

William grabbed papers and shoved them inside the case.

Papadopoulos turned and yanked the case from William's grasp. William glanced inside, hoping that the nuke wasn't visible.

It bulged out of the small fabric compartment, looking so obvious that William gasped.

Papadopoulos's black eyes narrowed.

"I'm sorry," William said again. "Let me help you."

"I do not need your help." Papadopoulos shoved papers inside the case, then slammed it closed.

William's heart jumped, even though he knew the harsh movement would have no effect on the nuke.

The train continued to slow, hurting William's balance. Other passengers stumbled into him, one telling him in German to stand up or he might be trampled.

William started to stand, but Papadopoulos leaned over the closed case and caught William's arm, holding him down.

Papadopoulos's black eyes glittered, and his mouth, barely visible beneath his oversized mustache, was firmly set.

"You have been following me." Papadopoulos spoke so softly that he didn't even try to mask his fluent Russian with his fake Greek accent.

"No," William lied. He was having trouble catching his breath. He never expected to talk to this man. "I was just sitting behind you."

"I saw you in Krakow. You were following me."

William shook his head, unable to make up a plausible story.

"You know enough to speak Russian to me," Papadopoulos said.

"I didn't at first," William said, hoping that Papadopoulos wouldn't realize that the first language William had spoken was English. "I saw your papers. They're in Russian."

Papadopoulos's grasp tightened on William's arm. "You read them?"

"Of course not," William said. "I didn't have time."

Papadopoulos pulled William close. There was a coldness in Papadopoulos's eyes, a ruthless intelligence that William had never seen before.

It made William's heart beat harder, and he started to tremble. He couldn't help himself.

"Take care that I do not see you again," Papadopoulos said, and let William go.

William had to put a hand on the filthy floor to keep himself from falling. He didn't try to get up—he wasn't even certain if his legs would hold him.

If Papadopoulos had chosen to hurt him, William wouldn't even have been able to use the handheld to vanish.

Papadopoulos stood, then leaned his case on the back of the seat. He latched the case closed, then held it under his arms. He turned away from William, facing the front of the train, waiting, just like all the other passengers, to get off.

"Stand up," said the passenger behind William.

William clutched the side of a seat and used it to pull himself up. His breath was still coming in short gasps.

The train slowed even more, and through the grimy window, William could see the Prater's Ferris wheel, a large gaudy circle against an impossibly blue sky.

Almost there.

Just a few more minutes, and he could go home.

Safe.

A hero.

Alive.

2005

IT TOOK SOFIE TWO DAYS to make sure the evidence was catalogued and in some kind of order. Initially, she thought of keeping each item in the boxes she originally found them in, then she realized that the boxes were put together haphazardly. She had a hunch Johann Runge compiled them from even more boxes in storage, bringing them down to a manageable number so that no one thought he was stealing drugs, money, or precious jewels from the evidence room.

Sofie cleared out a section of the basement study for the evidence. With Anton's permission, she moved the boxes for the other cases into the main basement room, and promised she would move them back into the study as soon as she possibly could.

But she wanted clear access to the filing cabinets, and with all the boxes stacked all around, such access wasn't always possible.

Sofie kept Greta Thaler for several days longer than planned. Sofie made Greta open and photograph each file drawer. Sofie wanted proof of where everything stood before she delved into each file.

Then, while Sofie began her research in earnest, she had Greta photograph the contents of the other boxes. Greta lingered over several of them, saying that they seemed as interesting as the Sniper boxes, only just not as complete.

Sofie wouldn't be sidetracked. As each extraneous box left the office, as she opened file drawers, she realized just how much work was ahead of her.

Runge's files were frighteningly complete. He had constantly updated files on the witnesses and on the survivors, checking where they lived, what their occupations were, how they treated their children.

He even kept track of siblings and grandchildren, people who had no real association with the Sniper at all. Sofie found many of the files creepy in their depth—down to photographs of the niece of the Mannerheim victim, Hietler, a girl who hadn't even turned ten when her uncle had been murdered. Runge had an entire biography of the girl, up-to-date as of the mid-1950s, even though he noted in one of the analysis pieces he taped to the back of each file that he doubted the niece even remembered her uncle, let alone had anything to do with him.

Sometimes Runge's overabundant research proved useful. Anna Freud wrote a dissertation on the effects of trauma on children, and Runge managed to get a copy of the document. Even though the dissertation was the basis for the rejection of her doctorate—by then, nearly a decade after Freud's death, psychoanalysis had fallen into disrepute—the document would make interesting reading.

But Sofie put it off. Runge's notes made her leery. He said the document was an autobiography of the breakdown Anna Freud had after her father's murder.

By the end of the week, Sofie realized that Anton had been right—the amount of material here was overwhelming. Even working every day for the next month, Sofie wouldn't get through half of it.

She would have to work more efficiently, find ways to lump together information. First, she decided to read all of the police reports, just to refresh herself.

Then she planned to go through the files murder by murder, in order of death. Finally, she limited her study to 1913. After all, the point of her book was to find the Carnival Sniper, not write about the way that murder left a gaping hole in each survivor's life.

That way lay madness. She understood too well how murder altered a family in the space of an instant.

The work had its own rhythm. After Greta left, Sofie spent most of her time in the basement alone, reading and making notes.

Sometimes Anton would come down for an update, and she found herself looking forward to those moments, not that anything special happened. He had found a chair that wasn't broken and had brought it into the room. He would sit on it, and ask her what she'd found, and seem interested as she told him about the smallest details.

Most of the time, though, she was by herself. She would listen for the piano upstairs, the soft notes keeping her company as Anton worked on his commission for the Vienna Boys Choir.

Sofie had had no idea that he still made money as a musician. She had been embarrassed that she hadn't heard of his compositions, but Anton had shrugged it off.

Composers are meant to be anonymous, he said, and she got a sense that he liked being unknown. Perhaps that, more than the money, was the reason he didn't want to go through the files.

He already had enough renown from his great-grandfather's legacy.

The legacy was incredible. Even though Sofie had only been at the work for a week, she had found a large pile of things she hadn't known.

The police reports alone were a treasure trove. She had no idea that Runge believed that Bronstein had been shot before Adler. All the newspaper accounts, all the books assumed that Adler had been the target. *Death at Fasching* had lumped the two victims together as if they were inseparable.

Sofie was beginning to sense that she would have to reread the book after she reviewed all of Runge's files. It seemed that *Death at Fasching* had several layers not obvious to the casual reader.

Runge had written a book that left out three-quarters of his notes, and had downplayed the assumptions Sofie found in every file. It was almost as if he had written the book to keep the case alive for future generations, as if he felt there was a stake in not letting anyone forget about the Carnival Sniper.

The order of death between Bronstein and Adler was the first surprise Sofie found in the cases. If Adler was merely an afterthought, as
Runge thought, then all of the Vienna-based conspiracy theories collapsed. Only Adler and Freud were Viennese. The other victims were
outsiders, and none from the same place: Bronstein from Russia, Hietler from Austria (where, on the birth records, his name had been
spelled Hitler), and Papadopoulos from Greece.

The other surprises in the police report were just as confusing. Sofie had had no idea that Hietler was well-known in the Mannerheim
for giving long, rambling speeches, often about politics. Twice he'd
been warned to stop making anti-Semitic comments—comments that
might have gotten him thrown out of the home.

Hietler hadn't stopped; he had just stopped making those comments in front of the manager of the Mannerheim. No one reported
them, except to Runge in follow-up interviews, much later.

But if Hietler had died for his anti-Semitic views, then the deaths of
Adler, Freud, and Bronstein made no sense. They were Jews, although
not all of them practiced.

The ties between the victims were tentative at best.

And then there was Papadopoulos, who always threw the equa-
tion out of whack. Some theorists had assumed he was an accident,
the victim of a stray bullet, that someone else in Wein Nord had been
the target.

But Runge's police notes had details in them that shook Sofie's cer-
tainties about the case even more.

Papadopoulos had carried a case filled with handwritten notes in
Russian. They were for an article on social democracy he was to write
while in Vienna.

Papadopoulos, then, had links to socialism, like Bronstein and
Adler. But so far as anyone knew, neither Hietler nor Freud shared
those links.

The fact that most interested Sofie about Papadopoulos, though,
was one that took her completely by surprise.

The silver ball that Sofie had found in the evidence had been inside Papadopoulos's wooden box—the peasant suitcase he had carried off the train.

Somehow Sofie had thought the sphere was connected to the Sniper, but according to the notes, it was not. Yet it had English writing on it.

The more she learned about Papadopoulos, the more of a cipher he became.

The Sniper case became more intriguing as she read, not less. She had a hunch she could spend her life on it—as Runge had—and never be certain of the answers she found.

Was that why he had searched for the Sniper for his entire life? Or was there something in the notes, something that led Runge to believe that the Sniper would attack others, somehow do something worse?

Sofie didn't know, and she wasn't sure that was a question she could answer—at least, not for this book. But she was already generating a list of other books to write, books about Runge, books about the related cases—books that could keep her searching through files in this basement for as long as Anton Runge would tolerate her.

1913

THE HALLWAY SMELLED of onions, beer, and vomit. The assassin winced as he stepped out of the stairwell. The stench was powerful, something that he doubted he could have lived with from day to day.

He hoped he was on the right floor. He was going from an old memory. There had been no way to check *Mein Kampf* before he left.

Even though the walls were freshly painted, and the floor clean, there was a feeling of despair here. It was clear that the men who found refuge in the Mannerheim were, for the most part, not here by choice.

The assassin walked as quietly as he could. In the damp cold of the previous night, his shoes had developed a squeak, and no matter what he tried, he could not make it go away.

The squeak sounded doubly loud in the quiet hallway. He couldn't hear anything through the thick doors even though, he would assume, some of the residents were still in their rooms, preparing to leave for the day.

He had seen a number of them in the kitchen—too many to use it as a site for the shooting. He hadn't completely made his location choice until he peered through the open double doors and saw men, wearing scuffed shoes and dingy suits, trying to cook their own breakfasts on the makeshift stove.

The door in the middle of the hallway looked no different than any other. It was large and painted a dark brown. Behind it, he knew, was a metal cot, a chair and table, and a storage area, too small to call a closet.

He also knew that if he didn't stand to the side of the door, he would be blinded by the light coming in from the large window that dominated the far wall.

He knew all these things. The only thing he wasn't certain of was whether or not this room actually belonged to Hitler.

The assassin stopped before it anyway. He took the Glock from his coat, pressed off the safety, and held the pistol at hip level. Then he held up his left hand to knock, hesitating for only a moment.

If he waited a few more minutes, until 9 a.m., Hitler would come out of the room on his own accord. He would turn, head toward the stairs, and go down toward the kitchen.

It would be easier to escape from the stairwell. But the sound echoed there and the *thwep* of the silencer would be twice as loud, almost loud enough to bring in a crowd before Hitler's body fell on the metal floor.

The assassin knocked.

He thought he heard a faint sound from inside the room, a response, a guttural answer, but he wasn't certain. Then something clanged, a lock turned, and the door banged open.

Adolf Hitler stood before him, impossibly young. He had no mustache, and his features hadn't yet formed into a permanent frown.

He was shorter than the assassin, and he smelled of hair tonic. Only his eyes were familiar. Dark, beady, glittery—they were the eyes of the man in the photographs, the man in the newsreels, the man whose speeches still sent chills of horror down the assassin's back.

"I do not know you," Hitler said in German, which sounded raw and guttural after the soft tones of the Viennese.

"No," the assassin said, as he brought the Glock up. "But I know you."

Hitler understood the assassin's intent too quickly. He grabbed the door and started to push it closed, but the assassin blocked it with his gun arm.

218

Hitler stumbled backwards and the assassin fired, the shot missing and pinging into the nearby wall. Hitler ran for the window, and this time, the assassin had time to target him.

The laser site found the center of Hitler's back, the vulnerable spot just below the left ribcage—and the assassin fired again.

This time, Hitler fell forward, arms upraised, body slamming onto the edge of the metal cot. He pushed himself off, not dead yet, and tried to crawl beneath it, but the assassin reached him, placed one foot on Hitler's buttocks, and fired, point-blank, into the back of Hitler's skull.

The hair split wide, revealing the bullet's path, and Hitler's face—what the assassin could see of it—went slack.

He was dead. Finally, truly, completely dead. Dead at age twenty-three, long before one of his girlfriends committed suicide by flinging herself through a closed window, before another killed herself by shooting herself in the back.

Dead long before he slaughtered millions of people to satisfy his own hatred.

The assassin's shoes were growing wet with blood. He thought he heard voices in the hallway. He pushed the door closed, and waited, breathlessly, hoping no one would come in here.

The voices faded away.

Even so, the assassin made himself count to one hundred before he opened the door and started his escape.

2005

BY THE END OF THE FIRST WEEK, the music in Anton's head had shifted from the march to something soft and lyrical.

The march was mostly complete. He had only to rescore the entire piece for orchestra, and he would be done. Rescoring was something he could hire out if he wanted to—and on some pieces, he wanted to— so he felt he could leave the composition until later.

He had to turn his attention to the lyric piece. Part of him hoped he finally had the song for the Vienna Boys Choir. Another part of him didn't care.

He worked in a frenzy, getting little sleep, spending what free time he had with Sofie. Her enthusiasm was infectious. He never realized how much working alone drained him.

It wasn't as if he were working on the same project that she was, although he had an interest in what she was doing. It was more like her excitement about her work transferred into his.

He always left her feeling invigorated, the lyric piece even stronger than it had been when he started his visit with her.

He was beginning to worry about a time when she wouldn't be in his basement, studying the records. He was worrying about months ahead, when she would be locked up in her own office, writing her book.

He didn't want to lose her presence in this house.
He didn't want to lose her at all.
And that was beginning to scare him.

1913

WEIN NORD, VIENNA'S NORTH STATION, was soot-covered and old, even though it couldn't have stood there more than fifty years, at least at this point in time. William didn't remember the building being so small and so ugly, but things had changed a lot in the intervening years.

He leaned against the passengers in front of him, crouching just enough to get a good view out of the nearby windows. The train had slowed to a crawl, and then it was plunged into darkness as it went inside the station.

His breath was coming in small gasps. It wasn't until he actually listened to himself breathe that he realized how nervous he was.

He had been wrong. The hard part hadn't been putting the nuke in Papadopoulos's case. The hard part would come now, when William set the remote and then fled back to his own time.

He had no idea what he would go back to—and that made him even more nervous.

If he didn't use the remote at all, nothing would change. He would go back to his own future (unless he had done something small, something utterly unnoticed) and continue with his life.

Feeling like a failure.

Knowing he had had one moment to change the history of the world, and he had let that moment slip through his hands.

He couldn't go back on his ideals now. Not when he was so close.

His hands were slick with sweat. The train was too hot, where most of the trip it had been too cold.

Papadopoulos had shoved his way even closer to the door, and hadn't looked back at all. He was shifting from foot to foot, favoring his left knee.

The history books said he had injured it learning to ride a bike. Such a mundane thing. It seemed impossible that men like Papadopoulos would do mundane things, but they did. They rode trains, they wore peasant boots, and they carried their own luggage.

They had a curious humanity, one the history books did not give them.

Perhaps that was why William's hands were covered with sweat.

This Vienna, the Vienna of the past, looked too much like the Vienna of his present.

And he hated that.

With a final squeal of brakes, the train stopped. The passengers lurched forward and back, clinging to whatever they could.

William's hand slipped off the seat back and he stumbled. The man behind him, the one who had been talking to him throughout the accident with Papadopoulos, grabbed his arm.

"First time to Vienna?" the man asked, and William did not know how to answer him.

Finally, he said with a little too much honesty, "Actually, I think it will be my last."

2005

TWO WEEKS AFTER she had given him the evidence, Sofie heard from Kolisko. He had finished his preliminary report, but he wanted to talk with her about it before he wrote up the final. He asked her to come to the office.

She did the next morning, on the way to Anton's. Sofie hated changing the routine, but she felt she had no other choice.

In the time since she had dropped the evidence off at Crime Research Labs, she had heard from Scotland Yard. They would let her use their forensic services, but their prices were ridiculously high. She might have decided that the prices were worthwhile if it weren't for the timetable—the Yard wanted to process the evidence on a low priority basis, with a deadline of no less than one year.

She couldn't agree to that and still complete her book on time. She thanked them for their bid, and decided to hire a different backup lab—another private one, whose priorities would be based on the client's schedule, not a government's.

Besides, she wasn't as disgruntled with CRL as she had been. They had managed to calm the Americans, claiming that they didn't know where the bullets had come from (technically true), and proving that the chemical composition of the green coating was slightly different than the American model.

CRL also had Kolisko, whose enthusiasm for the project seemed to grow every week. He had left several messages on Sofie's phone over the past few days, hoping to meet with her, and growing more and more disappointed when she didn't respond as quickly as he liked.

If he were anyone else, she would have been leery. But she knew Kolisko got very involved with his work; he probably wasn't thinking about his lack of tact at all.

He was waiting for her in the same lab where she had left the evidence. The large evidence box was on the floor beneath the windows. Items from the box sat on various tables, with white sheets of paper beneath them, as if they were part of a demonstration.

In the center of the room, the sphere caught the light, reflecting it like a disco ball at an American dance club.

As Sofie stepped inside, Kolisko shut the door.

"I have to say, this is the most intriguing thing I have ever worked on." He was wearing his lab coat and a pair of gloves. He handed her a pair as well. "I want you to hear what I have, and then if I'm not clear, you can ask questions. That way I'll get closer to the version you want."

Sofie smiled. "You need me to help you by being dumb."

Kolisko grinned in return. "You got it, sister."

He led her to the bullets, displayed on their own sheet of paper. Most of the bullets were still in their boxes, but two were not. One was a flattened round from the Café Central; the other the original bullet from Adler's body.

"Okay," Kolisko said. "I've checked every database we have access to. I even got a friend to use the Russian system to see if China had bullets like these. No one does. The Americans are really thrilled by them and hope to start developing them. Apparently no one there had thought of using tungsten as the core for a bullet before."

"Great," Sofie said. "Nice to know I'm of help in building more ways to kill people."

Kolisko gave her a withering look. "It's not like that, Sof. I'm just saying there is no one today working on bullets like this—not anyone, worldwide."

"But these weren't made today," Sofie said.

"Precisely," Kolisko said. "And I got it from at least four different experts that even if some genius were ahead of the curve on inventing plastics like this one, no one had the technology to coat it so thinly and so expertly on each bullet—not and have it last after being propelled out of a gun and run into walls."

He picked up the flattened bullet. And gave it to Sofie.

She stared at it.

He had to turn it on its side so that she understood his point.

"See?" he said. "Just a little bit of coating remains. But it's enough to show what a great procedure this is. The other bullets that were flattened on impact still have a bit of coating as well."

"They couldn't have appeared out of thin air," Sofie said. "Somebody obviously made them."

"Yes," Kolisko said. "Somebody did. But no one we know of."

"But does that mean that this Sniper, whoever he was, couldn't have done this?"

Kolisko gave her a disappointed look. "I suppose anything's possible."

Then he moved to the next table. The long hollow tube he had called a silencer sat alone on its sheet of paper.

"First, let me tell you that the silencer was modified to fit the gun." He waved at the handgun, which sat on its own table. "It's pretty clear from the tests I ran that some of the bullets went through the silencer and some of them didn't."

"Which ones?" Sofie asked, although she had a hunch she knew. The Mannerheim—the shooting no one heard.

"These," he said, pointing to the boxes. She had been right. They were the bullets removed from the Mannerheim shooting. "They all have the same mark, which you can trace to this right here."

He picked up the tube and pointed, with his little finger, and something on the edge.

"I don't see anything," Sofie said.

"It's a land," he said. "It cuts—"

"Just take a picture of it for the report, and tell me how to describe it correctly," Sofie said. What mattered to her was not what caused the mark, but that the mark could tie the bullets to the silencer.

Kolisko nodded. "Like I suspected, this thing does use a dry technology that we don't have. The writing on the side here is, I think, a company logo and the name of the product itself. I'm assuming that the number is some kind of order number, but it could also be instructions on the kind of weapon this silencer is best suited for."

"Assuming?" Sofie asked.

"Yeah." Kolisko set the tube down. "Again, no one I know of has even seen this technology, and most thought it not very effective—despite what I learned in our tests."

"You learned that it is effective?" Sofie asked.

"Very," Kolisko said. "Especially with high-velocity weapons, which this one clearly is."

He looked at the gun again.

"The company didn't exist in 1913?" Sofie asked.

"Not that we can find," Kolisko said. "And the writing on the outside is some kind of vinyl stamp, again not something normally done ninety years ago. Then there's this little notation."

He rolled the cylinder over. At the very bottom of the vinyl stamping were three small words.

He pointed to them. Sofie squinted. She couldn't read them.

"The first two words are English," Kolisko said. "'Made in' is usually followed by the place on the globe—the city, the country—where this silencer had been manufactured. But this one's impossible—it's got to be some kind of joke."

"Why?" Sofie asked.

"Israel, Sofie. It says 'Made in Israel.'"

She felt herself grow cold.

"There's no such place," Kolisko said. "At least, not any longer. If I read my Bible right, the Kingdom of the Jews disappeared a long time ago."

"Could someone have put that on there as a joke?" Sofie asked.

Kolisko raised his hands, leaving the palms up and open in a gesture of confusion. "Sure. Anything's possible, like I said. But I have no idea why they would."

Sofie shook her head. "The word 'Israel' had so many meanings. It was the name Jacob received after he wrestled the angel. It was also the Biblical Holy Land, established for the Jews by Abraham. The Bible said it existed until the Romans conquered it—right? And made it Palestine?"

"I don't know," Kolisko said. "Religion has never been my strong suit."

Sofie shook her head. "I don't understand it. One of the victims was an anti-Semite. Three of the others were Jews. Papadopoulos wasn't. There can't be a religious angle, can there?"

"I'm only telling you what I've found," Kolisko said. "Thank heavens it's not my job to have it all make sense."

She threw him a reluctant smile. Then she sighed. "The words are smaller than the rest. Were they added later?"

"Already checked," Kolisko said. "No. That's one single stamp. I would assume every silencer this company made of this type had the same wording on it."

Sofie took a deep breath, feeling very unsettled. It felt as if she had taken two steps forward and five steps backward. Israel. What next? Atlantis?

"The thing is," Kolisko said, "I figure a company like this had to make something other than silencers. So the company should show up somewhere. I couldn't find it—but again, that's not my area of expertise. I figure the company has to be a small one, since none of my sources know about it, and it isn't in any databases."

Sofie nodded. She didn't like the uncertainty. One reason she had decided to do forensic testing was for certainty. Now he was telling her that his assumptions, which he had initially presented to her in a fanciful manner, might be correct.

"Now," he said, "let's look at this handgun. It is the weapon the Sniper used. Or at least, these bullets were shot out of this gun."

"You tested it?" Sofie said.

He nodded. "We didn't have the same kind of bullets to use, but we did our best. This thing was a joy to shoot, let me tell you. I'd love to have a pistol like this one."

He walked over to it and put his hand on it possessively. His eyes sparkled. The handgun still intrigued him.

"It's a semi-automatic pistol that has some owner modifications," he said. "It's fired by pulling on the slide—here—and that chambers the round. Then each shot rechambers the round, until all the bullets are gone."

"Allowing the shooter to fire off a lot of bullets quickly," Sofie said.

"You got it," Kolisko said.

Sofie crossed her arms. She hated weapons like that. She remembered what it was like trying to get away from one, sliding beneath the bench, gravel scraping her knees.

"Sof?" Kolisko asked.

"Sorry," she said. "What else?"

"The design of the semi-automatic pistol has been pretty standard since 1911. An American company named Colt invented the first one," Kolisko said.

"So it wouldn't have been uncommon to have a semi-automatic in 1913," Sofie said.

Kolisko shrugged. "Who knows? I'm not sure who would have had one and who wouldn't have. That's your job to figure out, but I can tell you that when we find an unusual gun—maybe a rare one—it often leads us to the criminal."

Sofie's breath caught. She was focusing on the negative phrases he had been using—*impossible to find; hard to find*—and not thinking about what they meant. When she did find these things, she would most certainly have the killer—even without DNA.

"This pistol has a lot of unusual features," Kolisko was saying. "The first is this."

He pointed to the square box near the trigger.

Sofie made herself concentrate.

"Watch when I press the side." He pressed a place on the side of the box.

Nothing happened.

"What am I supposed to see?" Sofie asked.

Kolisko pointed to the wall. There, on a map of Vienna, was a dot of red light. As Kolisko moved the gun, the light moved as well.

"What's that for?" Sofie asked.

He looked at her, surprised. "Sometimes I forget how little you know about guns. It's a sight. It shows you where your bullet will hit."

"My God." Sofie breathed the words.

She walked to the map, and peered at the small red dot. Then she stuck her finger beneath it. The dot was on her finger, making her skin an orangey red. She turned and saw the light projected from the pistol itself, little dust motes floating in the red beam.

"That's horrible," she said.

Kolisko shook his head. "I think it's fantastic. It's some kind of laser, but I've never seen one this small. I'm not sure they even have lasers outside of labs yet."

"But they did in 1913," Sofie said.

"If your evidence box is to be believed," Kolisko said. "And apparently they had plastic guns, too. This entire thing is so light that I had to weigh it three times before I accepted the number I got. The grip is also plastic, with some kind of rubber on the sides so that your hand won't slip."

"That's all unusual?" Sofie asked.

"This kind of rubber grip is pretty common now. I don't know anyone who did it ninety years ago. The rest of it is stuff I've never seen, not now, not then." Kolisko let go of the light and it faded, leaving a momentary echo of itself in the air. "This is a pistol designed for people who love weaponry. I mean, a gun is a gun is a gun for most purposes. But this—this has the kinds of alterations you make when you sell to a connoisseur. Guns have always had their proponents, but over the past century, we've used them less rather than more."

"Except in the United States," Sofie said.

Kolisko shrugged. "They've always had a love affair with guns. Which brings us to the writing."

He tapped the slide. Sofie looked at the gun once more. The writing was engraved on the side.

"I'm guessing that the first line is the manufacturer's name, and the second line is the name of the weapon, but those are just guesses. What intrigues me is on the other side of the slide."

Kolisko turned the gun over, showing Sofie the writing she had initially noticed on the gun.

"Again, we have the English words 'Made in,'" Kolisko said. "But this time they're followed by the word *Austria*. Made in Austria."

Sofie felt a chill. "Here?"

"Well, sort of," Kolisko said. "Only you're the historian. Seems to me there was no Austria proper in 1913. The Austro-Hungarian Empire, maybe, but not Austria. And it certainly wouldn't be listed officially that way."

"Unless it was made by a nationalist," Sofie said, more to herself than to Kolisko.

"Well, I think it's odd," he said.

Sofie nodded. She felt unsettled.

"Is this all you have for me?" she asked, hoping it was. She wasn't sure what to do with these pieces.

"A few more things," he said. "There's blood all over this pistol. I swabbed it down and got blood from at least four different people. One donated quite a bit. The rest were just spatter."

"If I give you other samples, you can match them?"

Kolisko smiled. "I can't, but the lab can. I'm curious as to who donated all the blood. I didn't think the Sniper got close enough to his victims to douse the gun. And one entire side had been in a pool of blood."

Sofie shuddered. She had touched that. "I didn't see it."

"You wouldn't," Kolisko said. "Someone tried to clean it off. But not really well. The gun wasn't cleaned. It was just wiped."

"Fingerprints?" Sofie asked.

"A few. None of them match our database, but that means nothing. Old prints are purged once a person dies. You'll have to ask the print experts if there's a base of hundred-year-old prints that someone could use."

Sofie nodded. That one she understood. She knew it would be very time consuming even if she found such a database. The old prints were on index cards, and had been photocopied once that technology became available. She had no idea how many prints were copied in those days before someone had the idea to scan the prints into the large Cray computers.

"I think that's it for the pistol," Kolisko said. "But we have one item left."

He swept his hand toward the sphere.

Sofie let out a small sigh. She was almost afraid to find out what that was.

"We need to do a lot more testing on this thing," Kolisko said. "It's got a metal shell that's completely unfamiliar to me. We can't open it, we can't break it, we can't do anything with this thing. It's going to need a lot of study."

"Can you tell me anything about it?" Sofie asked.

"Only that it gives off a small amount of radiation. I wouldn't even have it out of the little lead box we made for it if you weren't coming this morning."

"Is it dangerous?" Sofie asked.

"The radiation?" Kolisko's face was reflected in the sphere, round and very pink, distorted like in a fun-house mirror. "Probably not, unless you stood close to it for some time."

"Close?" Anton had been living above that thing for decades. Sofie had touched it repeatedly. "What do you mean by close?"

"I'm not an expert. The same room, touching it, something like that. You want me to check?"

"Please," Sofie said, "and put it in your report."

"Done," Kolisko said.

She stepped closer to the sphere. She saw another pinkish shape move in its silver coating. That had to be her.

"Actually, though, I wasn't asking about the radiation. I was asking about the sphere itself. Do you think it's dangerous?"

"I wouldn't expect the word 'danger' on it otherwise," Kolisko said dryly.

"No," Sofie said. "Radiated items often carry the word 'danger.'"

"Now," Kolisko said. "And in this country. I can't vouch for the English-speaking ones."

Sofie gave him a sideways glance. He was studying the sphere.

"If I had to guess," he said, "the word 'danger' is on there for another reason. We didn't know a lot about the harmful effects of radiation until well after the nuclear power plants were online. Remember those watches with the irradiated paint on the numbers so that they glowed in the dark?"

"I remember reading about them," Sofie said. "They were before my time."

"They still turn up now and then. And those glow-in-the-dark balls they had around the same period. All had some kind of irradiated something-or-other. We get them in here now and then for testing."

"For crimes?" Sofie asked.

Kolisko smiled. "We do a few other things here. You know that. The benefits of being a private firm."

She felt a slight shiver run down her back. Did he know she'd checked with Scotland Yard? She wouldn't put it past him. Or anyone else at CRL could have sources there.

"So this could just be a toy," Sofie said.

"The Americans are crazy-cautious," Kolisko said. "They put warning labels on everything. They might have done that decades ago."

"You think it's an American toy?" Sofie asked, wondering how it got into the hands of a Greek man who wrote about Russian government.

"I don't think anything. It unnerves me that I can't figure out how to pry the thing open. I would think, if it was a toy, it would be easy to disassemble."

Sofie would have, too, but she knew little about toys. Or other practical matters.

"Have you shown it to anyone else?" Sofie asked.

"Meaning, do you think someone smarter than me might figure this out?" he asked.

Sofie grinned at him. It felt good to smile; she had been too serious during the last half hour. "If you want to take it that way."

"Yes," he said. "Of course I have. We're going to keep studying the thing, but so far, it hasn't revealed any of its secrets."

Like the Sniper case. How many people had tried to figure it out over the past few decades? The case had yielded a few secrets to her, but she felt like she was in deeper now. All the proof she wanted was becoming something else, something a lot more twisted.

"You'll tell me if it does," she said.

"You'll be the first to know," he said. "But I'll be honest with you. We can't even x-ray the thing. We've given it the most time of all the items in this room, and we are no farther along with the thing than we were when we started. I'll be surprised if we ever get much more for you. You might have to come at it some other way."

"Historically," Sofie said.

"Catalogues, drawings, photographs, anything," he said. "If we have a clue what it is, we might be able to work it properly."

She nodded. "I'll look."

But she wouldn't make it a priority. She had other things to do first. The gun provided her with more than enough research questions. So did all of those files in Runge's office.

If the sphere had come from the Sniper, the way she had originally thought, then she might spend more time on it. But now that she knew it had come from Papadopoulos, she felt it wasn't as important.

Perhaps that was one of her incorrect assumptions. But, as she had realized earlier, she only had so much time to finish her work. She had to streamline wherever possible.

Kolisko shrugged. "That's all I've got."

"It's plenty," Sofie said. Too much, but she didn't want to tell him that. "I'm ready for the report whenever you can finish it."

"Part one," Kolisko said. "Part two'll come with the blood and maybe if I can find out some more stuff from my sources."

"I hope you can," Sofie said. "This case is driving me crazy."

"Isn't that what it does?" Kolisko asked. "Once it has you, it doesn't seem to be able to let you go."

Sofie grabbed her purse and pulled open the door. "Call me," she said, and stepped into the hallway.

Then she let out a large breath of air. It hadn't been stuffy in the room, but she had felt squeezed in. Too much information, too many things she still didn't understand.

At least she knew the gun fired those bullets. All the strange things she found—with the exception of the sphere—were tied to the Sniper. That was something, at least.

All this new evidence, all these new facts. Amazing that none of them led anywhere. But, she knew, even the dead ends would help her book. The Sniper enthusiasts would have more things to talk about.

But she wanted facts, answers. She wanted the solution.

The information from the lab might give her that solution, but she wasn't as optimistic as she had been when she'd arrived with the box. This book was becoming more and more complicated with each new piece of information.

She finally understood how Johann Runge had dedicated his life to the Sniper case.

She felt the same impulse herself.

1913

THE ASSASSIN RAN down the hallway toward the stairs. The hallway was empty, but that wouldn't buy him much time.

Because he had waited in the room, because he had stood so close to the body, because he had shot from point-blank range, his pants were spattered with blood.

And his shoes—his shoes left bloody prints on the nice clean floors. Even though he had pulled Hitler's door closed, the prints would lead someone to the crime scene very, very soon.

The assassin ran toward the stairwell. At least he had remembered to reset the safety and shove the Glock back under his coat.

The stairwell door was open—had he left it that way? He couldn't remember—and he hurried down, using the railing to swing himself down five stairs at a time.

He had been right: The stairwell echoed. His panicked footsteps sounded like bangs against the metal steps, and he knew he was drawing attention.

It just might take the residents a moment to reach him.

The assassin glanced back up the stairs. He was still leaving prints, but they were irregular now, and not recognizable as blood. Someone would have to follow him from the top floor to know what he had done, to know why he was running.

He reached the ground floor to find that group of men from the kitchen peering into the stairwell. They had gaunt faces and large eyes, and looked amazingly similar.

"Excuse me," the assassin said, shoving his way past them, his German guttural, his accent atrocious. "Pardon me. Let me through."

He managed to get through the tangle of bodies and head toward the exit. It seemed impossibly far away—and it was only at the end of a corridor.

His heart was pounding. He looked over his shoulder.

The men hadn't followed him. A few of them were staring after him, the rest still peering in the stairwell as if it held answers to questions they hadn't even realized they were asking.

He shoved the double doors open and stepped outside, taking deep, rich breaths of the morning chill. His lungs ached and he was panting.

He scraped his shoes on a small pile of snow, cleaning off the rest of the blood. Then he went southeast, toward the Prater, and his very last stop.

2005

ANTON WASN'T AS WORRIED about the radiation as Sofie had been. When she finally arrived at his house, three hours later than usual, she told him about her meeting with the scientist at CRL. Not everything, of course—Anton had the sense that Sofie rarely told him everything—but enough to keep him interested.

They were sitting in his kitchen. Anton had developed the ritual of making Sofie lunch. Lately, she had been bringing some of the ingredients, claiming she had to pay her fair share of their meal costs.

Lunch this day was simple, because he had been too preoccupied waiting for her to plan anything complex. Bread, several kinds of cheese, some wine.

Simple, and very good.

"My understanding of long exposure to radiation is that it causes cancer," Anton said as he cut himself a slice of bread. "My great-grandfather died of heart failure. My grandfather died of complications from pneumonia. My father, who never lived here, died of lung cancer, but I think his cigarettes had something to do with that. So I'm not really worried. No one in my family has ever gotten the kinds of cancer that would come from long-term exposure to something irradiated."

Sofie's entire body relaxed. "I was worried about you."

He smiled, then looked down at his plate. "I was worried about you," he said. "This morning."

Sofie's hand tightened on her glass of wine. "Why?"

He shrugged one shoulder, trying to pretend nonchalance. "You were late. You've never been late before."

"I never set a time. I didn't realize—"

He reached across the table and put his finger on her lips. "We have no agreement," he said, letting his finger linger a moment too long before moving it away. He liked touching her. "You didn't do anything wrong."

"Then I don't understand," she said.

He felt cold and too warm at the same time. It was the same feeling he had just before he had to go on stage to perform with an orchestra, a small version of the stage fright that haunted him during his solo performances.

"I've come to care for you, Sofie," he said softly.

She didn't respond, but her expression was enough. She was surprised. Obviously, she didn't reciprocate. Obviously, she thought of this place as a library, a place filled with research materials and nothing else.

And the librarian, whom she had never really noticed, had just expressed his feelings for her. Clearly, she was trying to figure out a way to let him down gently.

Anton picked up his plate and carried it to the sink so that he didn't have to look at her. He didn't want to see the expression of surprise turn to pity.

Finally, he couldn't take the silence any more. He turned back toward the table.

Sofie's head was bowed, her hair covering her face. He could no longer see her expression.

"It's not like I expect anything," he said.

She lifted a hand. On anyone else, it would seem like a queenly command for silence. From Sofie, it looked like a feeble protestation.

Then she ran her other hand through her hair, pushing it away from her face.

To Anton's surprise, her cheeks were red.

"I don't know what to say." Her voice was soft.

"You don't have to—"

"Please," she said, turning toward him.

He stopped trying to speak. She had something to tell him, and in his nervousness, he wasn't letting her.

Her eyes were wide and filled with an emotion he'd never seen in them before. Fear? What would she have to be afraid of?

"I've never—no one's ever—." She stopped herself, shook her head, and smiled. The smile was rueful. "I've been alone my whole life. I'm not used to being noticed."

She wasn't angry at him, then, or disgusted at him. Anton slid back into his chair and reached across the table. He took her hand, and she didn't pull away.

Then she covered his hand with her other one, capturing his fingers under her palm.

"I care for you too," she said. Her flush grew even deeper. "But I didn't say anything because…you know."

"You've been alone your whole life," he said, wondering if she didn't want to change that.

She shook her head. "I've been unwanted my whole life."

His gaze met hers. Now he understood the expression in her eyes. She was naked. He was seeing the real Sofie for the first time.

"You're not unwanted anymore," he said.

1913

THE TRAM LET RUNGE OFF near the Votivkirche. He could have gone another stop, but he wanted to walk.

And to think.

His meetings with the widows had disturbed him.

The gothic spires of the church rose against the blue sky. The sunlight still seemed odd to Runge. He was used to Vienna's grayness in the winter. The sun's presence added to the unreality he had been feeling since he had been called to the Café Central the afternoon before.

The streets were filled with people going about their business. The mid-morning trade seemed as brisk as usual—men in their heavy coats and hats, women carrying muffs as they scurried along the ice-covered cobblestones.

Hard to believe these were the same people who had celebrated into the early morning hours, playing at Carnival. Everyone looked so serious, so intent.

And yet, not frightened at all, despite the headlines in the morning papers, despite the conversations he had heard on the tram, the discussions of the shootings.

Perhaps the people thought themselves too unimportant to die in such a flamboyant manner. They hadn't realized that Bronstein and Adler had more in common with them than with the kings and queens of Europe.

This killer was different. He had different reasons for his killings, reasons Runge had yet to discover.

When Runge reached the Ring, he found one of the young officers standing outside police headquarters, arms crossed. Other officers went inside the building, going about their work, talking excitedly.

Runge's stomach clenched. Something else had happened.

"The killer." He did not ask a question of the young officer. Instead, Runge simply made a statement.

The officer looked surprised. "How did you know?"

"I believe he is not finished with us," Runge said. "What is it this time? The Asylum? Or another socialist dead in a café?"

A frown crossed the officer's face. "Neither," he said. "We have just received reports of a shooting in the Mannerheim."

"The Mannerheim?" Runge asked. He had expected many things, but not that. The Mannerheim was a poor place in a poor neighborhood. He doubted he would find anyone of the same consequence as Freud, Adler, and Bronstein in such a place.

Although Bronstein had been poor. He had simply found a way to provide for his family.

Perhaps this new victim had no family. Perhaps he was as well known as the others, and yet without means.

"One victim?"

"We don't know," the officer said. "It's too new."

"How new?" Runge asked.

"We got the call just a few moments ago."

Runge felt a surge of excitement. If he was able to use the department's automobile, he might get to the scene fast enough to catch this killer.

There weren't a lot of places to go in that district.

Finally, Runge felt like he had a chance.

2005

WHEN SHE GOT HOME THAT NIGHT, Sofie went to her office, where she did her best thinking, got into one of her favorite chairs, and sat in the dark, replaying the entire day.

They hadn't fallen into each other's arms after Anton made his announcement. They hadn't done much more than stare into each other's eyes.

But Sofie knew that he meant what he said. He cared for her. He had worried about her. He had thought of her before thinking of himself.

And that unnerved her.

She sat in her chair, knees against her chest, arms wrapped around them, surrounded by her books and her research and all the things she knew.

She had been alone her whole life. She hadn't even gotten a pet. Not even fish. Fish died, like everything else. And that was the real risk, for her. The deaths. Not the life, not the sharing—which would be difficult all by itself.

But the death.

Death was a sniper. Sometimes the shot hit an artery on the first try, killing the victim instantly. And sometimes, the shot hit a limb or an organ, maiming, but not killing immediately. Instead, the shot set up a long, slow process whose end was inevitable.

Either way, long and slow or fast and surprising, death changed the people around the victim forever.

She had lost more than her parents that sunny summer afternoon, more than her willingness to go into parks, and more than her capacity to be comfortable in crowds.

She had lost her ability to laugh. Not just her will to laugh. She couldn't remember how to do it.

Her minders used to comment on how serious she was, how worried they were that this small child didn't even smile. Over time, she realized that smiling was as much a protective device as huddling in a corner. People didn't notice you if you smiled. They noticed when you frowned.

Sometimes she watched little children laugh—that from-the-gut, no-holds-barred laughter that seemed so unaffected and so true. Children would roll on the ground when they laughed. They'd cover their mouths and chuckle so hard that tears would fall.

Sofie couldn't remember laughing like that. She could almost touch a memory of that kind of laughter—and it would fade, in a series of colors, as if she were watching balloons through a kaleidoscope. Half a memory, along with a gunshot, and the scraping of gravel against her knees.

Death changed everything, and she wasn't really willing to experience that change again.

She wished her past had never happened, that her parents had never died. She wished she knew how to love the way someone like Anton deserved.

She wished she could be someone else.

She rested her cheek on her knee, feeling the twill fabric of her pants bite into her skin. She didn't know how to tell Anton that. She liked the way he had smiled at her, liked the touch of his hand against her face.

She had told him to go slow, that she needed time. And he seemed to understand.

But what if she needed more than time? What if she could never face that kind of loss again? Because that was what love was all about. It was about endings.

It was about loss.

Every relationship ended, whether in divorce or death or simple loss of affection. Her reading had taught her that.

It had also taught her that every relationship gave its participants an illusion of immortality, one that she had never had. A love that would survive time was not possible, as far as she was concerned, because love protected no one.

Love didn't stop the inevitable.

It didn't prevent death.

Sofie pulled her arms tighter around her knees. How to tell Anton all of this when he had never experienced it? How to let him know that while she cared for him, she wasn't sure she would risk the connection, risk the loss?

Or did she even have a choice? Had she made the connection without knowing it?

Would she have worried about him this morning the way that he had worried about her?

Probably.

She was already feeling something. And that frightened her more than she could say.

1913

THE MANNERHEIM'S MANAGER was a slight man who moved with exaggerated importance. He was former military, and treated everyone else like a subordinate.

Runge disliked him at once.

The manager met Runge at the main entrance and immediately started in on a list of complaints. The officers on scene would not let him near the room. No one would allow him to clean the floors, and why had no one disposed of the body?

Runge ignored them all, passing the manager to yet another officer, and went up to the murder site, taking the stairs three at a time.

Runge had been to the Mannerheim before. The building, finished in 1905, had become a sought-after refuge for men down on their luck. What always struck him about the Mannerheim was its tidiness, and that wasn't in evidence at all this day. The hallways smelled faintly of burned bread—apparently a small fire had started in the kitchen when someone had left his breakfast to see what was happening upstairs— and the stairwell was filled with dried bloody footprints.

When Runge saw a complete one, he stopped and examined it. Pointed toe, square heel, shoe size slightly larger than his own. The heel seemed to hit the floor firmly—no wear rounding an edge—and so did the toe.

Expensive shoes then, or perhaps boots, and relatively new.

Finally he had a bit of information about this killer. But he had no idea what that information meant.

The hallway leading to the dead man's room was crowded. Residents who lived on the floor were standing in their doorways, which had been one of the many things the manager complained about: They weren't supposed to be in their rooms this late in the day, watching the police officers come and go.

Half a dozen officers were already here, guarding the scene, one of them talking to a reporter for one of the local newspapers. The reporter had his back to Runge, and Runge hoped he could sneak into the crime scene before the reporter cornered him.

Runge had nothing kind to say about that morning's reporting. It was sensational, and while it did not seem to alarm Vienna, it would—particularly now that one of the dead was clearly down on his luck.

Several of the policemen touched the bills of their caps as Runge passed them. He nodded in acknowledgement but said nothing.

He didn't want to contaminate his own examination of the crime scene. He had heard too much already—a painter shot in the Mannerheim; a vicious murder with so much blood that it had dripped to the room below.

Part of the fault for his overhearing lay with him. The department's only automobile was on a joy ride. Runge had been in such a hurry to get here that he had decided not to wait.

He took the tram, and on the way, heard more rumors than he had wanted to. He had no idea how information had gotten all over the city so quickly, but it wasn't his job to trace leaks.

It was his job to find this killer. When the automobile had been unavailable to him, Runge knew he had lost his chance to catch the man in the neighborhood. Now he would have to do it through detection.

He only hoped he would get enough evidence here to lead him to this clearly deranged man.

The door leading to the victim's room was partially closed, probably to keep prying eyes from seeing inside. Runge stepped past one of the officers, then pushed the door open and stopped as the fetid smell of blood and loosened bowels reached him.

The room was smaller than he had expected, and brighter. Sunlight fell across the narrow cot pushed into the room's right side. A table on the right was covered with competent paintings of Vienna's landmarks—St. Stephen's Cathedral, Messepalast, and even the Riesenrad at the Prater.

Runge looked at the body last. The rumors had one thing right: There was a lot of blood. Footprints covered the floor, all of them different sizes and all of them made of blood.

Runge cursed silently. Someday he might win the battle to teach his people how to handle a crime scene, at least the way he wanted them to. Fortunately there were other prints farther away from the body, the prints in the stairwell, which clearly had not come from the police.

Runge would have to have someone sketch them before the manager got his way and washed the floors.

Runge crouched over the body. The back of the man's skull was gone, his black hair slick with drying blood. The man was small and young, perhaps thirty, perhaps younger than that. His hand clutched at the floor, his fingers curled.

There was another entrance wound in the middle of the back, and then, on the buttocks, a strange imprint. Runge peered at it. The impression looked like a square boot print.

The killer had stood on this victim and fired into his skull at point-blank range.

Runge rocked back on his heels. "How did the killer escape?" he asked the nearest officer.

The officer looked at another man, one Runge didn't recognize, obviously the first to arrive.

"The stairwell, sir."

Runge shook his head. "I mean, considering all the noise from the shooting, someone should have understood what was going on. Surely at least one man in this place knew what a gunshot sounded like."

"That's the strange thing, sir," the officer said. "No one heard the shots."

"How many shots?" Runge asked. He saw evidence of two, but he hadn't had much time on the scene.

"Three that I can count, sir," the officer said. "Two in the victim, and one in the wall."

He nodded toward the table. Runge turned. From this vantage, he could see the hole in the plaster, big enough to keep a bullet.

He felt a surge of excitement and tried to tamp it down. Two pieces of evidence, then. The footprint, and the bullet. Perhaps the bullet would even be intact.

"Are these walls so thick, then, that no one can hear gunshots?" Runge asked.

"We haven't tested it, sir," the officer said, "but they don't seem so thick."

Runge nodded. That was his sense. Probably the other men were lying. They had enough trouble, and probably had not wanted to get involved. He did not approve of that attitude, but he had seen it before, especially in places like this.

"Do we know who our man is?" he asked.

"The registration papers here identify him as Adolf Hietler," the officer said. "He has lived in this room for some years."

"Is he a socialist?" Runge asked.

"He talks a lot of politics," the officer said, "particularly late at night. Apparently, he spends much of his time ranting. I have heard of his opinions on Jews from the other residents, but I have not heard what kind of politics he espouses. Only that he does, at great length and at great volume."

Runge let out a small sigh. "So he's not a psychoanalyst, either."

The officer laughed. "I would think, from the people I have talked to, that he would be in need of one rather than be one."

The hair rose on the back of Runge's neck. "Is he a former asylum resident?"

"I do not know, sir," the officer said. "But I don't believe it would be hard to find out."

"Have someone try," Runge said.

The officer nodded and waved his hand. Another officer left the room, tracking, Runge noted, blood with him.

"Tell him not to use the far stairwell," Runge said. "He has blood on his shoes."

At that comment, every officer in the room looked at his shoes. The officer to whom Runge had been talking crouched beside him.

"We have witnesses." the officer said.

"To the shooting?"

"To his escape."

"Did they follow him?"

"No," the officer said. "They had no idea who he was or why he was here. They remembered him because he was running."

Runge could barely catch his breath. "And? What did he look like?"

The officer shrugged. "Normal, I guess. Thin, average height. Large coat."

"Hair color?" Runge asked. "Eye color?"

"They couldn't tell me. Some think he was wearing a hat."

"Some *think*?" Runge couldn't believe this. People had finally seen the killer and they couldn't remember him?

"He was making a lot of noise coming down the stairs, but no one knew what was happening until they saw the blood. Then everyone went upstairs to find out what was going on."

"And no one thought to follow him." This time it wasn't a question. This time, Runge couldn't believe these people's indifference.

"Apparently not, sir," the officer said.

Runge sighed and stood. "If the man was making bloody footprints inside the building, then he was making them outside. I suppose no one thought of that, either."

The officer flushed. "No, sir."

Runge nodded once in irritation. He checked his own shoes—amazingly, he was one of the few who hadn't stepped in the blood—then headed into the hallway.

Maybe no one had tracked more blood down the stairs. Maybe—and this might be too much to ask of his people—no one had tracked blood outside.

Maybe, for the first time since the shootings began, Runge might have a lead.

Somewhere out there was the killer.

Somewhere close.

2005

AT THREE IN THE MORNING, Anton finished the lyric piece. He worked as if he were in a fever, the music pouring out of him as it had never done before.

He didn't remember finding the notes; he barely remembered transferring them to paper. He just remembered the white-hot moment, the way he felt as the music flowed from him, as if it were being sent through him from somewhere else.

Not until he had finished, one hand on the bench, bracing himself, the other holding the musical sheets, studying what he had written, did he realize what he had done.

For the first time in his life, he had written a piece of music as a gift for someone else.

He had written a love song.

For Sofie.

1913

THE ASSASSIN STEPPED inside the station at Wein Nord. The air was warm here, probably caused by steam from the trains pulling into the station.

He resisted the urge to unbutton his coat. He was sweating from his walk to the Prater. He had used the Ferris wheel as his landmark, seeing it tower over the city. Somehow the round familiarity of the wheel calmed him.

He needed to be calm to finish his work.

The assassin stopped in front of the large board on which the station's staff posted the arrivals and departures. He knew what time the train arrived from Krakow, but he did not know how to get to it from this part of the terminal.

He finally saw the listing, then looked for some kind of map so that he could find the terminal.

Of course, there was no map. This was 1913: No one thought to help commuters along in those days. He would have to ask, or rely on his somewhat faulty memory. There was no guarantee that what he remembered would actually be accurate.

Time changed things.

He had learned that all too well.

The assassin stopped near the entrance to one of the terminals. Green-capped customs officials searched passengers entering Vienna.

Ever since the Middle Ages, Vienna had charged a tax on goods bought outside the city.

In this time period, it had been the only city in the world to do so.

The assassin felt his breath catch.

He touched the Glock as if it were a talisman.

One more victim.

Just one more.

And then he would be done.

2005

THE NEXT DAY, everything was different. Not greatly different, but subtly different. They touched more.

They smiled more.

And Sofie was as nervous as she had been that very first day, uncertain what to do, what to say. She knew Anton noticed, but she didn't know how to talk with him.

So she did what she had always done.

She retreated to her work.

The basement had become a haven. The files no longer struck her as overwhelming, but as a safety for the conflicting emotions she felt. She lost herself in past lives—all of them gone now, all of them untouchable—and let herself forget about her own.

She learned that Hietler had been staying in Vienna to avoid the draft. A year after his death, German conscript officials finally located him and closed the file. If he had lived, he would have been sent back to Linz in Upper Austria and served the entire tour of duty that he had avoided.

She learned that Bronstein had a wife and two children in Vienna, but he had abandoned another family in England at the turn of the century. Bronstein wrote under the name Trotsky, and had some identification made up in that name as well. His writings were political, just like Papadopoulos's were, but Bronstein, it seemed, acted on his convictions; he had served time in a Russian prison for crimes against the state.

She learned that Freud's protégé, Carl Jung, was plotting a rebellion against the old man, hoping to split the psychoanalytic community away from Freud's doctrines. Freud's death enabled Jung to make the split without embarrassing Freud. It also guaranteed that Freud's work would become marginalized, since no one bothered to reprint his books, considering them out of date.

And she learned that Runge could find no record of Stavros Papadopoulos's existence before he boarded the train in Krakow. It seemed that Papadopoulos was an assumed name, but Runge had never found out what Papadopoulos's real name had been.

All that work pleased her. She knew these files would add depth to her book. Even if she didn't deliver the identity of the Sniper as promised, she would at least have a new text, one the other Sniper writers had never explored.

But she had only touched the surface of the files. She continued to dig through them, hoping to find more.

And she did.

One afternoon, while searching for background on Viktor Adler, she lifted an entire accordion file out of a middle drawer. There, lining the bottom, were a series of notebooks.

At first, she thought they'd fallen out of other files. And then she realized they'd been taped down there to keep them out of sight. If she hadn't moved the correct file, she would never have noticed them. They would have looked like the bottom of the file drawer.

But she had seen the yellowing tape, and reached down, touching the unmistakable cardboard top of one of the notebooks.

Then she detached it, pulling the notebook out of the drawer.

It was labeled Number Two in a confident hand that she had come to recognize as Johann Runge's.

Her breath caught.

She opened the notebook and saw the date: January 1913.

Then her eyes caught the opening line:

I have become convinced our sniper is a ghost. Every time I feel I have
him, he slips past me. He has as many masks as Carnival itself. I fear
that we will not catch him, that he is too smart for all of us....

Sofie pulled out the other notebooks—five in all—then sat cross-
legged on the floor and began to read.

1913

RUNGE STOOD BESIDE THE OLD MAN on the street. The old man had been sitting in the doorway of the building opposite, and had smiled when he had seen Runge come toward him.

"So," the old man had said, "you are the only one smart enough to ask me questions."

The old man thought he had seen the killer. He had said so the moment Runge introduced himself.

"He did not seem like the usual customer of the Mannerheim," the old man said with a formality that most of Vienna had lost. "I had seen him before he went inside. He stared at the building for a long time, as if he did not know where he was, and then he disappeared. When he reappeared, he stopped and wiped off his shoes."

Runge could almost see it. Of course the killer would study the building before entering. He probably realized at that point that there was no escape through the windows.

So he decided to risk the stairwells.

Obviously he had known who his victim was, and even where his victim lived. He had known that about the others as well.

If this shooting had been random, the killer could have just as easily shot the men making their breakfasts in the kitchen. Some of them reported that the killer had looked inside before heading up the stairs.

"Did you see where he went?" Runge asked, hoping that his luck would hold, yet doubting that it would.

The old man nodded. "He walked quite deliberately toward the southeast."

"Walked," Runge said. The killer had done the same thing on Berggasse. He had walked away from the shooting.

"Running would call attention, don't you agree?" the old man asked.

Runge nodded absently. "Southeast," he repeated.

"Looking up." The old man's eyes twinkled. "As if he saw something he recognized."

Runge turned toward the southeast and looked up. Just barely visible over the tops of trees was the Riesenrad, the sixteen-year-old Ferris wheel inviting people to play in the Prater.

Who would the killer be targeting there? The Prater was just an amusement park. No one famous lived nearby.

But this last victim hadn't been famous.

It was, Runge thought, like guessing where the first drop of rain would fall in a storm due three days hence.

He had no idea and if he guessed, he would probably guess wrong.

2005

THE NOTEBOOKS RAN FROM 1913 TO 1953. And then they stopped, with a few cryptic notes at the end, notes that made no real sense to Sofie, at least not yet.

The first notebook had a strange little annotation at the beginning, and it wasn't until Sofie started reading it that she realized Runge had always kept a journal. These were to have been his 1913 journals, but they had gotten filled with the Sniper case, and he had placed them with the files.

Her heart pounded as she read, and once she smeared a page because her palms were sweating. In these notebooks, Johann Runge wrote things he wouldn't dare put in police reports—his feelings, his hunches, his hopes.

All the things he couldn't officially say, but that he believed. Somewhere in here might even be the very thing Runge had refused to do throughout his life.

He might have speculated on who the Carnival Sniper had really been.

With Runge's speculation, Sofie would have even more to go on. She would have names, possible dates, ways of tracking. She had more resources available to her. There had to be Sniper DNA on some of the materials. If she found that, she could get familial DNA from some of the names and rule out entire suspects.

She might even figure out who the Sniper was, just from Runge's notes. After all, the man knew the case better than anyone else. Even without modern forensic techniques, his hunches were probably accurate.

Knowing how meticulous Runge was, his evidence simply might not have been good enough for him to arrest a man—suspect one, yes. Arrest him, no.

Sofie read, page after cramped page. And as she read, she found that everything she had assumed about Runge, everything she had come to believe, was wrong.

1913

WILLIAM COULD NOT STAND STILL. He rocked back and forth as he waited to get off the train.

Papadopoulos had just exited. He took the steps carefully and clung tightly to his case. As he stepped onto the platform, he had looked in the windows, probably checking to make sure that William couldn't follow him.

William didn't need to follow him, not anymore. So long as they stayed within five hundred meters of each other, William could still use his remote.

His stomach cramped. He hadn't eaten in a long time. But he didn't want to eat here, where food hadn't been pasteurized or processed, where germs lurked and unsanitary cooking methods abounded.

He wanted a good healthy meal.

He wanted to go home.

Only a few more minutes. Just a few.

The line moved forward, and he finally reached the front of the train car. The air blowing in the door was hotter than he expected, and the smells, even after a week, still seemed unusual to him—the stench of burning, the unwashed bodies, the perfume.

He grabbed the railing and stepped down, his feet landing on the wooden platform. People had moved away from the car, some of

261

them hugging loved ones, others striding with purpose toward the main door.

At the door, he saw green-capped men. They wore uniforms and looked official. They were stopping passengers, searching their belongings.

Customs? Here?

William had thought customs a modern invention, something to do with airplanes and border guards and world wars—not anything to do with this more innocent time.

What would they make of the nuke? Would they confiscate it? They certainly would find it.

His stomach cramped again.

Papadopoulos still had several meters to go before he reached the line for the officials. If William was any judge of lines—and he wasn't, not really—then Papadopoulos would be standing there maybe ten minutes.

If the officials found the nuke, the worst they could do was take it away, keep it here. They wouldn't be able to make it work. They wouldn't know how to use it.

And it wouldn't make any difference, not in the scheme of things.

He shivered.

He didn't need the symbolism. Papadopoulos could die here or in the tram. It didn't matter. William just needed to finish and leave.

He hurried down the platform, then stopped as Papadopoulos approached the line.

If the customs officials found the nuke, then Papadopoulos would know who put it there. Papadopoulos would turn, would see him, maybe even attack.

There were so many stories, so many unproven stories, of the way Papadopoulos had killed with his bare hands. Some of the histories speculated that he had stomped a man to death over a missed order.

What would he do when he learned that William had put the nuke in his case? Because if anyone could figure out what that device was, it would be Papadopoulos. He would know a bomb—even a not-yet-invented bomb—when he saw one.

William's stomach cramped for the third time.

He wouldn't get privacy. He would have to do this before he left the station.

He stepped to the side, away from the flow of people, and brushed up against the soot-covered walls.

Then he felt inside his coat for the remote. It was small, barely big enough for his thumb to play on the keys. Still, he cupped his right hand around it, and turned away from the people still pouring out of the train.

He had to do three things in rapid succession. He had to make contact with the nuke. Then he had to set the timer. And then he had to program it to detonate.

Thirty minutes should give Papadopoulos enough time to exit the building. Not that the roof would make much difference, but William wanted the blast to be as strong as possible.

Thirty minutes would also guarantee that, no matter what happened, he would be able to use his handheld to return to the future.

His hand trembled. He checked the wireless connect.

The nuke responded.

Phase one was done.

He set the timer. Then he programmed the nuke to detonate when the timer went off.

Thirty minutes.

Thirty short minutes.

He had to get out of here before the mushroom cloud rose against that pale blue sky.

2005

ANTON HAD GONE BACK to the Boys Choir piece. The love song he had written was only for Sofie, and the march wasn't appropriate—not for the kind of holiday piece the director had wanted. Anton had to get into the holiday spirit, even though it was summer, and he needed to think in five parts.

He was having trouble thinking at all.

Mostly he plucked at the keys, and concentrated on Sofie, one floor below. He was treating her like a frightened animal, trying to give her a chance to get used to his presence. He hadn't found the right time to play the love song for her.

He hoped it would be tonight.

He planned to ask her to dinner, and not just a home-cooked meal like they had been having at lunch. He would take her to a nice restaurant—not too nice so that she would feel like they were on a date—but nice enough that it wasn't a common, everyday occurrence.

Then he would bring her back here, play her the song, and see what happened.

Maybe nothing.

Maybe everything.

He played a series of arpeggios, but they didn't inspire him. He had no idea why he took commissions when his music usually didn't come on demand. If he was supposed to write a Christmas piece, his mind gave him waltzes; if he was supposed to write waltzes, his mind gave him folk tunes.

Finishing a commission always meant winning a war with himself, a war he never really wanted to fight in the first place.

It was the middle of the afternoon before he completely settled in—the lunch with Sofie had been pleasant, but she had seemed distracted, probably from the work below. She had said she was making new discoveries, but she wasn't ready to share them yet.

He wished she would get ready to do something; he wasn't very good at waiting.

Five-part harmonies with boys' voices meant writing mostly for the upper ranges. Using Austrian tradition gave him the gamut of classical music from Mozart to Beethoven to Strauss. Anton could even throw in Arnold Schönberg or Alban Berg if he wanted to, although he doubted that such "modern" music was what the choir director had in mind.

Still, Anton was playing a variation on *Adestes Fideles* in the style of Schönberg, using the dodecaphonic rigor Schönberg had perfected toward the end of his career, when Anton realized he was being watched. He stopped, the atonal chords still buzzing through the piano wires.

Sofie was standing in the arch to the main room. She hugged a notebook to her chest.

"You didn't have to stop for me," she said.

"It's all right," Anton said. "I was just playing around."

"It sounded serious," she said.

"The school of modernism always sounds serious," he said.

"That's for the Boys Choir?" she asked.

"Heavens no," he said. "They might accept it, but no one would like it, least of all me."

She smiled at him. He liked her slow, radiant smile. It felt like a gift. And the more he got to know her, the more he realized that it was.

"Did you find something?" he asked.

"I don't know," she said. "Do you have a minute?"

He nodded and stood up from the piano bench. He put the lid down over the keys, picked up some composition paper that had fallen to the floor, and walked toward Sofie.

They had to go into the kitchen, which was his only real room for conversations. He hadn't realized the lack until Sofie had come into his life. Until then, he had always met his non-musical friends in cafés or at their homes, never at his.

His musical friends always gathered around the piano. There was rarely any discussion when they were around. They brought their instruments or sang, and held an impromptu, and usually enjoyable, jam session.

But it had been a long time since he had done that. Mostly he entertained outside of the house, and spent his time alone inside.

By now, he and Sofie had their places at the kitchen table. He was surprised when she didn't sit at hers, but instead pulled up a chair next to his.

"I know you don't know a lot about your great-grandfather," she said, "but maybe you remember hearing a few things."

Anton shrugged. "I'll see what I can recall."

She nodded. "Was he a fanciful man?"

Anton raised his eyebrows. "My great-grandfather?"

He thought, trying to remember the stories his grandfather and father told. They often said he believed impossible things, but they never said Johann Runge was fanciful. If anything, Johann Runge had sounded like a humorless man who was too focused on his own past.

"I don't think so," Anton said after a moment.

Sofie bit her upper lip, a sign that she was concentrating. "Did you ever hear of him trying to write fiction, maybe making up stories?"

"My great-grandfather?" Anton's voice rose. "Are you kidding?"

"No." Sofie hadn't changed her posture. She was still clutching that notebook. "I'm not kidding. He was a writer, after all."

"He might have written that book, but he might not have," Anton said. "They had ghost writers, even in 1955."

"I know that," Sofie said, "but I found early drafts, and I found other examples of his writing. I'm pretty convinced he wrote the book himself."

Anton studied her. She seemed very uncomfortable. Her entire body was hunched together as if she were protecting herself against something.

"What did you find, Sofie?" he asked.

"I'm not sure," she said again. "I thought they were his contemporaneous journals, but now I'm really not sure at all."

"In the files?" Anton asked.

"Beneath some of them," she said. "As if they'd been hidden."

Anton looked at the notebook clutched in her arms. "Is that one of them?"

She nodded, but didn't give it to him. "It's got some strange things, Anton."

"Like what?"

"Like—." She stopped herself and shook her head, as if she couldn't quite say what she wanted to. "I've spent the last few days reading the files, which are pretty dry, and the police reports, which are also dry. But you get a real sense of the crimes—or at least I did. Your great-grandfather had a gift of expression. He kind of put you in the crime scene, with all the blood and the bodies and the scared people."

Anton nodded. He'd read a few of the reports himself, until he decided he didn't want those images in his brain.

"But these journals, they're almost like his impressions of the crime scenes—not the dry facts, but the emotions."

"You're kidding," Anton said.

"Apparently, he'd done this all his life," Sofie said. "Somewhere around here are journals that go up to 1912. These start at 1913, and then they have some really strange notations for each year after that."

"Strange notations?" Anton asked.

Sofie set the notebook on the table. It was old, the cover frayed, but not from age. From use.

On the front, it had a large number 4 written in black ink.

Anton ran a hand over it. "Wow," he said. "How many are there?"

"Five that I've found so far. Probably more, unless he destroyed them." Sofie opened the notebook.

The first page had his great-grandfather's handwriting. Anton recognized it from files he'd seen below.

"Look," she said, running her hand alongside the page.

Anton leaned close enough to her to smell her vanilla shampoo. He wanted to lean even closer to Sofie, to put his arm around her, but he didn't dare. Not when she was being this serious.

He forced himself to focus on the paper in front of him.

The notations were odd. They made no sense, at least not to him.

January 13, 1932: No
January 13, 1933: No
January 13, 1934: No
January 13, 1935: No

"Are all five notebooks like this?" Anton asked.

"This one is," Sofie said. "Every page, a different group of years, but the same date, all followed by the word 'No.'"

"And that's not in the others?" Anton asked.

"It begins in the third, and ends in this one. The last date is January 13, 1952."

"1952," Anton said, frowning. 1952. The date brought up a memory, and he wasn't sure what it was.

"He had scrawled the date for 1953," Sofie said, "and then crossed it off in a different color ink."

"Do you have any idea what it means?" Anton asked.

Sofie swallowed visibly. Her hand shook as she closed the notebook. "January 13, 1913, is the date that the Carnival Sniper killed his last victim or, at least, the last one that we know of."

Anton frowned. He took the notebook and carefully looked through the pages. Sofie was right: They were simply a series of dates in different color inks, all ending with the word "No."

"But there's no clear reason why he's doing this?" Anton asked.

Sofie gave him a pained look. "I didn't tell you everything about my visits to the Crime Research Lab."

Anton had known that, but her change in topic had caught him off guard. "I don't understand."

Sofie sighed. "You will."

1913

THE LINE WAS ALREADY several meters long when the assassin entered the terminal. The train from Krakow had arrived several minutes before.

For a moment, he thought he was too late. How ironic that would be. Too late, when he had time-traveled all this way.

Then he saw the man whose name he had once memorized as Stavros Papadopoulos. Papadopoulos was heading toward the line, his square, pockmarked face looking determined.

He walked with a limp and he carried the case that the assassin had held another lifetime ago.

Stavros Papadopoulos, the name the target had traveled under in 1913. Joseph Dzhugashvili, the name he was born with. Joseph Stalin was the name no one yet knew.

If the assassin acted quickly, no one ever would.

The assassin reached inside his coat for his gun. He had to wait just a few more seconds.

He searched the crowd for his own face, then remembered: His other self hadn't been walking. He had been huddled against the soot-covered wall, typing the codes into the remote.

It only took a moment to find his other self. His other self's hands were shaking—but with excitement or nerves, the assassin couldn't remember. He couldn't remember much about what had driven him here then, even though it had been less than six months ago.

So much had changed.

He had changed.

His younger self looked up and for a moment, their eyes met. His younger self flushed and looked away, and the assassin knew that he had not been recognized—he was so fundamentally different that his younger self had no idea that he had been looking into his own future.

Papadopoulos...Joseph Dzhugashvili—dammit, it was time to use the name he made infamous—*Stalin* had almost reached the line.

The assassin couldn't let him do that.

The assassin glanced at his other, younger, stupider self in time to see him pull out the handheld time travel machine—

And vanish.

DATE UNKNOWN

As William spun and whirred and shifted, he wished he could have stayed for the explosion. Papadopoulos's face would show a moment of surprise, and be obliterated forever. Around the city, Hitler, Trotsky, and Freud would look at the whiteness, wonder what it was, and then die—their legacies dying with them.

No Holocaust, no purges, no one to destroy a man's faith in his own mind.

Vaporized in an instant, a mushroom cloud taking them and their horrors away.

William smiled even as he shifted back to his own time. He floated, then landed—

—and stumbled.

He extended his hands, scraping them on hard dirt. He landed on his belly, against ground. Above him, a pale sun shed thin light on an empty landscape.

He rolled, wiped his face, and frowned. He was supposed to be in Wein Nord—the Wein Nord of his own time, bullet trains zooming past and passengers zipping by on their own personal passageways. Floating ads should have greeted him, not a barely blue sky.

Behind him, a sign in German warned him that he was trespassing. A few yards away, a slender man wearing some kind of hazmat suit hurried toward him, shouting.

The man shouted in German—not Viennese German, but Russian German, harsher than any other form of the language. William had once described it as hawking and spitting along a three-note scale.

"How did you get here?" the man shouted. He had a thin protective covering over his face, obscuring his features. "This is a protected zone. You need radiation gear."

William stood up. His knees ached from the fall. He had no idea what he could say without sounding stupid. "I thought I was in Wein Nord."

The man pointed at curled and rusted train tracks some distance away. "Satisfied? Now leave. No one is allowed here without permission."

William's mouth was dry. This couldn't be Wein Nord. He had been to Wein Nord in his own timeline. It was a beautiful station, remodeled from its old shell. He had loved it.

He shook his head, then turned. Brown dirt as far as he could see. More warning signs. Barbed wire protecting a perimeter. A single road, made of dirt.

Nothing more.

"Where am I?" he asked.

"You are in the forbidden zone. You know that. Stop playing and leave before you are arrested."

"I'm not playing," William said. "I thought I was coming to Vienna."

"Vienna." The man laughed. "You are in Vienna, fool."

"No," William breathed.

The man grabbed William's arm and pulled him toward a small hole. Inside, others were working an archeological dig. Just beyond it sat a vehicle with an obvious combustion engine. It couldn't be his own time period. Such things had been phased out long ago.

"What happened?" William asked. "Here. What happened here?"

The man looked at him as if he really were crazy. "You don't remember your schooling?"

William shook his head.

"Vienna," the man said as if William were a certified idiot, "was leveled in the worst bomb blast ever. We are trying to find clues, to see if we can solve once and for all who planted this thing that nearly destroyed the world."

"Destroyed the world," William whispered, feeling cold. "World War One started in 1913?"

"The Great War started in 1913," the man said. "Are you finally remembering? Or are you playing? Because if you're here to photograph our research site, be warned we will not tolerate it."

"No," William said. His mind reeled. A bomb that had flattened Vienna. Could he have done that? The simple nuke he held in his right hand only a few moments ago had destroyed one of the most beautiful cities in the world?

"You have to leave," another man said.

"What year is this?" William asked.

A third man stood. "Get rid of him."

"Please," William said.

But they didn't answer him. The man holding his arm led him to the vehicle. William stumbled along, looking for something, anything, familiar. He couldn't even see the Danube.

This couldn't be his time, could it? Setting off his nuke couldn't have caused this. Could it?

Not this.

Oh, please, God. Anything but this.

1913

THE ASSASSIN'S BREATH CAUGHT. He had less than thirty minutes to undo everything his younger self had done.

People hurried through the train station, oblivious to their horrible future. He had started to sweat, remembering.

What a mistake that first trip had been.

What a stupid mistake.

He had thought it would be so easy. Remote-detonate a nuclear bomb and time-travel out of the past—not realizing what detonating a nuke actually meant.

The inhabitants of Vienna, more than two million people, all died in an instant, and the world never recovered. He didn't even manage to prevent World War I—just like his friends had warned.

Most of his friends believed that war was unpreventable, and the assassin's younger self—Arrogant William—had said that didn't matter. The war to prevent was the second one, the war of Hitler, the war that guaranteed Stalin's power for the next eight years—the war that had become cold, over time.

Arrogant William had set a remote detonator on a nuclear bomb, and then time-traveled home to a place he didn't recognize. Even when he left the forbidden zone—the place where Vienna had been—he entered a world that he didn't recognize.

There were no exotic coffees, no twentieth-century classical music—no Schönberg or Alban Berg—no Vienna Boys' Choir, no modern architecture, because of the loss of Wagner and Hoffmann and Loos.

Not to mention the loss to art and culture and history. The buildings, the museums, and the churches had great value in this city. And all the intellectuals who had been here at that moment, some of whom he wouldn't discover for months.

Maybe those intellectuals had just been visiting Vienna; maybe they had lived there. The assassin no longer had any way of finding out because all records of Vienna at that moment in 1913 had been obliterated. No one could ever know the exact death toll. People could only guess at how many had died.

The First World War—now known as the Great War—had started almost two years early, and went on for nearly a decade longer, ravaging Europe in ways that the assassin had initially thought unimaginable.

The world Arrogant William had returned to was so different that he couldn't stand it. Even the good things were gone—the Moon colonies, all the genetic research.

And finally, he realized what he had done.

The Great War had started with the destruction of Vienna.

His idea had been right—right enough, anyway. Get rid of the major players and the Second World War would not happen. European Jewish culture thrived, and the fact that the Russian Revolution had never happened had at least allowed Russia to flourish.

There had been a few good things.

No one psychoanalyzed things to death. No one looked for hidden meanings or believed that man's sexuality was the only thing that governed his mind. Freud was gone, and with him, the poisonous one-on-one sessions with shrinks who thought they understood other people when they really didn't.

The assassin's mission now was to make sure those good things remained, without the Great War to hold them back.

He just hadn't realized it would be so hard.

He had never shot a man until yesterday. And now he had shot four. And this wasn't going to be any easier.

First, he had to make sure he could shut off that bomb. He reached into his inner coat pocket and found the remote. It was there, with the prototype, waiting for him to complete this last task.

He let out a small sigh of relief. Seeing the remote in Arrogant William's hands had made the assassin worry that he had lost it—that somehow the remote had not traveled back with him, making all this for naught.

But it wasn't. He could prevent the explosion if he acted fast enough.

Stalin had reached the edge of the line. He pushed too close to a young woman who was in the final spot. She shot him an angry glare and then took a slight step back, as if she didn't like what she had seen in his face.

The assassin found his Glock, thumbed off the safety, and moved the weapon to the edge of his coat. The moment he revealed the Glock, he would have to act—someone would see it, someone would try to stop him, and he didn't dare let that happen.

"Herr Papadopoulos!" he yelled.

Stalin did not turn. Of course, he wouldn't turn. He was just traveling under that name. He probably didn't recognize it. He certainly wouldn't answer to it.

"Joseph!" the assassin yelled.

Stalin turned his head ever so slightly to look for the source of the voice without being obvious.

"Joseph Stalin!" the assassin shouted.

This time, Stalin turned, his thick black eyebrows raised in surprise. Then he saw the assassin and frowned.

The assassin hadn't been able to recognize himself, but Stalin had. Stalin somehow knew that the two men he had encountered—the one on the train and the differently dressed one in the station—were the same.

"You!" Stalin snapped in Russian. "I knew you were following me."

"Yes," the assassin answered in the same language. "I've been following you all over time."

Then he raised the Glock and fired several times, hitting Stalin in the chest. Blood sprayed behind him, and a woman screamed. The officials looked up.

Stalin fell to his knees, his expression filled with hatred.

For a brief, desperate moment, the assassin thought Stalin would be impossible to kill. He was too powerful, too strong.

But the assassin had killed Stalin once. He should be able to do it again.

This time, the assassin held the Glock steady in both hands and fired at Stalin's dark, empty eyes.

The bullet hit just above them, in the wide plain of Stalin's forehead, and Stalin leaned backwards, then sideways, his skull splatting against the platform.

Bile rose in the assassin's throat, and he swallowed hard.

People were staring at him, at Stalin, at the officials. No one was moving.

And Stalin's eyes were open.

The assassin had been wrong.

Stalin's eyes hadn't been empty before. They had been filled with a cold intelligence, which was finally gone.

The assassin kept the Glock in his left hand. With his right, he groped for the handheld and was about to press it, using the preset codes to take him back to his future, when he remembered the remote.

Sweet Jesus, he had nearly forgotten the nuke.

The officials were running toward him. His hands were sweating just like Arrogant William's had on the train. The assassin removed the remote and stared at it, unable to remember the code to shut off the bomb.

He should have written it down. He should have realized what kind of trouble he'd be in. He should have understood the stresses.

But he had always underestimated the power of history.

The officials had nearly reached him.

The assassin held up the remote as if it were the bomb.

"One step closer," he said in his bad German, "and I'll blow us all up. I swear."

His voice was shaking as badly as his hand. The officials apparently believed him. They stopped, palms extended, as if they weren't going to harm him.

If they were like cops anywhere else in the world, they would take any chance they could to shoot him. He didn't know if old-fashioned Viennese customs officials carried guns.

In his world, his new world, everyone did.

His grip tightened on the remote. He had no idea how much time had passed. Everyone was just staring at him, and him at them.

And Stalin hadn't moved.

The code, the code. The assassin needed the code, and he couldn't dredge it out of his memory.

He had made it something easy, something he couldn't forget. So stupid. He should have preprogrammed it in.

But he hadn't wanted to touch the remote since he had come back from Vienna the first time. As if the remote had caused all the deaths, not him.

As if the remote were the problem.

The assassin looked at Stalin and finally knew why he hadn't felt any righteous anger when he'd killed that man.

They weren't that different, after all. They had both killed by remote.

The only differences were that Stalin had used soldiers, and the assassin had used a device. That, and the number of people they each killed. And those numbers might be closer than the assassin wanted to admit, if he factored in the extra deaths in the prolonged Great War, all the unnecessary lives ruined forever by a single bomb.

The code, the code, he needed the code.

And he had absolutely no idea what it was.

1913

RUNGE STOPPED AT THE CROSSROADS at Praterstern and whirled around in a circle. He had been heading almost blindly toward the Riesenrad, without a plan at all.

He just had a feeling that his chance, his only chance to catch this killer, was about to run out.

The Praterstern crossroads was a confusing intersection. The seven broad avenues that crossed Leopoldstadt met here—and the assassin could have taken any of them.

Or he could have gone further east, into the trees that hid the bottom of the Riesenrad, the trees that marked the edge of the Prater.

Or, worst of all, he could have gone to Wein Nord—caught a train and left Vienna to continue his deeds elsewhere.

Runge studied the roads—all of them—and knew he had reached the end of his.

He would have to go back to the Mannerheim, find what clues he could, and begin the long tedious task of police work, knowing he had lost again.

He turned back toward the Mannerheim when he heard the scream. A woman, fleeing the train station, yelling that someone had been murdered.

Runge was running toward Wein Nord before he even registered a thought. His instincts had been right. The killer had gone to the train station, maybe trying to leave, and had gotten in trouble somehow.

The killer had shot someone else.

And that someone had died.

2005

As she explained the mysterious weapons and bullets to Anton, Sofie felt lightheaded. She probably hadn't eaten enough the last few days, and she certainly hadn't slept. She had been worrying about Anton, about her relationship with him, and about his expectations.

When she did sleep, she dreamt about the files, and all the information in them jumbling up until she didn't understand it.

Maybe the dreams had been prophetic.

When she paused for breath, Anton shook his head. "You're telling me that the bullets and the gun don't exist."

"No," she said. "I'm telling you that we can't find who made them or what they're made out of."

"But they're more sophisticated than anything we're familiar with now," Anton said.

"Yes," Sofie said.

"And they're nearly a hundred years old."

Sofie nodded. "You were there when we opened the box."

Anton leaned back, his fingers pressed together. He tapped his lips with his fingertips, and frowned. "Then there's the radioactive sphere."

"Yes," Sofie said. "Although that didn't belong to the Sniper. It belonged to the mystery victim, a man named Papadopoulos."

"You call him the mystery victim because—?"

282

"Because that's not his real name." Sofie ran a hand over the notebook. She didn't know how to explain most of the things she had read; they sounded so preposterous. "In the fifth notebook, your great-grandfather postulates that Papadopoulos used the name Stalin as an alias. That name was on some of the papers found in his briefcase, but your great-grandfather hadn't realized they referred to Papadopoulos, at least in 1913. Stalin means 'man of steel' and your great-grandfather thought it was some kind of cryptic reference to someone in Russia."

"It's not?" Anton asked. He seemed fascinated.

Sofie's mouth was dry. She got up, opened the cupboard, and grabbed a glass. She had become quite at home here. It surprised her. She rarely felt comfortable outside of her own apartment.

She filled the glass with water and returned to the table.

"In the fifth notebook," she said, "your great-grandfather related some of the work he did tracing the author whose byline was Stalin back to Russia. Apparently the man was a friend of a V.I. Lenin, who considered himself a revolutionary. He wanted the socialists to revolt against the government, but after an abortive attempt in 1907, he failed. He spent most of the Great War trying to find a way into Russia, but Germany wouldn't let him travel through the country, so he never did get inside. He just sort of disappears from history."

"That 1907 coup, was that connected to Bronstein's?" Anton asked.

Sofie looked at him in surprise. She thought she was the only person who had a mind for that kind of detail.

"Yes," she said. "This Stalin was a friend of Lenin's, but not Bronstein's. So far as we can tell."

"But they were both in Vienna," Anton said.

"And both shot by the Sniper."

"Fascinating." Anton looked at the notebook.

"Your great-grandfather traced what he could find of this Stalin—and there wasn't much. Apparently, he was to publish his first real article with that byline in the next year or so and never did. Anyway, your great-grandfather used some of Lenin's documents to help him find this Stalin. He was a peasant named Iosip Vassarionovich Dzhugash-vili, and became well known among the socialists for his willingness to use violence as a means to an end. They thought that he was the muscle to Lenin's brains."

Sofie sipped the water. She was still unsettled, but it felt good to be discussing these things—better than she had expected.

"What's so important about him?" Anton asked.

"Nothing, really," Sofie said. "If he was Papadopoulos, he was trav-eling under the assumed name to avoid Russian authorities, just like Bronstein. Both were known enemies of the state."

Anton nodded. "But there's a reason you're telling me this."

"Yes," Sofie said. "In the notebooks, we go through this assessment of the case in Numbers One and Two. Three starts to get strange, and then we have the notations that I showed you in the rest of Three and Four."

"Strange how?" Anton asked.

"I'll tell you in a minute." Sofie wasn't ready to get into that yet. "Then in Five, your great-grandfather tries to research the future lives of all the victims, postulating whatever he can based on who they were. He thinks that Adler, Bronstein—who also went under the name Trotsky—and Papadopoulos might have banded together to join this Lenin, or even alone, to try to overthrow the Russian Tzar."

Anton raised his eyebrows and leaned back in his chair. "How does Freud fit into this?"

"I don't know," Sofie said. "And neither did your great-grandfather. He thought maybe some of Freud's later theories might have helped them. Or not. He was not certain at all about Freud, or Adler for that matter. Adler had never shown an interest in Russia. Only in Vienna's politics."

Anton shook his head. "This *is* strange. What about the fifth guy?"

"Hietler? Your great-grandfather was even more stumped by him. Hietler was an eccentric. He was an artist who was running from the compulsory military service of the time, hiding in Vienna and pre-tending to be broke, even though he had a family inheritance. He was a coward and a liar and a bigot, not well-liked by anyone, and very much a loner. No matter how hard your great-grandfather tried, he couldn't figure out how Hietler fit into the picture."

"Can you?" Anton asked.

Sofie shook her head. "But I've never been trained to postulate forward. My training comes from imagining backward."

Anton drummed his fingers on the notebook, as if tapping it would reveal its secrets. "Is that the reason you came to me, asking if my great-grandfather was fanciful? Because he had postulated forward?"

Sofie looked down. Her heart was pounding. She hadn't told Anton everything. She hadn't told him about the other snipers, about Johann Runge's suspicions.

She wasn't sure she could—at least, not yet.

"That's not the only reason," she said. "There are others."

"There's more?" Anton's fingers stopped drumming. "Like what?"

Sofie ran a hand through her hair. She made herself look up. His blue eyes had crinkled around the edges, as if he were concentrating. He was a handsome man. She forgot that sometimes.

Sofie closed her eyes. She didn't want him to think she was stupid. She didn't want anyone to believe that. Her intelligence had always been her protection and her guard.

Now she was jeopardizing it with the one person she really wanted to impress.

She felt her cheeks heat, and she wished she could control her blushes. She opened her eyes and sighed.

Anton was watching her closely.

"In Notebook Three," she said. "Your great-grandfather…."

Her voice trailed off. She couldn't do this.

"What?" Anton asked. He seemed impatient. "What did he do?"

Sofie bit her lower lip. She had started this. She had to finish it. She couldn't think about these things by herself. For the first time in her career, she truly wanted someone else's opinion on something important.

"Your great-grandfather wrote what really happened at Wein Nord that last day."

Anton's eyes lit up. "Really?"

Sofie held out a hand. "It's not what you think."

"He has a record of what happened? Why didn't he write about it? Do you know how many people over the years thought he let the Sniper escape? Thought maybe my great-grandfather was in on the whole thing?"

"Yes," Sofie said softly. "But you're not going to like this, either."

Her heart seemed to be pounding even harder.

"Why?" Anton asked. "What is it?"

Sofie shrugged. There was no good way to say this. "He claimed that the Sniper disappeared."

1913

RUNGE HAD TO DODGE TRAFFIC—a few horse-drawn carriages, a Model A—but he made it to the edge of the station, only to have more screaming people head toward him.

He felt like he was going to be trampled. He put his arms out, pushing the bodies away from him, and plowed his way into the terrified crowd.

As he hurried into the terminal, he caught bits of what had happened. A madman with a gun had shot someone getting off the train. Which train, Runge couldn't tell, but he didn't need to know. It was clear from the yelling people which platform the train had stopped at.

He ran toward it, and skidded to a stop when he saw a crowd ringing a young man. In the front of the crowd, customs officials stood, hands up, sheer panic on their faces.

A man wearing a cheap overcoat and peasant boots was sprawled on the platform. His hands still clutched a wooden case as if it held all the treasures in the world.

He had been shot in the head, but his face was still visible.

Runge did not recognize him.

"Stay back!" said the young man. He was holding up a device that Runge did not recognize. "Or I mean it. I will blow us all up."

He was smaller than Runge expected—shorter, thinner, but wearing the coat everyone had described. He held in his left hand a pistol of a make that was unfamiliar to Runge. It seemed inordinately shiny, and too frail to do the kind of damage Runge knew it had done.

The young man's German had an accent Runge did not know. Obviously the young man was not Viennese.

His hands were trembling. The young man was as terrified as everyone around him.

Runge could use that to his advantage.

He pushed through the crowd, past the customs officials. As he did, he took one of their guns. The official looked at him with great shock, but Runge raised his eyebrows, signaling quiet, and kept moving until he reached the front.

He kept his hands behind him.

"Young man," he said as gently as he could. "Put your weapons down."

The young man—the killer—shook his head. "You don't understand. We'll all die if I do that."

"I do understand." Runge kept his voice soft. "My name is Johann Runge. Detective Johann Runge. I've been following you all over Vienna, and I'm so very curious about what you're doing. Perhaps you'll tell me?"

The killer shook his head. He glanced at the body still sprawled on the platform, and then at the device in his hand.

"Detective," the young man said. "I had no idea there were detectives in 19—"

He stopped as if he were having a realization.

"Holy son of a bitch," he said in English. "Detective. Oh, my God."

2005

"*I KNOW THAT THE SNIPER DISAPPEARED,*" Anton said. "My great-grandfather wrote that in his book."

Sofie rested a hand on the notebook. She shook her head. "He used the word 'disappeared' on purpose."

Anton looked at her, clearly not understanding.

Sofie felt her cheeks grow even warmer. "Disappeared," she said. "Vanished. As in, one minute he was lying on the platform bleeding, the next he was gone."

Anton frowned. "Gone?"

"Leaving the gun and a pool of blood," Sofie said.

"But the witnesses—"

"Claimed he ran away, I know," Sofie said. "But your great-grandfather wrote that the Sniper had been badly injured and couldn't move. He took a device out of his pocket—your great-grandfather thought it was some kind of bomb—pressed a few buttons, and disappeared."

"Disappeared," Anton said.

"Your great-grandfather was right in front of him." Sofie's cheeks were on fire now. It felt like she were making up the story, not repeating something Johann Runge had written. "I can show you the passage if you want. The whole notebook, if you'd like."

"No," Anton said. "I believe you."

289

She let out a breath that she hadn't realized she'd been holding. "You do?"

Anton nodded. "He always said that he touched the Sniper, but I never saw how. Not in the book, not in the way that the escape was described."

Sofie felt her blush fade. Anton had mentioned that the first day they met, that his great-grandfather had touched the Sniper.

"I just don't get it," Anton said. "I don't understand why he would write that."

Sofie sighed. Anton didn't understand after all.

"Because," she said softly. "He believed it."

1913

OF COURSE IT WAS SIMPLE. Too simple. All he had used for the code was the year. One-nine-one-three.

1913.

The assassin typed the numbers into the remote with his thumb, then hit enter. He glanced at the display on the remote. It blinked red for a moment, and then it signaled the all-clear.

The nuke had been disarmed.

"Oh, thank God," he said, and let his arm drop. He slipped the remote into his pocket and reached for the prototype.

"I'd rethink that, son," the man who had introduced himself as a detective said in German. "Take your hand out slowly, and then set your gun down."

The assassin found the prototype. The menu scrolled along the screen, reminding him he held a prototype, that it did not belong to him, and then, in that perversity of most MIT devices, invited him to read the instructions.

He didn't need to. All he needed was the preprogrammed *Enter* key. A simple press of the thumb and—

He spun backwards, slamming into the wall. For a moment, he couldn't catch his breath, and then he heard it—not the air, but the gunshot.

The damn detective had shot him.

The man was holding a pistol like it was the Old West.

The assassin looked down—arm, chest—he couldn't tell where he'd been shot. Only that he couldn't breath very well. He was coughing and he tasted blood.

He was already dizzy.

And that, he knew, was a bad sign.

He couldn't stay here. They had no medicine here. They couldn't heal him. They'd kill him.

Besides, he couldn't leave the remote here. The remote, with its codes and five-hundred-yard range. The detective would take it and Stalin's case and the assassin's gun and the prototype, and they'd put them together and someone might hit the wrong numbers, and then what?

Then it would happen anyway, the explosion.

The assassin couldn't get to the nuke. Not now. But they'd never figure it out, anyway. No one could reverse engineer that.

It was too advanced.

But everything else. Everything else, the Glock, the prototype, the remote, had to go home.

With him.

He had to go home.

He followed the line of his arm. His hand, apparently, was still trapped in his pocket, still holding the time-travel device.

The detective was hurrying toward him.

And the dizziness was growing worse.

The assassin pulled the prototype from his pocket. It took all his strength to move. Then he saw the blood, glistening on his stomach.

He was getting cold.

That was a bad sign, right?

The prototype's display was blurring. He had to press the automatic *enter*.

Press, and then he'd be home.

Wherever home was.

Whatever it had become.

2005

ANTON LEANED BACK in his chair. It creaked as he moved. Then he stood up. The news made him restless, made him feel as if he were disconnected somehow.

He had never once heard anyone claim that his great-grandfather was crazy. No one who had met the old man ever thought he had lost his faculties.

But his behavior had gotten odd toward the end of his life. He refused to solve a few crimes that crossed his path, even though he was still on salary with the police department. They even wanted to have a hearing about one—a mugging gone wrong. His great-grandfather had been at the crime scene, but refused to participate.

It's unimportant, he had told the papers, as if he could bother himself only with "important" crimes like assassinations and snipings.

That was the beginning of his bad publicity, and Anton's great-grandfather did nothing about it.

He became a recluse, refusing to travel, and he became obsessed with writing the book.

When he finished it, he refused to give interviews about it. *The book stands for itself*, he would say. *If it interests you in the Sniper, so be it. I just want the record as clear as I can make it.*

As clear as he could make it. He had always said the book was incomplete.

Sofie was watching Anton closely. Clearly this entire section of the notebooks disturbed her, and repeating it to Anton disturbed her more. But there were some things she wasn't telling him.

As usual, he had a hunch that it was those things that bothered her the most.

"He believed that the Sniper just disappeared," Anton said.

"Yes," Sofie said. "And it's not like he wrote these notebooks years later. I'm pretty sure they're contemporaneous. I'll have to get an expert to check inks and paper age, and things like that, but I would wager my entire advance that he wrote this the day of or the day after the Sniper's last shooting."

"Was it dated?"

"No," Sofie said. "The next entry was. Three days later. He was trying to get someone to figure out what type of weapon he had."

"The gun again," Anton said. "The one you can't figure out."

Sofie nodded.

"And all the bullets. I suppose my great-grandfather had a theory?"

Sofie's cheeks flamed even more. Her entire face was red now. "Time travel," she whispered.

"What?" Anton raised his eyebrows. "You're kidding?"

"No." Sofie put a palm against her cheek as if she were trying to cool it off.

"That explains the postulating forward," Anton said. "He was trying to figure out motive."

Sofie nodded. "In Notebook Five, he goes through a whole bunch of the cases he worked on in the years after the Sniper, and he cites all sorts of anomalies. He thought some of them were time travel, too."

"Someone's coming back and shooting people for no reason?" Anton asked.

Sofie shook her head. "It's so crazy, I know. But he didn't think it was one someone. He thought it was several."

"And the fact that the Sniper 'disappeared' was proof?" Anton had to work hard to keep the sarcasm from his voice. It wasn't Sofie's idea. She was just reporting what his great-grandfather had written.

"He didn't have proof," Sofie said. "In fact, early on, he made fun of himself for even thinking it, maybe convinced he'd read too much H.G. Wells."

Anton started. *The Time Machine* was one of the books he had found in the various boxes—he found an English and a German edition, and seeing how early they had been published, had wondered if they would be worth money.

"But Wells wrote about a big machine, and your great-grandfather said this was a little tiny one." Sofie pushed her hair away from her face again, something he'd never seen her do. "So here's the strange part."

Anton smiled. He couldn't help it. "The rest of it wasn't strange?"

"No," she said. "I mean…oh, hell. You understand."

He did. They were running out of words for the oddities of this conversation.

"Your great-grandfather talked to a whole bunch of physicists over the years. He wanted to know if time travel was even possible, and if it was, how it would work. Then he wanted to know if a machine could be made small instead of large," Sofie said. "Most of those people went on to work on a series of experiments that later got classified by the Russian and German governments."

"Experiments?" Anton hadn't expected her to say that. "What kind of experiments?"

"Time travel," she said. "I think they figured it out, and your great-grandfather believed they were ahead of schedule when they did."

"Schedule?" Anton was getting confused.

"The other timeline—apparently if you change something in the past, your timeline splits from the other one. So if a man lives in this timeline, and you go back into the past and kill him, then that man is still alive in this timeline. But you start a new timeline in which that man is dead."

Anton had to think for a moment before he understood what she was talking about. "Like branches on a tree."

"Yes," Sofie said. "The tree starts at the trunk, but the branches fork and break off, often without ever touching the trunk. Does that make sense?"

"As much as this conversation can," Anton said.

Sofie winced, and he wondered if he had hurt her feelings. He hoped not. He reached for her hand, but she didn't see him. Instead, she stood.

"Anyway," she said as she went to the sink, her water glass in hand, "your great-grandfather believed that the other timeline, the one the Sniper came from, didn't develop time travel until the twenty-first century. Here, we had it—briefly—in the late 1950s."

Anton's head was spinning. "Okay," he said. "Let's assume we accept this crazy premise. If time travel was possible, then how come our guys from the 1950s didn't go back and change things? Maybe figure out who the Sniper was?"

"They might have," Sofie said. "But if they changed one thing, they had a new timeline. They couldn't come back to this one."

"It's a one-way trip?" Anton asked.

"Other reading I've done suggests that," Sofie said.

"Other reading…" he let his voice trail away. "How come I've never heard of this?"

Sofie shrugged. "There's a lot of things that happen that you've never heard of. I may know about some of it because of the work that I do. It's the nature of government. From what I can tell, on the whole time-travel thing, they thought it was too dangerous, and banned it."

"Banned it," Anton said. "But someone came here and shot people?"

"From a different timeline," Sofie said. "And not just one someone, if your great-grandfather is to be believed, but several."

"Several." Anton shook his head. It did sound crazy. No wonder she had asked him if his great-grandfather was fanciful.

Sofie remained by the sink. She had her head bowed. She was still visibly upset. Then she seemed to shake it off, and used the tap to fill her glass again.

Anton wished he knew her better. He wished he understood her.

He leaned back in his chair. "You can write your book without mentioning this, right?"

She blinked up at him, as if she hadn't heard him. He was about to repeat the question when she nodded. "Of course I can."

"Then why does this theory of my great-grandfather's upset you so?" Anton asked.

She looked down at the glass of water in her hand. For a moment she didn't move at all. Then she set the water on the table and sat down.

"It upsets me," she said slowly, "because I think he might be right. I've seen the gun, and the bullets, and there are a lot of things in this case that are impossible to understand. Like, where did the Sniper go?"

"But you don't have to espouse the time-travel theory," Anton said. "Your reputation will be fine."

Sofie nodded. "It's not my reputation I'm worried about."

She folded her hands around the glass. Anton watched her. Her expression seemed calm, but he could sense great agitation inside her. She seemed to be considering her next words.

"Then what are you worried about?" he asked after a moment.

She looked at him, her eyes lined with tears. "My parents," she said. "They were killed by a sniper, too. One who never got caught."

1913

RUNGE DIDN'T RECOGNIZE the device in the killer's hand, but it looked just as menacing as the other device had. The killer's face was unnaturally pale, going that grayish white that accompanied severe blood loss.

The killer would die. He would die without telling Runge why, what the plan was, what the murders all meant.

The killer looked up at him. Impossibly young. Why were these killers always so young?

Then the killer smiled.

"Found it," he whispered.

And disappeared.

Runge stopped in front of the space where the young man had been. There really and truly was no one there. No young man. No killer.

No one.

Runge glanced behind him. People were gaping, shocked. The killer had disappeared.

There was a gun in a pool of blood—too much blood. The killer had clearly been dying.

It must have slipped from the boy's fingers, that gun. That strange and unusual gun.

The crowd near Runge was murmuring, calling out. A few officials ran toward the exit, as if they were searching for the killer, as if they hadn't just seen a miracle, as if the young man hadn't just vanished right in front of their eyes.

But there were no footprints, and the blood, the blood was real enough.

Runge looked at the other body, the killer's victim.

That body remained. It was real, too.

Runge crouched, picked up the gun, and knew instantly he had never touched material like this. There were no sights—not as he knew them—and the barrel was too perfect. The gun was too light. No gun weighed this little and worked.

Runge held it. Solid proof that the killer had been there. Solid proof that the killer was gone.

It was over. It was done.

And it left him with questions.

More questions than he'd ever had in his life.

2005

AT LEAST HER VOICE hadn't quivered. Sofie had finally spoken the words, for the first time in her life, and her voice hadn't quivered at all.

It took her a few minutes of steady breathing to get her emotions back under control, though. During that time, Anton didn't say a single word.

She wondered if he hadn't understood her, if he hadn't known what she meant.

Then she looked at him. He was watching her, his face filled with compassion. She had to blink hard again, just to keep her eyes from tearing up.

"I'm so sorry," he said. "That's why you want to go slow with this relationship."

She frowned, trying to see the connection. She had told him about her parents' murder, and he had jumped to the feelings they had for each other.

But he was right. She had even thought of it. Just not at this moment, not while she'd been thinking of Runge.

She couldn't get close because of the loss, the death.

"Yeah," she said. "I've never been normal. My parents' death and all the years after, I—I never—I don't—"

She stopped. She knew if she told him that she wasn't willing to love anyone because that person might die, he would give her empty assurances that he wouldn't. He would lie, just like everyone else had.

"You're afraid everyone will go away," he said softly.

She shrugged. "Everyone does," she said. "Eventually."

"Eventually," he said. "But that's the given. We love despite that. Human beings. It's the only way we show courage."

She shook her head slightly. She had no courage. Courage came from delusions—a willingness to believe in happily-ever-after, a willingness to believe that death wouldn't happen to such a perfect couple, a willingness to believe in life everlasting.

Anton's hand hovered over her shoulder. She couldn't bear it if he touched her now. He seemed to know that. After a moment, his hand returned to the table.

"Okay," he said, his voice different, businesslike. It was as if he knew that she couldn't talk about the personal issues any more. It had taken quite a toll from her to tell him as much as she had. "Let's go back to my great-grandfather. If his theory is right, then you're worried about what? That your parents were killed because they might have done something awful if they had lived?"

It sounded ridiculous when he put it that way. But that had been her fear.

She said, "His theory is that everyone who died would end up like Papadopoulos—this Stalin, if indeed that's who he was. Someone bad."

"I don't know how he could know that," Anton said. "What you consider bad and I consider bad might be two different things."

"I suspect we'd agree on a few," Sofie said. "Like the assassination of the Archduke."

Anton didn't answer that. "Most of the time, people do things for their own good, not for the common good. If they had the ability to time-travel, they'd go back and shoot a rival for a lover's affections or prevent a mistake that they'd originally made. They wouldn't do something on a grand scale. That's intellectualizing, Sofie. Most people don't live that way."

She tugged at her bottom lip with her teeth, then tasted blood. She hadn't even felt the pain of breaking the skin.

"Some of us do," she said.

Anton looked at her. "If you had the chance, you'd go back, wouldn't you? You'd save them, whatever it took."

Sofie blinked. Save her parents? What would it take? She didn't know who the sniper was. No one had. Had he disappeared, too?

She could imagine herself walking to that apartment they'd had in Munich—it had seemed so grand at the time—and knocking on the door, telling her parents not to go to Palace Park that day. What would she have done if a stranger showed up and told her not to do something?

She would obsess over the stranger. But if she had a reason, an appointment or something important to do at the park, she would still go.

"I couldn't stop them from going to the park," she whispered.

"But what if you could stop the sniper?" Anton asked.

"By getting him away from the bathhouse?"

"If you could." Anton's voice was very soft. "Or shooting him."

"Shooting him." She felt the blood drain from her face. "Become a sniper myself?"

"So to speak," Anton said. "Would you? To save your parents?"

"And all those other people?" She didn't have to think about it. She knew. "Yes, of course I would."

Anton extended his hand on the table, palm up so that she could place hers in his. He'd done that once already and she had pretended not to notice.

She didn't want to pretend this time. She put her hand in his.

He didn't hate her for having these feelings. He understood. Maybe he understood better than she did. Those policeman genes, carried down from generation to generation.

Or maybe he just understood her.

"If you're right, and these snipers are going back for a personal reason…." She shook her head.

"Then your parents wouldn't have done something wrong if they had lived," Anton said.

Tears filled her eyes. She nodded. "It would be just as inexplicable as it was," she said.

Only preventable—something that hadn't happened in at least one timeline—the one before the sniper had arrived.

She was shaking.

"Even if I don't think of my parents," she said, "I don't want your great-grandfather to be right."

Anton's hand tightened around hers. It felt comforting. She was still shaking, and he was soothing her.

"Why don't you want him to be right?" Anton asked. "I would think it would be the other way, that time travel would be a relief to you."

She bit her lip again, and tasted the blood. She had actually wounded herself. With her free hand, she wiped away the moisture. If only she could calm down.

But she wasn't sure she could. This was life-changing for her. No matter what she ended up believing, it was life-changing.

"Because," she said carefully, "if your great-grandfather is right, I'll never know the Sniper's identity. He may not have even been born yet."

"Which is why," Anton said, "my great-grandfather wrote the book. So that someone in the future could prevent this man from coming back and doing all that killing."

Sofie shrugged. "Maybe. Or maybe he rejected all the things he wrote in the fifth notebook. Maybe they were just fanciful thoughts."

"But you don't think so," Anton said.

"I don't know what to think," Sofie said. "Except that I have to proceed as if he were wrong. I have to keep doing what I've been doing as if the Sniper got away in that crowd, and lived out his life in 1913 and beyond. I can't do anything else."

"I have a hunch my great-grandfather felt the same way," Anton said. "Some things are just too impossible to believe."

But Sofie didn't agree with that. People would believe anything, given enough time and preparation. She would never have considered the possibility of time travel a month ago. Now, with the gun and the bullets and the sphere, with Kolisko's reminder about Asimov's writings, with Johann Runge's notebooks, she was predisposed to consider time travel as an option.

However, it wasn't her only option.

She would finish her book even if she didn't discover the sniper's identity. She would present a lot of new, never-seen-before evidence. Some reader might identify the bullets and gun that Kolisko said couldn't be identified.

Maybe there would be a rational explanation after all—one that Sofie might not get if she didn't publish her book.

After all, Johann Runge hadn't given his readers a chance to help. He had withheld all the questionable information.

She had no need to do that.

Her choices would be different than his, all the way down the line.

1953

JOHANN RUNGE WAS LATE.

He couldn't run any more, but he did his best, leaning on his cane and swinging his bad leg into wider and wider steps. People gave him a large berth, a few shooting him that *crazy-old-man* glance he was getting more and more these days.

He hated being old.

He hurried down the steps to the platform, now numbered A1, soon—someone told him—to go out of commission, although he wasn't sure he believed it. He had heard that the platform was going out of commission a decade ago, and nothing had happened. He suspected rumors like this were the only thing that gave the train station any life.

The large clock above the arched entry said he still had five minutes. Maybe his watch was off. Or maybe he was as crazy as people said.

For forty years, he had come down to the Wein Nord on the anniversary of the assassin's disappearance. Runge waited near the spot where the assassin had been, where he had vanished while Runge watched, leaving only the gun and a pool of blood behind.

The blood stain was long gone from the platform, which had been resurfaced five times in the past forty years. The walls were tiled, then plastered with posters; benches were added, benches removed, and benches added again, this time bolted to the wall.

Still, Runge saw that spot as it had been forty years before—a dirty floor and even filthier wall, people crowded around, and the assassin in the middle of it all, holding a device that Runge thought would blow the station apart.

He had been wrong.

He had probably been wrong about a lot of things. But his instinct told him to come here for all those years, and instinct couldn't always be off.

Besides, there were all those hints, those clues. The strange bullets from the assassin, the even stranger gun. The other snipers over the years, using technology that Runge could never trace. Or, in a few of the early cases, technology that was developed later—from the high-powered scopes to the plastic grips.

Too many details that didn't add up. Too many unexplained details.

Johann Runge shivered despite the station's heat. The exhaust from the trains, the overextended heating system, the press of bodies, made this place more unbearable in the winter than in the summer.

He never came here any more except in January, except on the anniversary. And now, after forty years, it felt like a vain hope.

Even if he were right, the Sniper might not show up in Runge's lifetime. For all Runge knew, the Sniper could have come from one hundred, two hundred, three hundred years in the future, and for all his waiting, Runge would never live long enough to see the man return to this station.

Or his assumptions might be wrong, and all that writing the physicists did on time travel—some to Runge's request—might have been wrong as well.

Perhaps it was possible to travel in time *and space*. No one thought so, but scientists had been wrong before. If that were possible, the Sniper would have left Wein Nord in 1913 and surfaced somewhere else in some other future.

If that was the case, Runge would never find the man. Runge wouldn't be able to predict where or when the man would show up.

Not that Runge knew what to do with him, anyway.

Runge hurtled down the platform, nearly tripping on the new steel step guards someone had installed. The customs officials had moved to the main doors, but in place of the tables, the authorities had built a shoe-shine station and a newsstand.

Runge did not feel the change was an improvement. But then, at seventy-three, he didn't believe most changes were improvements.

Finally, he stopped on the platform.

The spot where the Sniper had vanished was beneath a large poster advertising Marlena Dietrich's latest film. She still looked like a goddess, one leg bare as she placed her foot on a chair, a Berlin nightclub behind her. She had never gotten past her *Blue Angel* image, and Runge, for one, believed she should have moved past it—at a certain age, even a beautiful woman should no longer play the seductress.

Runge looked up at the clock. Still a few minutes to spare. His heart was pounding—he had been so convinced that he was late.

Not that it mattered.

It hadn't mattered in the past.

Now it had simply become a ritual, one that he was loathe to give up. He would pace down here for the next two hours, maybe even get a request from security to leave, and then he would go home, feeling as tired and discouraged as he had in previous years.

The ironic thing was that even if the Sniper returned—appeared— whatever word he chose to describe such a magical event—Runge no longer knew what to do with the man. In the first few years after the Sniper vanished, Runge imagined arresting him, figuring out some charge, some way of showing that this man was tied to the killings.

A few years after that, Runge knew the arrest would no longer work. He brought his gun for nearly a decade, believing that perhaps he would have to kill the man.

But for twenty years, Runge hadn't carried his gun. He couldn't arrest the Sniper should the man appear, nor could he kill him. Runge was no longer certain why he was here, except that some part of him hoped—some part of him believed—that all of this was a bad dream, and if he saw the Sniper again, he would wake up: case solved, bad man arrested after the first two murders—or even before—and everything would be as it was. Vienna during Carnival, before the Great War and all that horrible, ruinous death.

Runge had to lean on his cane. He was no longer young, no matter what he wanted to believe. The sprint he had made to the platform left him light-headed.

He leaned on his cane, and looked at the Arrivals board. A train was due in half an hour. Soon the platform would fill with anxious people.

He would have to find a position that guaranteed him a view of the spot before all those people arrived.

But first, he wanted to rest. Just for a minute. A short rest before he had to move again.

2005

THAT NIGHT, ANTON invited Sofie to come upstairs after she finished her work. He made it clear that there would be dinner, and she had the sense that this was going to be some sort of special occasion.

She was still a bit shaken from the journals, from her own confession, and from Anton's understanding. She hadn't expected anyone to see her as well as he had.

When she reached the main floor, she frowned. The lighting was dim and the air smelled fresh. As she went into the piano room, she gasped. Anton had cleaned it, and candles were strewn on all surfaces except the piano itself.

He was sitting behind the piano. He stood as she came into the room. He was wearing a gorgeous black tuxedo, complete with tails.

This was the Anton Runge of the album covers, the handsome man who had won the Chopin competition. The performer, the famous pianist.

He bowed, then flipped his tails behind him, reseated himself, and played a quick arpeggio.

"Please sit," he said, not looking at her. She glanced around, saw a red velvet chair that had come from the basement. The chair had been repaired, and it looked inviting. She sat in it, feeling self-conscious.

Anton raised his head. He seemed nervous, too. No, he seemed terrified, and she remembered what he had told her during one of their many conversations. He got debilitating stage fright.

Even playing for her? Even in his own house?

"When you arrived," he said quietly, "you apparently brought my muse with you. And ever since, I've been composing a record of these events. I'd like to play the pieces for you, if I could."

She didn't want to speak. She couldn't speak. He'd been inspired by her work? That stunned her.

"The first day," he said, "when we found the room, it was so overwhelming. I wrote this."

He played a march. It had elements of Sousa, of course, but it was all Anton—gaiety and triumphant with just a touch of melancholy. It was magnificent.

She would have applauded when he finished, but he didn't let her, talking to her in that nervous voice, explaining each piece before he played it.

She heard it all—the triumph of the first day, the regularity of her visits, the panic that morning she was three hours late. The excitement over the bullets, the dark worry about the radiation, the air of mystery throughout.

He had written a masterwork. Each piece—the march, the fugue, the sonata—all had motifs from the other pieces, and yet stood alone.

Just when she thought he couldn't have done any more, he raised his hands with a flourish, stood halfway so that he could see her face, and said, "And this, Sofie, this piece is for you."

The music was gentle, almost tentative. Something in it reminded her of Schubert, and that was when she knew what she was hearing. It was a *kunstlied*, a love song, a poem put to music, designed to be sung. Only Anton did not sing. There was no poem here, no words. Yet somehow the poem was there, the words suggested, almost audible in the breathy way that he played the piano's upper register.

Tears filled her eyes, making the candlelight blur and the evening seem even more magical. He had done this for her, all of it, and told her, with everything he had, how he felt.

She actually felt an ache in her chest, as if something she'd held rigid was relaxing. The light blurred and the music continued and the man at the piano watched her as if her reaction meant everything.

When he finished, neither of them moved. Applauding felt wrong, somehow, as if she were demeaning what he had done by making their relationship that of audience and performer. Instead, she stood, wiped her eyes, and walked to him.

She took his face in her hands, studied each line, each angle, and then kissed his forehead, his cheeks, his beautiful eyes.

"Thank you," she whispered.

He pulled her into his arms. "I love you, Sofie."

"I know," she said. "I finally know."

1953

THE SPINNING, WHIRRING, SHIFTING sensation made the assassin
dizzy for the first time. And the bright light from the time shift hurt his eyes.

It felt like it always felt, as if he had been lifted, buoyed up in salt water,
blinded by the sun, and set back down, somewhere familiar yet unfamiliar.

He was very cold.

The assassin blinked, and his eyes cleared. Still in Wein Nord. The
wall still supported his back. His legs ached. His pants were wet with
blood, but no blood pooled around him—at least that he could tell.

The crowd was gone. In its place, people scurrying to catch—not a
bullet train, but something else, not quite as sleek. Almost like a sub-
way car, but that wasn't right. Metal, painted a strange blue, large windows and wheels on a track.

A train, then, but not the trains he was used to.

The men wore hats—no beards or very few—suit coats tailored
wide, pleated pants, shiny black shoes. A shoe-shine station was only
a few yards from the assassin, an elderly man leaning on it, running a
polishing rag through his fingers.

Travelers hurried by him, like they hurried by the assassin. The
women wore high heels and wide-skirted dresses, no pants, and the
women all seemed to be heavier than he remembered. With cinched
waists and large busts, accented by pointed bras.

He had seen that before. Where? Movies, photographs. When? When?

He was so cold.

He shivered. No one seemed to notice him, sprawled next to a wooden bench attached to the tiled wall with metal struts. He wanted to use the bench to pull himself up, to ask for help, but he wasn't sure he could move.

His hand still clutched the prototype. He brought the device up, glared at it, saw the LED—it said he was home. It said he had returned to his time. But he didn't think so.

It had been wrong before.

The wall across from him had life-sized posters of cigarettes, the ads written in German, the company unfamiliar. No one had hand-helds or cell phones. Every man carried a briefcase, it seemed, and every woman had a purse.

A big oversized purse, with a clasp.

Like in Marilyn Monroe movies.

The assassin groaned and leaned his head against the cold wall. Only halfway this time. Or even less. The 1960s? 1950s? He had no idea. He was out of his element.

And he wasn't sure they had the medical technology to save him here.

He wasn't sure they could save him at home, either—whatever home was—but there was a better chance.

The prototype felt very heavy. His entire body felt heavy.

He was going to die alone, in a train station, in a Vienna he never planned to see. No one would know what he had done. No one would understand the changes he had made in their lives.

For the better.

It had to be for the better.

He had to believe everything he had done was for the best.

2005

IT TOOK TWO MORE WEEKS for the test results on all the blood spatter to come in. Two weeks in which Sofie went back and forth between being a giddy woman in love for the first time, and a professional historian who was working on the find of her life.

She and Anton spent every moment together. Sometimes they worked at their various places in the same building. Sometimes they watched each other work. And sometimes they held each other in his narrow bed upstairs, coming together in complete and somehow perfect silence.

She had never experienced anything like this before. She doubted she ever would again. She was trying to memorize the emotions, so that when the inevitable loss came—whatever it was—she had something to hold on to.

Of course, she would always have her work. And she focused on it anew when the spatter test results came back.

First, the report mentioned that some of the blood was testable. Apparently new techniques had been devised to get DNA from decayed blood. She hadn't even realized that might be a problem.

The report went on to tell her that the blood residue on the gun showed traces from all five victims, although there appeared to be more spatter from Hietler than anyone else. However, the large volume of blood, the entire coated left side of the gun, had no obvious source.

The CRL even tested Anton's DNA to see if the blood was from Johann Runge. It was not. That gun had lain in a pool of blood, and the pool belonged to a person unknown.

The fact that the gun was found in a pool of blood only appeared in Runge's third notebook. The pool of blood was mentioned in the police report, but the way that report was written, it sounded like the Sniper dropped the gun as he ran through the crowd, leaving it on a dry portion of the platform.

Sofie read between the lines, of course. The report never exactly said that. It never exactly said anything.

Just like the other reports. Just like Runge's book.

Sofie would send the blood work to the Swiss lab, but she knew the results would be the same. The problem wasn't the decomposition of the samples; the problem was that no one knew who the Sniper was. His DNA was not on file—at least, not in any accessible way.

She worked on the tests, worked on the files, and listened to Anton's music. Sometimes, she found herself thinking about her parents. Not as they had been, but as they had died.

She wondered what Runge would have thought of their case. Would he have classified it as unsolvable, like the Munich police had? Or would he have assumed poor detective work resulted in the fact that the sniper wasn't caught?

She wished Runge had lived long enough to investigate—not that it would have been possible. The shooting had occurred in 1975, and Runge had been dead for twenty years. He would have been nearly a hundred years old, even if he had lived. Not young enough or spry enough to investigate yet another case.

He probably wouldn't have even had an opinion about it. He hadn't had opinions about a lot of cases toward the end.

And that thought niggled at her as she worked.

It bothered her and bothered her—

—until she made one final discovery.

1953

AT FIRST, RUNGE DIDN'T BELIEVE WHAT HE SAW.

A man appeared in the spot. Simply appeared. He wavered in like a heat mirage, then solidified, his legs sprawled in front of him, his back braced against the wall.

In his hand, he held a device.

Runge's breath caught. He had been waiting behind a trash can on the far side of the spot, away from the bench, but not so far that he couldn't see. No one had noticed him here. This time, no one seemed to care.

They all seemed concerned with catching the train. Runge couldn't even remember where it was going. He had seen so many trains on this platform over forty years that he no longer cared. The people all looked the same, too. They glanced at their watches, hurried to the boarding area, checked the Arrivals board.

They never saw the strangers around them and would be hard-pressed to describe anyone should a crime happen.

Just like the last time. No one had even realized that Papadopoulos had been shot until the second shot was fired.

And no one else admitted to seeing the Sniper vanish. Everyone assumed he had escaped through the crowd.

Apparently Runge was the only person who realized the Sniper had been too injured to run.

Like the man leaning against the wall. He wore a wool overcoat and his pants were twice as dark as they should be, almost as if he wet himself. Then he moved ever so slightly, and Runge saw a blackish-red smear of blood on the floor.

Runge swallowed. This was not his imagination. The Sniper was here. He had finally made an appearance.

And now Runge had to decide what to do.

2005

SOFIE WAS LOOKING for something else—a secondary file on Papadopoulos, with all of the assumptions that Runge had made in his notebooks outlined in the file—when she found her answers. She hadn't even been thinking of her theories. She had been focused on Papadopoulos, on Runge's conclusion that Papadopoulos wasn't the Greek tourist that history made him out to be, but was, instead, a Russian revolutionary who had been born in the province of Georgia.

Even if she didn't believe that Papadopoulos would become a Russian revolutionary trying to overthrow the Tzar, she had to assume that Runge's information about Papadopoulos's past had come from somewhere.

So when she reached the Papadopoulos information in one of the last filing cabinets near the wall, she did what she had been doing since she discovered the notebooks. She lifted out the largest accordion file in the drawer and felt along the bottom for hidden material.

The notebooks had been the last thing she found, weeks before, so the search had become little more than a formality. When her fingers hit newsprint, she didn't notice at first, and almost put the accordion file back in the drawer.

But something did register, just enough to make her look inside.

There she saw a series of newspaper articles, all from Vienna and all from the same week. She pulled them out and set them on the desk, her hands shaking. She recognized the photograph accompanying the first story: She had seen that exact image sketched in the police reports filed in 1913.

Sofie made herself walk behind the desk and sit down. At the very desk where Johann Runge wrote his reports. And his notebooks. And *Death at Fasching*. Where he had woven his blend of truth and half-statements and maybe (she had been hoping) lies.

His lies.

She sat down, slid the clippings close to her, and started to read.

All of the articles concerned a mugging victim, found in Wein Nord, hands over his stomach, dead from blood loss. The victim, who remained nameless—no identification was ever found on the body—wouldn't have made news by himself.

No. He made news because of the man who stumbled across his body. Literally stumbled.

Vienna's most famous detective, Johann Runge.

And Runge made even more news by saying that, as far as he was concerned, the case was solved.

Sofie's fingers were moist. They left little smear-marks on the faded newsprint.

The case was solved.

Runge never spoke to the press. He refused to take the case, even though his so-called boss, the head of the Federal Police, demanded that he do so.

Runge retreated to his home and refused to give interviews, claiming once again that he believed the case was solved.

Although he would never say who or what the solution was.

With reluctance, Sofie looked at the dateline for the first clipping, even though she had a hunch—a hunch that Runge had prepared her for.

January 13, 1953.

Forty years after the Sniper disappeared.

To the day.

And, as she discovered the more she read, to the hour.
Of course Runge thought the case was solved.
For him, it was.

1953

THE ASSASSIN LICKED HIS LIPS. They were dry, chapped, and he was thirstier than he had ever been in his life.

"Hello," he called in German. "Pardon me."

He wasn't ready to ask for help. He didn't really deserve help, not after all he'd done, the millions he'd killed.

Funny, it was the last five that were the hardest. Face-to-face, even knowing he was looking at madmen, people who had ruined his life, his world. Shooting them had taken every ounce of discipline he had.

And, in so many ways, made him no better than they were.

"Excuse me," he called again, but no one seemed to hear him. They moved past him as if he didn't exist.

He wondered if something else had gone wrong, if he wasn't really all there. Maybe he hadn't materialized properly, like those people in old science fiction movies. Maybe he was a ghost, just like some of them were, and he hadn't even realized it yet.

"Someone, please!" He was getting closer to yelling for help. He would have to use all of his strength to scream for it in a moment.

After he rested.

But he couldn't rest. Not yet.

"Hello!" Louder this time. And now, maybe—

A hand touched his shoulder. An old man crouched next to him. The old man's knee cracked with such vigor, it sounded like a gunshot.

The assassin looked up—

And saw a face he'd last seen only moments ago. It had been younger then. Forty years younger, without the lines or the bald pate or the white, tufted eyebrows. But the eyes were the same sharp blue, filled with intelligence and hatred.

"You," the assassin whispered.

"Yes," the old man said. "It's me."

2005

THE CLIPPINGS EXPLAINED EVERYTHING, if Sofie was willing to accept the time-travel theory. The Sniper returned to 1953—only in the wrong timeline—and Runge had been waiting for him.

Sofie sat at the desk and read and reread the clippings. It took time for all of the information to filter through—and for her to realize that she could prove Runge right or wrong.

All she needed was the body; she already had the blood.

She scanned the articles again and felt her breath leave her body. The victim was buried in a pauper's grave outside the city. Vienna no longer used mass graves, but the grave labels had been poorly done, particularly in the 1950s and 1960s.

The undertaker at the pauper's cemetery sometimes buried corpses one on top of the other to save land space and work. The scandal broke when someone identified a pauper and wanted the body disinterred to be buried in a family plot.

The body had no casket and no embalming, and had decomposed along with the body below. Both bodies had to be buried in the family plot, since no one was able to distinguish one from the other.

Even if she located the victim's body, she wouldn't be able to prove—not well enough for critics and detractors—that the body was the Sniper's.

She needed to do something else.

And as she leaned back in her chair and looked around the cleared-out room with the wooden file cases pressed against the crumbling walls, she knew.

She knew.

Johann Runge kept evidence from all of his cases after the Sniper—all the cases where the authorities allowed him to keep the evidence, that is.

But this case was emphatically *not* Runge's. He never touched the evidence. He never dealt with the body.

He claimed the case was closed.

Because the other case, the case that had driven him all along, the Sniper case—that case was finally closed.

Sofie felt a chill run through her. The evidence was back where she had started in the first place: In the police evidence room in the museum on the Ring.

She would get her evidence; she would get her answers.

Whether she wanted them or not.

1953

THE SNIPER'S SKIN was the color of chalk, his eyes sunken in his face. Runge had seen men bleed out before, and knew that his assumption forty years ago had been correct.

This man would die soon.

Runge looked around. No one else seemed to notice. No one to call an ambulance, no one to send for help. No one who would come to their aid.

Not that Runge was going to ask.

He moved his body nearer to the Sniper's legs so that other people couldn't see the Sniper clearly.

"How did you know?" the Sniper whispered.

"I didn't," Runge said. "I do now."

The Sniper swallowed with obvious difficulty. "When are we?"

"Don't you know? Isn't this when you came from?"

The Sniper shook his head. The movement made him even paler.

"It's 1953," Runge said.

"1953." The Sniper smiled. "The year Stalin died."

"What?" The reference sounded familiar, but vaguely. So vaguely, in fact, that Runge wasn't even sure what the Sniper was talking about. "I don't understand."

"Joseph Stalin. You know. The Soviet Union. Poisoned, they think, by one of his friends." The Sniper coughed. His hand covered his stomach.

Runge felt even more confused. "I don't know what you're talking about."

"Russia," the Sniper whispered. "Who heads Russia?"

"It depends," Runge said. "The Tzar still lives, but is ill. And the Duma is run by—"

"Duma? You mean Parliament?"

"Yes," Runge said.

"And the war? Was there a war?"

Runge nodded, frowning. Had this man killed people to prevent a war? "Yes, there was a war. It lasted for more than ten years."

"Ten years?" The Sniper's voice was little more than a whisper. "The Second World War lasted ten years?"

"The Second World War?" Runge didn't know that reference, either. "I was talking about the Great War."

The Sniper let out a small breath, and then he smiled. The device fell onto his bloody lap. He reached up a hand and caught Runge's.

The Sniper's fingers were ice-cold.

"You should thank me," he whispered, the smile still on his face. "You all need to thank me."

"For what?" Runge asked. "For killing five people?"

The Sniper nodded, then extended his hand toward the platform. "Thank me...for this."

Runge glanced at the people still milling about the train. He wasn't sure he understood. Somehow the Sniper believed he was responsible for what? Averting a war? For the station? For the people here?

If the Sniper hadn't reappeared like that, Runge wouldn't have listened to any of it.

He turned back toward the Sniper. The man's eyes were open, but they were glazing.

His lips moved and he spoke without sound. "Thank me."

And then he died.

2005

ANTON INSISTED ON GOING WITH HER, and Sofie didn't mind. It felt as if he had been part of her work from the beginning—and in a way, that was true. The work really hadn't started until she had stepped inside his house.

The Sühnhaus looked imposing in the midday sunlight. The square building, made of stone, with its spires and its religious icons, seemed somehow inappropriate on this day.

Anton gaped at it, and she realized that even though he had walked past this building all of his life, he had probably never been inside of it.

She led him through the main door. The guard greeted her, peered at Anton, and then nodded. Anton, startled, nodded back. The guard had him empty his pockets, which Anton did, and then waved him forward.

He waited as the guard had Sofie empty her purse (there was her notebook—small, unlike Runge's, but filled with the pertinent details in case this evidence file, like the others, was "lost") and sign her name. Then she smiled at him, and slid inside into the cool air-conditioning, kept at the same dry temperature so that the evidence within wasn't ruined.

Anton let Sofie lead him to the evidence room. He hung back as she spoke to the clerk, trying to keep the excitement from her voice. For once, she actually had a case that might be in the files.

The clerk found it quickly and led Sofie to the police reports. Anton followed, looking at the walls of filing cabinets, the piles of boxes that disappeared into the dim fluorescent lights.

The reports were sketchy. Sofie would read a page, then hand it to Anton, who read with an intensity she hadn't seen before.

No one had seen the man on the train. No one had seen him get off. In fact, no one had noticed him until Runge bent over him.

One woman—Sofie felt her hands start to shake again—one woman claimed over and over—unwaveringly—that Runge had been in that spot alone. Then, seconds later, the other man was on the floor, injured.

The woman seemed to think that Runge had injured him. The police surreptitiously checked, but believed that impossible. The victim had been shot twice, and had lost a significant amount of blood (although there wasn't much on the platform—suggesting that he had been injured somewhere else), but Runge hadn't carried a gun. He hadn't even tossed one away.

And when the officers suggested that maybe Runge clear his own name by allowing forensic tests, Runge let the crime lab people test him for gunshot residue.

He had none.

Because he knew he would have none.

The ironic thing was that he had shot the man forty years in the past. The residue was long gone. The police had the right man at the wrong time.

Sofie felt lightheaded. Anton kept shaking his head. The evidence clerk, who hovered, asked them if everything was all right.

"This isn't what we expected," Anton said, but Sofie wasn't so sure. Hadn't they expected something like this when they found the clippings? Hadn't they known?

The clerk continued to hover, and Sofie finally asked where the evidence for a case with this number would be. The clerk sent them to a part of the evidence room that Sofie hadn't been in yet.

And this time, the clerk didn't follow them.

The evidence room seemed even darker than usual. Or maybe that was because Anton kept the basement so well lit. Sofie wasn't used to thin fluorescents anymore, or uncomfortable tables, or dust—all this dust.

Anton gaped at everything, his fingers brushing against boxes; all of them had dates from the 1950s. Sofie had only been as far as the 1930s sections before.

But this area did have the same tables, the same storage shelves, stacked high. Boxes and boxes.

"This is impossible," Anton said.

He had no idea. She had never told him about her previous evidence search. It had never come up.

Part of her worried that this would be the same. But it wasn't.

This box was easy to find.

One small box, smaller than any that housed Sniper evidence, and filled with almost nothing.

Anton took the box off a high shelf without getting on one of those creaky ladders. He handed the box to Sofie. Her hands were steady as she carried it to the examining table. They remained steady as she set the box down and removed its lid.

The faint iron scent of old blood rose out of the box, along with the stench of mold. Sofie resisted the urge to sneeze.

Anton moved the box closer to the light. She stepped with him, her breath catching. The items in here were stored in evidence bags—thick plastic that seemed strange to her, like shower curtain plastic instead of thin plastic bags.

But plastic like this was better than the paper bags she had found the Sniper evidence in.

She picked up the first bag. A formerly white shirt: black with blood. A second bag: trousers, color indeterminate, but also stiff with blood. A woolen vest: black with blood. And on, and on—a suit coat, an overcoat, and long underwear, all coated with blood.

"DNA," Anton said.

Sofie nodded. Now she would know. She could match the blood on the clothing to the blood found on the gun. She could have even more proof.

She still dug bags out of the tiny box. One bag had matches from a long-gone bar in Vienna, as well as a sheet of blood-colored paper, with notations so smeared that Sofie couldn't read them.

Another bag had a small device, the size of her thumb. It glowed redly against the darkness of the box.

"What the hell?" Anton reached for the device, but Sofie—remembering Kolisko's warnings—pushed his hand away.

She could hear her own breathing. That was enough, really: the redness, the glow, like that light she had seen that came out of the mysterious gun, the same sort of thing—directed at something. Maybe some kind of weapon.

She wouldn't know. She would let Kolisko figure that out.

Then she pulled out the last bag. Anton leaned against her, his body warming hers. She could feel his heartbeat. It seemed faster than usual.

Hers certainly was.

The bag was heavier than all the others, but the item inside wasn't that big—about twice the size of her hand. It was rectangular, with a flat front panel. She ran her finger across the plastic covering it.

Her finger triggered something. The panel turned red. Anton gasped behind her.

Then the redness formed into words. They scrolled, first in English, then Spanish, then French. Red letters as magical as the red light she had seen in CRL's lab.

Finally, the letters appeared in German:

> STARTING PROTOCOL: TIME COMMAND [TR]
> TIME COMMAND [TR] IS A PROTOTYPE OF
> MASSACHUSETTS INSTITUTE OF TECHNOLOGY.
> DO NOT USE WITHOUT PERMISSION. IF FOUND,
> RETURN TO MIT, CAMBRIDGE, MA.

Sofie stared at it as the screen blinked white, then displayed several pictures. Beneath each were the four languages—strange languages to choose, she thought.

The German word said: **INSTRUCTIONS**.

Instructions. For a time machine.

Her mouth was dry. Anton put his arm around her waist, holding her against him, as if he was afraid she would vanish.

Maybe he was.

"I didn't think it was possible," he said.

But she had. The time-travel part. She had never thought she would find the machine.

"It has instructions," she whispered.

She looked over her shoulder. Anton wasn't looking at the machine. He was looking at her.

"You have your chance now," he said.

He knew. He knew what she wanted to do. She could go back. She could save her parents. She could make everything right.

"You do remember," he said, "that going back and fixing things won't change you. You'll be the same."

"I know." They were whispering. No way could the clerk hear them. No way could anyone know what they had.

And yet it felt like the whole world knew, now that they did.

"But they'd be alive," Sofie said. "And that little girl, their little girl, she'd have a chance to be better."

"I like this girl," Anton said.

Loss. It was finally here. In its own shocking way. Sofie swallowed. "I'm going to go back," she said.

"I know." He squared his shoulders. "I'm going with you."

Her light-headedness seemed worse, and then she recognized what it was.

Panic.

"You can't. You could die." She said that louder. Almost too loud.

"So could you," he said.

"No," she said. "I won't let you."

"You'd rather lose me this way?"

She frowned at him. His grip on her waist was too tight.

"You said it before," he said. "It's a one-way trip. If you change anything, you'll never come back here. I'd never see you again."

"But your house, your career—"

"I don't care about the house. It's given us its secrets." He smiled. "It gave me you."

"But the piano—"

"Is something I can do anywhere. Think, Sofie. This'll work better with two of us. We need to do some planning, a little research. Thirty years isn't so long ago. We can get the right clothing, some old money, maybe even some old identification. And we'd have to go to Germany, right? Munich?"

She nodded, feeling overwhelmed. He'd already thought of this. Probably since that day she said she would go back. He had thought beyond the Sniper case to Sofie, and realized that if the time-travel theory proved true, they might get this chance.

"It'll work better with two," he said again.

He was right. It would.

Two to investigate. Two to plan. Two to flank that bastard in Palace Park and make sure he never hurt anyone again.

She reached up and touched his face. She didn't want to lose him, either. Not yet. Not now.

Not like this.

"I love you," she whispered.

He looked frightened. It was the first time she had spoken the words, and she scared him. Did he think that was a prelude to leaving him?

"You're right," she said. "We can do this."

"Together?" This time, he was asking.

"Together," she said, and then she kissed him, clinging to him with one hand—and to all of time with the other.

ABOUT THE AUTHOR

BESTSELLING AUTHOR Kristine Kathryn Rusch's award-winning fiction includes many historical stories, including "G-Men," and "The Gallery of His Dreams." The London *Daily Mail* called her novel *Hitler's Angel*, published by Max Crime, "a little gem of a thriller." She also writes highly acclaimed mysteries under the name Kris Nelscott. For more about her work, go to kristinekathrynrusch.com.

Also by
KRISTINE KATHRYN RUSCH:

The Retrieval Artist series (novels and novellas)
The Diving series (novels and novellas)

Recovering Apollo 8 (novella)
The Tower (novella)
Show Trial (novella)

The War and After: Five Stories of Magic & Revenge (collection)
Five Female Sleuths (collection)
Five Diverse Detectives (collection)

*WMG*PUBLISHING

CPSIA information can be obtained at www.ICGtesting.com
Printed in the USA
LVOW06s1908210813

349003LV00007B/702/P